HIDDEN IN SIGHT

HARRIET KNOWLES

Edited by JW Services

Proofreading by Mystique Editing

ISBN-13: 978-1976197093

ISBN-10: 1976197090

CHAPTER 1

Fitzwilliam,

*I am writing this letter in a great deal of
 haste; I have a duty to do so because
 we share Georgiana's guardianship.
 But I am also writing this to you as
 my friend.*

*I have to take Georgiana away at once.
 We will have to quit Darcy House
 and Pemberley for the time being and
 take a small country house under
 assumed names.*

*I cannot take any possible risk with
 Georgiana's well-being and future,
 and I am sure you know of my great
 devotion to her as my sister, and also*

our shared responsibility to her in memory of my own beloved father and mother.

I must explain to you in full the reason why I have made this decision and I will have this letter delivered securely to Matlock House for your attention.

As you know, Georgiana has been in Ramsgate this summer, in the care of Mrs. Younge. I understand now that there was some connivance between that lady and Mr. Wickham.

He also went to Ramsgate. It was Georgiana's natural affection for her childhood friend, together with the strong recommendation of him by Mrs. Younge, which led her to consent to an elopement.

Georgiana was uneasy enough about the circumstances to write to me and I hastened down there at once, as you can imagine.

Unfortunately, there was some difficulty which I had not anticipated, and although I was able to recover Georgiana safely, I was set upon by a group of men. Were it not for the

*intervention of the Earl of
Sandwich, who had brought his wife
and daughters for the sea bathing;
and some of his servants, I might
have received worse injuries than
I did.*

*It transpires that Mr. Wickham — of
course — has very considerable
gambling debts, and these thugs are
the face of those to whom he owes
money. They are determined that he
will obtain Georgiana's fortune and
thus be able to pay his debts.*

*We are presently at Darcy House, while
the physician is dealing with my
injury, but Georgiana is much
affected by the threat to Mr.
Wickham now that I will not permit
her elopement. She still fancies herself
deeply in love.*

*As we both know, she has no knowledge
of what the man is really like, and
all my attempts to inform her are
falling on deaf ears.*

*I am sufficiently aware of those behind
the attack to be concerned that there
might be significant attempts to*

3

*continue to inveigle Georgiana to
Scotland from Pemberley. It is too
close to that border for my peace of
mind, should my protection fail.*

*Unfortunately, I no longer believe London
is a safe place, either; there are far too
many places and crowds to hide
within.*

*I have, this morning, received an
anonymous note, written in a rough
hand, not Wickham's. It states:*

*"We know where she is. Miss Darcy and
her fortune will be ours."*

*It cannot be long before it occurs to the
organisation behind Wickham's
creditors that he is not required. She
might be forced to marry any one of
them and once they have access to her
fortune, her life may well be in
danger, and will certainly not be
worth living.*

*I am indebted to the Earl — as you
know, his estate at Sandwich is less
than ten miles from Ramsgate — for
the information which has led me to
this knowledge.*

But by going into hiding, which is what

we shall effectively be doing, I am very much aware of the need for great secrecy in order to prevent us being discovered while we are less protected than we could be at Pemberley.

I have one man whom I will take with us, and whom I trust absolutely. He is currently in a part of the country chosen by me mainly as being utterly unfamiliar to Georgiana and myself, where nobody would think of us going, and is attempting to find a small but hopefully comfortable estate which he will then rent using the assumed name we will be living under.

I can only ask that you do not make any attempt to find us, which might draw unwanted attention our way.

I will, of course, continue to keep you informed as to our well-being as soon as I judge it safe to do so. I would urge you to contact the Earl of Sandwich, with whom I believe you are already acquainted, and he will be able to inform you as to the nature of the threat to Georgiana, and the

professionalism and utter ruthlessness
of the forces against us.
But now I must finish, the physician is
waiting to do his work.
I remain, sir, your friend,
Darcy.

~

*H*e threw down his pen and grimaced. Even now, he hadn't said what he really wanted to. But he had managed not to give anything away, should the letter fall into the wrong hands.

He swivelled round in his chair, scowling, and watched as the physician got swiftly on with his work.

He was most fortunate the leg wasn't broken. The stick that had been thrust out to trip him up had certainly caused enough damage, but it would not stop him being able to walk.

He watched with detached interest as the doctor worked. A long gash, surrounded by dark, swollen bruising. At least the bleeding had stopped, and his breeches had prevented the wound being contaminated too much.

"What is the risk of infection?" he demanded, suddenly.

"There is always a risk, sir. You must be very careful. I must insist that you use only a highly qualified physician to change the dressings when necessary."

"I doubt that will be possible." Darcy scowled. "I shall just have to hope that there is a good man where I am going."

"I could write a letter outlining my treatment regime, sir?"

"Thank you, that shouldn't be necessary." Indeed not. Darcy wanted to hide from his real identity, not broadcast it.

He shook his head. "As fast as you can, please." He pushed away the risks of infection from his mind. It could change nothing, except that he must make an arrangement for Georgiana's safety should he become more incapacitated.

He frowned and winced.

"I am sorry, sir."

"Do not be. You must do what is necessary." He turned his mind to that of luggage. A certain amount would be expected. However, he did not want any servant from here knowing where it went, nor any servant from there knowing where it had come from. He puzzled over the dilemma until the wound was bound.

"Thank you." He stood up and tested his

weight on it. It throbbed cruelly, but he had to endure it as best he could. It was time. Mr. Thomas would be back soon and he, Darcy, would become Mr. William Hudson, with his sister, Georgia.

CHAPTER 2

"Oh, Jane!" Elizabeth sighed as they walked around the gardens. "I wish our lives were more interesting. You are so patient and tranquil. But I cannot be like that."

"But what else would you wish for, Lizzy?" Jane stopped to smell one of the early roses. "Indeed, we have a very pleasant life here. We do not have lives of drudgery like the servants and farmhands do. And neither do we have too much to manage in the way that those of higher birth seem to." She smiled over at her.

"In fact, I can think of no other life better than that we have now."

Elizabeth raised her eyebrows and smiled. "Except perhaps, a home of your own, with a family?"

Jane blushed a becoming pink and looked down. "Perhaps." She glanced up. "Is that what you are pining for, Lizzy? A husband and children? You are not yet twenty."

"I don't know." Elizabeth swung her arm against the lavender hedge, sending a shower of tiny scented petals fluttering to the path. "Perhaps it would keep me busier than I am now and I would not feel each day so ..." she made a face. How could she explain her feelings to her sister?

"What is each day to you, Lizzy?" Jane seemed genuinely puzzled. "Do you not find interest enough in each day? Are there other things you wish to be doing?"

"No," Elizabeth sighed. "At least I don't know what I want." She swung round to her sister. "But it doesn't help us if we do want marriage and children. In this small place there are no manner of suitable men for us to meet — at least none with the means by which we can have this settled life you enjoy so much."

She placed her basket on the ground and went onto one knee. She forced herself to start picking the lavender stalks properly, so they could be hung for drying. "Even Charlotte, who is five years older than you, has met no one remotely in a position to marry."

When Jane did not answer, Elizabeth glanced

up. Her sister's face was troubled and her lips trembled.

"Oh, Jane, I'm sorry." Elizabeth jumped to her feet. "I should not talk about my thoughts so much. I know you prefer to allow time to cure all problems."

Jane tucked her hand in Elizabeth's arm.

"You know you must tell me what worries you, Lizzy. I wouldn't like to think you had no one to confide in." She carefully picked some stems and laid them in her basket. "Why don't you go for a walk? You know it always cheers you up."

"Indeed it does. I think when we have finished our task here, I might do that."

She moved further along the flower border. "But do you not think it a pity that there are so many empty houses here? So many men gone to war and their families choosing to live in London where they can know what is going on?"

"While the French crouch the other side of the Channel, things will never change, Lizzy." Jane seemed perfectly calm and matter-of-fact about it and Elizabeth forced herself to be equally calm. She could do nothing, she knew that.

AN HOUR LATER, she was walking fast along the

lane towards Lucas Lodge, having decided to call on Charlotte. Her friend would help her, and she began to marshal her thoughts together. Perhaps she should learn something new. She thought Father would buy her a book about whatever subject she decided on studying, in fact, he already had quite an extensive library. She might find something of interest there.

Charlotte greeted her affectionately. "Have you come to discuss the news, Lizzy?"

"What news, Charlotte? I have heard nothing."

"Perhaps it hasn't reached Longbourn yet." Her friend led the way into the house and Elizabeth hurried after her.

"What news, Charlotte? You must not keep it from me."

"Oh, it's nothing very exciting, Lizzy. Let's have some tea and I will tell you."

Elizabeth swallowed her curiosity and followed her into the sitting room. The younger Lucases swarmed around her, and she smiled.

Perhaps her own home ailed her. Now that her sisters were all growing up, the conversation was all about clothes, new bonnets and men. None of them were subjects that could hold her interest for very long.

"So, what is the news you told me of?" She raised her voice above the hubbub.

"I think you might not find it so very interesting as all that, Lizzy." Charlotte poured the tea.

"But I have heard that a gentleman is to take Bayford House. A single gentleman, and his sister is coming to keep house for him."

"Oh." Elizabeth thought about it. "Well, it will be nice to have a new face or two in the country. Your father will have to call on him and invite him to the assembly."

"I am sure he will." Charlotte smiled affectionately. "He is always enthusiastic to ensure no new arrival feels unable to join us."

"And is he a gentleman of fortune?" Elizabeth knew Lady Lucas would have a sharp eye for suitable single gentlemen for her daughters.

"Mother has not yet ascertained that." The glint in Charlotte's eye showed she knew what Elizabeth wasn't saying.

"But I don't think he can have a very good income. Bayford House is quite modest, and Netherfield Park would surely be the choice of a richer man."

"Yes, you're right, Charlotte." Elizabeth sipped her tea. Netherfield Park had been empty for nearly two years now, and she wondered if it would ever be let.

"But he might well be an amiable man, and good company. It will be interesting to see whether he is a young man. Has anyone seen him yet?"

"No. His steward came yesterday and signed for him. He engaged the housekeeper — the one who used to work for the old Bayford ladies before they passed. She has been tasked with engaging staff and the house is to be ready by this evening."

"This evening!" Elizabeth could scarce believe it. "Why, that seems most precipitate. I wonder why he is in such a hurry?"

"I don't know, Lizzy. I heard the attorney could get nothing out of the steward. So we will have to compose our curiosity until tomorrow, when I am sure my father will call upon the gentleman." She laughed. "Whether he is ready for callers or not."

Elizabeth put down her teacup. "Well, he will no doubt find himself fully engaged with callers. I am sure that once Lady Lucas has ascertained his fortune, my mother will be insisting my father calls on him, too."

She stood up. "I wonder whether he is aware he will be such an object of interest?"

CHAPTER 3

*I*t was not a good way to start a new life. Georgiana's eyes were reddened and while she was quiet and still, her misery was attracting attention.

But Darcy could do nothing. They were sitting in the post coach on the way to Hertfordshire. He hoped to God that at Hoddesdon there'd be a reasonable hack chaise for hire to take them on to Bayford. He tried to stay expressionless, not let his distaste at travelling this way show. He must play his part, as if he had never lived better.

Georgiana was stiff and self-conscious in a simple lawn dress befitting her country status, and her fine gowns had all been left behind. She looked miserably out-of-place.

He wondered if he had been too precipitate in

taking her away like this, but his heart hardened. If she had eloped and been married as she half-wished, he knew for sure that her life would have been immeasurably worse. It might do them both good to discover how one lived with economy in mind.

Mr. Thomas must also be wondering what his life would be like now. He was sitting outside, as befitted the servant of a merely comfortable gentleman, and would undoubtedly be very glad to arrive at Hoddesdon. Mr. Darcy had instructed him to be on the lookout for vehicles or riders who seemed to be following the post.

Darcy's leg throbbed, and with it, his temper. But he knew he had to be gentle to Georgiana. He must remember she was young, and that she had told him of the planned elopement. It meant that she wanted to be prevented from marrying, whatever she had said to him in her present state of disappointment.

He knew she felt unprotected, she didn't even have a maid with her, and she had no idea where they were going. He would have to be strong for her.

But, damnation! His whole life put on hold and all comforts cast aside for he knew not how long. And his reprieve would only come about at the actions of other men. He could do nothing except protect his sister.

He glanced out of the window. It was to be hoped that Bayford House had a reasonable library. He would die of boredom otherwise.

He wondered absently how the Pemberley estate would be after a prolonged absence. He was glad his steward there — and the housekeeper — were excellent at managing, it meant he didn't really have great concerns. He leaned back and stared at the roof of the coach.

A few minutes later, it began to slow. Mr. Darcy sat up and looked over at Georgiana. She was staring out of the window, squashed against the side by a large lady with a small child on her lap. At least the child hadn't misbehaved or been noisy.

AN INTERMINABLE HALF-HOUR LATER, their two trunks stacked on the back, the hack chaise was bowling through the bland Hertfordshire country-side towards Bayford House.

Mr. Thomas was sitting next to the driver. They were alone, briefly. Mr. Darcy exerted himself to be sociable.

"I expect you will be glad to get there,

Georgie." He might as well get used to her new name.

"Yes, William." She sounded subdued, and he smiled, making an effort to cheer her up. He leaned closer, keeping his voice quiet.

"We must treat this as an adventure."

She turned to him. "Yes, William. I will try."

"That's the answer, Georgie. And so will I. I expect the experience will do us good." But he didn't believe it.

She laughed. "You haven't called me Georgie so much since I was five years old. It makes me feel very babyish."

He smiled. "I would wish that you felt as protected as you were then, dear sister. But remember, Georgie is short for Georgia, and we must play our parts all the time, because servants are much inclined to gossip in the neighbourhood."

"I understand, William." Her voice was small. "I am sorry I have caused you so much trouble." She peered down at his leg. "I cannot believe Mr. Wickham has friends who would cause you harm."

"We will not talk of it again, Georgiana — Georgie." He cursed under his breath. "But I am doing this for both our sakes and I hope you will do your best not to raise any suspicions, and always tell me before you leave the house."

"I will," she promised meekly.

Mr. Darcy sat back and thought of the morning. His Cousin Richard had turned up unexpectedly, obviously still hoping they would be there. He had sat down very seriously with Darcy.

"You cannot vanish into thin air without someone knowing how to find you. For Georgiana's sake if nothing else. What would happen if your injury goes bad and you became very sick?"

"Then Mr. Thomas is tasked with leaving me and getting her back to you." Darcy had growled. "I am not so thoughtless as that, Fitzwilliam."

And if he is incapacitated while protecting you?" The Colonel had jumped to his feet, pacing up and down. Then he turned.

"If I promise not to write or call, will you at least tell me where you will be in case of dire need?"

Mr. Darcy had given in. He trusted his cousin absolutely, and he'd talked about the organised gangs who seemed to be infesting the country now.

Colonel Fitzwilliam had taken in all he said, and promised to work with the Earl of Sandwich so that the power behind this particular gang would be discovered and they would be dealt with.

Finally he'd stood up. "All right, then. You look after Georgiana as you can do best. I will work to eliminate the danger and wait to hear from you." He scowled down. "You must be in touch at least every month, Darcy, or I will have to search you out."

Darcy had agreed reluctantly, knowing it only took one letter to lose everything.

"But you must promise faithfully not to write to me. Anybody I know might be observed. At least the origin of my letters coming to you will not be discovered."

"I agree." He shook his head. "Although I still think Pemberley would be better."

Darcy had shaken his head. "I cannot. It is too near the border. If she was taken, the journey would not be long enough to discover them, to head them off and recover her in time."

"I suppose you're right." His cousin had clasped his hand and then was gone.

THE HACK CHAISE turned into the narrow driveway and stopped in front of a small house. Darcy stared at it, keeping his expression impassive.

Beside him, Georgiana giggled and he turned in surprise.

"I think you'll always know where I am, William. We will be in very close company in that house."

He smiled reluctantly. "We must make the best of it, Georgie. At least the gardens are of a reasonable size."

The hack stopped, and Mr. Thomas jumped down. Several servants appeared from the house and helped him unload the trunks. Mr. Thomas paid off the driver and they were left standing in front of the house.

Darcy leaned heavily on his cane. He must try not to limp too badly. Georgiana was clinging to his arm and he could feel her trembling.

He smiled down at her. "Let us go and see what it is like, Georgie. We can have tea together, then, and ..." He could think of nothing else to say. What were they to do here? They knew no one and he would not be able to write to his family or his friends. There was no one he knew to ride with, and in any case, he could not leave Georgiana.

He spoke to her as they went to the door. "I think the first thing to do is to obtain a carriage. We must have transport available."

She nodded. But she was looking at the door. "Let's think of this as an adventure, William."

He forced a smile. Some adventure. He was not at all sure just how many servants, what sort of carriage, what sort of food even, a man on such modest means should be able to afford. Any display of unexpected wealth might lead to suspicion.

The housekeeper curtsied as they went into the hall.

"You're the housekeeper, I think?" he tried to keep his voice mild.

"Yes sir. Mrs. James. I hope you'll be very happy here."

"Very well, Mrs. James. Have you managed a full complement of staff?" He glanced around. The place was clean enough, and there were adequate furnishings.

"Yes, sir."

"Good. We would like to see round the house, please. Then we will take tea in the sitting room before dinner."

Mrs. James curtsied. "Yes, sir." She went over to a door on the right. "This is the library, sir."

They followed her round the house. Darcy was wondering how long it would be before he made an error. He'd so nearly said drawing room instead of sitting room, it could only be a matter of time.

Georgiana seemed brightly interested. Of course, she had been at school, then to a new establishment in Ramsgate before this. He had only lived at Pemberley and Darcy House, places he'd been born to, places that were as familiar to him as his own face in the glass.

But that wasn't quite true. He remembered his first days at school, and at Cambridge. He'd not enjoyed getting to know those places, but he'd survived it, and he would survive this.

At least it was a small house. There was not much to remember.

His leg ached abominably. He'd be glad to sit down for tea.

CHAPTER 4

The next morning seemed to start reasonably well. He limped down to breakfast and was joined by Georgiana, who already looked younger, more countrified.

"You've changed your hair," he commented. She giggled.

"Emily has never been a lady's maid before. She has tried her best to do my hair as I described it." She moved her head around. "But this is comfortable."

"Good." He watched her. She seemed quite cheerful, although it was abominable that she should have to look like this. She had been born a lady and should be able to live like one.

But he had decided that they could not appear to be too wealthy, or he would become an object of much interest in local society. Then it might be whispered of in town, too.

He drank his tea, and watched as Mrs. James brought in the eggs and meats. Mrs. Reynolds, at Pemberley, had never carried a tray in her life, he thought. Her job was supervising the small army of staff.

"Thank you, Mrs. James. Do you have everything you need now you are here?"

She curtsied. "Thank you, sir. Yes, everything is in place. I was here before, looking after the old Miss Bayfords."

"I see." He must not show too much interest. He put down the book he'd plucked at random from the library.

"Please arrange for the London News to be delivered each day." He could not be expected to forsake a newspaper but he had better not ask for the Gazette as well.

"And serve coffee as well as tea at breakfast."

She curtsied again. "Yes, sir. I will send for today's newspaper now, and arrange that it is here by breakfast time in future."

"Thank you." He turned to his sister.

"Perhaps we might take a turn around the gardens, Georgie, when we have finished eating?"

"Of course, William." She seemed quite composed and he was very proud of her. Even having new servants around must be quite unsettling.

He turned to the housekeeper as she was leaving the room. "Mrs. James, could you ask Mr. Thomas to see me, please?"

MR. THOMAS WAS A SOLID, reliable man. He stood deferentially inside the doorway. "You wanted to see me, sir?"

"Yes. We have much to do here, to find ourselves comfortable. First, I must have transport. We need a small carriage, if you can engage the men required." He knew Thomas would not have taken Bayford House if stabling wasn't adequate.

"Yes, sir."

This was no good at all. He could almost feel the very walls listening. He pushed himself to his feet and his leg almost gave way. Swallowing a curse, he reached for his stick.

"Georgie, if you care to join me when you have attired yourself, I will be in the gardens with Mr. Thomas, seeing what is to be done."

Taking a turn around the gardens, he waved the stick at the road. "Mr. Thomas, just how secure can we be here, without taking any measures which might raise suspicions?"

"There is not much, sir, I am afraid. I looked at a number of properties in the area you told me to look. Very many of them have near neighbours and lanes and paths aplenty. This house has only the road."

At that moment, several young ladies walked along the road past the house, chattering. They looked in the gardens curiously and Mr. Darcy was very thankful he was too far away from the road to have to acknowledge them. He turned his back.

"They are not accompanied by a servant, Thomas."

"No, sir. Things are different in the country."

Mr. Darcy was in a quandary. Would this mean Georgiana would be out alone?

His steward seemed to know what he was thinking. "The young ladies tend to walk in groups, sir, as you can see. Miss D — Hudson will not walk alone."

"That is a small comfort, at least," Darcy growled. "Although I suppose it means I shall have to approve her friends."

"I think you will scarce be able to avoid the local efforts to be friendly, sir." Mr. Thomas' voice was deferential, but open enough. He had been in Darcy's service many years and knew what was required of him.

"Your best security is your story. If Miss Hudson has no fortune and is very shy, she may make some friends among young ladies, but will not excite too much attention." His lips twitched.

"I am afraid you will be the object of greatest interest. Marriageable young gentlemen are scarce, with or without fortune."

Mr. Darcy growled. He wanted to stride away from such thoughts, but his leg hurt him too badly to be able to walk fast, and a lack of exercise would make him very irritable, he knew.

"Thank you for your observations, Mr. Thomas. They are appreciated, even if they aren't very welcome."

"Thank you, sir. I am sorry, because I know how difficult it must be to put aside the way you have always behaved. But that is not how a gentleman of limited means is used to behaving."

Mr. Darcy sighed. "I suppose I will be thought of as having fallen on hard times."

Mr. Thomas was silent for a few moments. "It would be easier for you to act, if you can bear the ignominy. Now, if you would excuse me, sir. I will see if I can find a chaise or something similar that does not look too expensive and yet is not too uncomfortable for you and your sister."

"Thank you, Thomas." Darcy stood, watching

the road as his steward vanished around the corner.

"I am here, William!"

He turned and saw Georgiana coming towards him. Her bonnet and overjacket were simple and her cotton dress blew behind her.

"You look perfect, dear Georgie." He offered her his free arm, and they began to stroll around the garden.

She bit her lip. "You are limping more than yesterday, William. Is your leg very painful?"

"I must confess it is not comfortable, but I am sure that I must walk a while." He smiled down on her.

"You know what I am like to live with when the weather is inclement and I can get no exercise."

"I remember," she said softly. "But we must call an apothecary to at least dress your wound each day, must we not?"

"You are right. I have sent Mr. Thomas to engage a coach or chaise for us. We must have some transport, although I am not sure whether we can officially afford it."

"Emily was saying that young ladies here are quite safe walking into the town and that most of them do that every few days. She says there is a milliners and a haberdasher in Meryton and it is not far."

Georgiana turned to him. "I was thinking that perhaps she could accompany me there and I can perhaps buy some needlework to do."

He grunted. He would prefer to go with her the first time, but almost certainly the walk might be too far — his infernal leg.

"Do you have none with you to last a few days until I can walk well enough to accompany you the first time?"

"Oh, yes. But I did not wish to trouble you."

He smiled at her. "It is not a trouble to me and I would be happier if I have seen the town first. Then I will try and be more at ease about you going to town without me."

"Of course, William. I would not wish to worry you."

The sound of horse and carriage had them both turning in surprise and they watched as the vehicle pulled up and the liveried servants jumped down.

"I think the local gentlemen are beginning to call," Darcy murmured to his sister. "I will receive him in the library so you may sit in the sitting room."

"Yes, William." Georgiana answered and

hurried back to the house to give instructions to the housekeeper.

Mr. Darcy turned and walked back to the house as fast as he was able, which wasn't fast enough.

An older man heaved himself from the coach, rotund and dressed as a country gentleman. He had a face creased with lines from habitually beaming with good humour and his figure showed he enjoyed his food.

Mr. Darcy decided it would seem very rude to go into the house and wait for his guest to be announced. He turned and walked along the drive towards the coach, trying hard not to limp too much.

"Good morning, sir." He must seem reasonably welcoming. His usual manners would get them ostracised and that would not help his sister.

The gentleman turned and beamed at him. "Mr. Hudson, I think." He bowed.

"Indeed." Mr. Darcy bowed in return. "And you are, sir?"

"Lucas, Mr. Hudson. Sir William Lucas."

"Delighted to meet you, Sir William." Darcy was amused at the slight accent on the word *Sir*. He would no doubt hear the whole story soon from Mr. Thomas, but he would see what he got from this man. "Please come in and we will have a drink."

He turned and led the man into the library. He sank into the worn leather armchair when his guest was seated with his whisky. It was not a moment too soon.

"It is good of you to call, Sir William." He needed say no more and his visitor launched into a rambling monologue of welcome. Darcy listened carefully. He would no doubt learn a lot.

CHAPTER 5

*G*eorgiana nervously entered the milliner's shop with Emily dutifully following behind her.

Mr. Darcy watched, waiting in the open chaise, which was what Mr. Thomas had hired for them, and scowled.

Already he was regretting the need to be here, the abominable slow pace of life, and the sense of being in someone else's shoes, of merely playing a part.

This morning he had returned Sir William's call as he was obliged to do and found Lucas Lodge to be all that he had looked down on all his life. He had made an effort, however, and his jaw ached with having had to smile so much.

Lady Lucas had sat with her husband and, as

he had feared, her sharp mind was much engaged in crafting pointed questions about his prospects.

He had discovered that she had several daughters of marriageable age and he had also heard a considerable number of younger children beyond the door of the sitting room. The older boys were in the Navy.

However, they were pleasant people and their daughters could conceivably be friends for Georgiana, so he had swallowed his pride and accepted an invitation to spend the following evening at Lucas Lodge with Georgiana.

When he had returned and told his sister, she was, of course, very anxious.

"You will be quite all right, Georgie," he had reassured her. "You will sit next to me and I will not leave you."

"But we might have to dance, mightn't we?" Georgiana bit her lip.

"Dancing means you will not have to make much conversation, little sister." He had smiled down at her. "With my leg, I will be quite available at all times as I am not able to dance at present." Trying to reassure her had been quite good for him, too.

He wondered what the Lucas daughters were like. He certainly didn't want to excite any hopes of theirs. Such hopes would be quite futile.

He watched the road idly while he waited for Georgiana. It seemed a pleasant little town, if you had to live in the country. But it wasn't his preference.

He stiffened to attention as he saw Georgiana coming out through the shop doorway. She seemed more relaxed and was smiling at a young woman who was with her.

The woman — not much more than a girl, really, made a remark to Georgiana, and she smiled a little more widely and commented back. He watched narrowly, then breathed deeply and made himself relax.

It must be common for young ladies to gossip in shops and it was a sign of friendship, not someone who was necessarily trying to discover them.

Georgiana glanced over at him, and then spoke to her new acquaintance, who glanced his way and nodded. They began walking towards him.

He needed to get out of the chaise. Sighing at the sudden stab of pain in his leg, he climbed down so that he was standing beside the chaise when they reached him.

He listened gravely to his sister.

"William, may I introduce my new acquaintance, Miss Elizabeth Bennet?" She turned to the dark-haired young lady.

"Elizabeth, this is my brother, Mr. William Hudson."

Miss Bennet's eyes were alight with mischief as she curtsied. "I am pleased to meet you, sir. It is always pleasant to have new faces move into the country."

"Miss Bennet," he replied, then stopped. What should he say? "I am pleased to make your acquaintance."

"I see you appear to have an injury, sir. That is disappointing."

"Disappointing?" He couldn't follow her train of thought.

"Of course. My friend Charlotte Lucas tells me you are attending the gathering at Sir William's home tomorrow. There is always dancing and gentlemen are in short supply." Her eyes looked mischievous. "But perhaps you have heard this and have invented an injury."

He heard Georgiana gasp, and almost smiled. She would be expecting Mr. Fitzwilliam Darcy to deliver one of his withering replies at a young lady taking advantage of him.

But he was Mr. William Hudson now. It would be possible to try and be more agreeable and see whether it was more comfortable as his old friend Bingley always told him it would be.

"I fear my inability to dance today is not able to be put aside for tomorrow." He smiled at Miss Bennet. "I am sure you have heard from Miss Lucas that her father told her I have been limping since we arrived in these parts. It is not a ruse to be aloof."

She was studying his face carefully. "I am happy it is not a ruse, sir. But I am sorry to hear that the injury is genuine. I hope that you will soon be fully recovered."

She had uncommonly fine, dark eyes, he noticed. It would be possible to — no. He pulled his gaze away.

"Thank you, Miss Bennet. Do I understand that you will be at Lucas Lodge tomorrow as well, then?"

"Indeed. The whole country goes, and they are great fun and an opportunity to become acquainted with many people." She was watching him carefully. There was a little tiny frown between her brows. What had he done wrong?

"There, Georgie, you will know someone other than me at the gathering tomorrow." He turned, with an effort, to his sister.

"Oh yes!" she smiled with evident relief.

"Miss Bennet, I am afraid I am quite a reticent person and I have been afraid of having to meet so many new people."

Miss Bennet squeezed her arm, and her smile was warm. Why hadn't she smiled like that at him?

"Miss Hudson, you must not worry at all. We will be so pleased to get to know you." She glanced at him before turning her attention back to Georgiana.

"I will ask my father to call on your brother very soon. Then he can return the call and you will be able to visit us at Longbourn." She leaned closer.

"No one can be shy at Longbourn. I am one of five sisters!"

"Five?" Georgiana couldn't believe her ears. "And — do you have any brothers?"

"No." Miss Bennet laughed. "Apart from my father, we are a household of ladies. So it is loud and uninhibited, and my father hides in his book room."

Mr. Darcy forced a smile, but he was appalled. He could quite imagine what it was like, but Georgiana seemed interested and perhaps it would not be as bad for her as he feared.

CHAPTER 6

"*O*h, Jane, you'll be so interested to see Mr. Hudson tomorrow." Elizabeth swung on the post of her sister's bed as she watched her brushing her hair.

"Do you think you are becoming partial to him, Lizzy?" Jane glanced up at her.

Elizabeth thought about it for a moment. "No, I don't think so. But something seems — not quite right." She chewed her lip. "It seems that he is a true gentleman, and yet he's not dressed like one, or driving in a carriage that seems appropriate." She made a face in the glass behind Jane.

"I think he's not quite what he tries to seem." She sat on the edge of the bed. "But his sister is really sweet. She's very shy and quiet. But I do think she wants to be friendly. She just seems to have no experience of people. How can someone be like that?"

Jane turned round. "How old did you say she is?"

"She's fifteen. Just one year older than Lydia. But she seems so much younger. And she's very ladylike."

Jane turned back to the glass and began to braid her hair for the night. "You must remember, Lizzy, that Lydia is certainly not what most people expect of a girl her age. She is very forward and confident."

"Indeed she is, Jane, indeed she is." Elizabeth sighed. "Sometimes I think that any man either of us begins to be partial to, Lydia tries really hard to capture their attention and affections from us."

Jane concentrated on her braiding. "I think it is understandable, Lizzy. The younger the child, the more shocking they have to be to get any attention."

"I don't care whether it is understandable or not, I think her behaviour is dreadful and she drags Kitty down with her." Lizzy got up and stood right behind Jane, watching.

"I wish Mama or Father would check her." She looked at her sister, a little desperately. "How would you feel if you were partial to a gentleman and Lydia frightened him away with her behaviour?"

"I don't know why you have suddenly become sensible of this, Lizzy." Jane smiled at her through the glass. "Unless you are secretly taken with this Mr. Hudson?"

"I am not." Elizabeth declared. "We talked about it yesterday, if you recall, before we even had the news of his arrival in the country."

"Oh, yes. I remember." Jane smiled. "But we can do nothing, Lizzy. You know that. All we can do is not let it concern us and cause us distress."

She stood up and embraced her sister. "Dearest Lizzy. I so want you to be happy and content with your life."

"And I will be, Jane. For you." Elizabeth forced an untroubled smile. "Goodnight, Jane. I will see you in the morning."

THE NEXT EVENING, the Bennet ladies all walked down the lane to Lucas Lodge. Mr. Bennet had said he would not go.

"For I have been as sociable as I can be today, and called on Mr. Hudson for you this morning. Now he may come here and bring his sister with him. That is what you asked of me, and I will do no more today."

"Oh, Mr. Bennet! You are so difficult!" Mrs. Bennet didn't care, really. She was looking forward to meeting Mr. Hudson and then having a good gossip about him to her sister, Mrs. Phillips.

There was not really any benefit to that new gentleman coming to the area, since he was obviously without fortune, but it was always interesting to have someone new to gossip about.

Elizabeth watched her mother, amused. Her feelings and opinions were always so obvious, even before she stated them.

But she already felt rather discomposed. She liked Georgie Hudson and didn't want the shy young girl to be put off coming to visit her at Longbourn.

And as she walked demurely behind her mother and Jane, she felt equally as discomposed on behalf of the aloof Mr. Hudson. Why she was anxious about the evening for him, she didn't know. He seemed the sort of person who was perfectly able to act on his own behalf, but she was uneasy, she admitted it to herself.

Certain in her own mind that he was acting a part, she almost felt herself part of the conspiracy to keep his secret. That was silly, she chided herself. She had met him only yesterday, briefly, and discovered he had an injury. She could see lines of pain on his face, but they were new. So his injury was recent.

She wondered how he had come by it, but it certainly wasn't her place to ask.

As they walked along, she heard Kitty and Lydia giggling and gossiping behind her. Her mother was haranguing Jane in front of her and as Mary was walking beside her in a disapproving silence, she had time to think.

So why was she thinking about Mr. Hudson? It must just be because they hadn't had anyone new in the area for a long time.

His face intruded into her thoughts. He had an aristocratic face, the face of someone with far superior breeding and she wondered what had happened in his past to make him end up here in a totally new, strange place with his sister.

"HELLO, LIZZY." Charlotte Lucas greeted her friend as Elizabeth entered the salon at Lucas Lodge. "It is good to see you."

"Indeed I am happy to be here, Charlotte." Elizabeth looked round the room. All the early regulars were there and the room buzzed with conversation.

Charlotte surveyed the room, amused. "As you can probably discover, Lizzy, much of the talk is about Mr. and Miss Hudson. I hope they are not put off by it."

Elizabeth agreed. "Miss Hudson is extremely shy. It might make her appear proud, but I hope she does not take fright."

"Have you met her then, Lizzy? Already?"

"Yes." Elizabeth took a glass from the servant's tray. "We met yesterday in Meryton. She was in the milliner's, buying some ribbons."

Charlotte leaned close. "And was Mr. Hudson with her?"

"He waited outside, in a rather battered-looking chaise. She took me over to introduce me."

"Tell me more," her friend urged. "What was he like? My father called on Tuesday and says he is very handsome, but when he called here, Father did not call us in to be introduced."

"Yes, I suppose he is handsome," Elizabeth said slowly. "He is very aloof, though. I do not think the company here will get much out of him."

"Oh, I believe they have arrived." Charlotte looked up. "If Miss Hudson is so shy, perhaps you will come with me to reassure her of your presence."

Elizabeth turned and followed her friend to the door.

Miss Hudson was clinging to her brother's arm. She looked completely overwhelmed. Sir William Lucas was greeting him pompously and the two girls had to wait a little behind him.

When Sir William had run out of steam a little, Charlotte put her hand on his arm, and he stepped back and saw his daughter. He pulled her forward.

"Let me introduce my daughter Charlotte to you, sir. She is very hospitable."

Charlotte curtsied, and Mr. and Miss Hudson returned her greeting formally.

She smiled at the girl. "I think you have met my great friend, Elizabeth Bennet?" and she pulled Elizabeth forward.

Elizabeth smiled at the girl. "Why not come with me, Miss Hudson? I know a quiet corner where there are some seats and I can tell you all the interesting gossip about the neighbours."

"I'd like that." But the girl's hand tightened on her brother's arm.

Elizabeth laughed. "We will allow your brother to come too, if you like, Miss Hudson. But I warn you, all the mothers will be descending on me to introduce him."

She happened to glance at his face. It was as

impassive as it had been before, but she could sense his distaste.

"This way then, please, Mr. Hudson." She had to do something, and she led them to the corner of the room she had noticed afforded protection from behind. She was sure that Miss Hudson would feel happier sitting in a corner.

CHAPTER 7

*M*r. Darcy followed Miss Bennet through the crowded room, trying not to limp too noticeably. Sir William Lucas obviously felt his little gatherings were the centre of the community and attendance almost seemed to be compulsory.

He frowned. It was not a good place for Georgiana to meet people. But there was nothing much he could do about it, and he was completely dependent on this Miss Bennet, whom he knew almost nothing about.

"There!" she'd reached the little corner and it was empty of people. "I think if we make our base here and then we can sally forth to be sociable if we have to and retreat back here when you have had enough."

He looked at the chairs. It was a good plan of hers, and perhaps they could get away after a decent interval if he played on his injury causing him discomfort.

He scowled. It would be true. Since the apothecary had called that afternoon and changed the dressing, his leg had given him nothing but a deep-seated ache with added sharp little stabbing pains which was difficult to cope with.

"Are you not in agreement with my plan, sir?" Miss Bennet was staring at him challengingly.

"What? Oh, yes. It is a sound plan, Miss Bennet. I thank you."

Her chin was tipped up defiantly. But she smiled. Her smile did not reach her eyes. "I thought, with your frown, that you disapproved."

He forced his face to a smile. Georgiana needed friendly young women around her.

"I apologise for my expression, Miss Bennet. The apothecary seems to have placed a thousand blades in my wound when he changed the dressings this afternoon. I was frowning at the discomfort."

"Oh, I'm sorry." Her challenging expression was replaced with one of concern as she peered down at his leg.

Taking complete charge of the situation, she

waved a hand at the chair in the middle, set back from the other two.

"Why don't you take that middle chair, Miss Hudson? Then we'll be between you and everyone else."

She waved at another. "Mr. Hudson, if you take that one, your injured leg will not be where any passer-by can knock it."

"That is thoughtful, thank you." He lowered himself into the chair, hoping against hope he wouldn't have to keep getting to his feet to greet people.

But she wasn't listening. She'd turned and was scanning the room. He watched. What was she looking for?

He saw her beckon a servant over. A few murmured words and then she sat down on the other side of Georgiana.

Darcy looked at his sister. She looked much better, and her breathing was beginning to return to normal.

The servant reappeared with a footstool, which he placed deferentially beside Darcy.

"Thank you." Miss Bennet nodded her thanks at the man, then she looked at Darcy.

"I thought raising your injured leg might reduce the throbbing, sir. And it will justify you not rising to your feet to greet every man, woman or child who might approach you."

Darcy smiled appreciatively. "I thank you for your thoughtfulness, Miss Bennet."

He watched her as she turned to Georgiana. "I hope this feels a little more comfortable for you, Miss Hudson?" She waved a passing servant over and they all took a drink.

"It is a great pity the gathering is being held so soon after your arrival, or you might have been able to get to know some of us in easier surroundings."

"I did try to say that we should perhaps come to the next occasion," Mr. Darcy said. "But Sir William is persistent."

She laughed. "Indeed he is, but a more genuine gentleman you could not meet." Darcy could not believe the way her face lit up as she laughed. Her eyes — he had to see her laugh again, and soon.

But he forced his gaze away and across the room. He must not allow himself to be distracted from his task. He was here to protect Georgiana, that was all. This young woman was able to help her by being a friend to her.

But that was all she must ever be. He would not allow himself to think of her playful liveliness, her dancing eyes, and her thoughtfulness in obtaining the footstool.

His bad leg stuck out in front of him, protecting Georgiana. And the pain was lessening now, she must know what she was talking about.

A plain-looking young lady took the pianoforte and began to play, accompanying herself in a dreary and tuneless song.

Some younger girls were loudly competing for the attention of a very few young men. The whole situation was insupportable and he sat there in silent indignation at having been brought to this.

Despite looking across the room, he could hear her talking to his sister.

"I was hoping you'd feel able to call me Elizabeth or Lizzy soon, Miss Hudson. I find Miss Bennet so very formal."

He heard Georgiana replying. "I'd like that, Elizabeth. My name is Georgia, though everyone calls me Georgie."

He let himself relax slightly. If she could keep her part going, things would be much, much easier.

He muttered slightly. He should not have looked around the room. Sir William Lucas was walking towards him, a gentleman in black garb beside him.

He couldn't remain seated, he felt at too much of a disadvantage. He levered himself to his feet.

"Mr. Hudson," Sir William said. "Allow me to introduce Mr. Stephenson. Mr. Stephenson, this is Mr. Hudson, who has just moved into Bayford House with his sister." Sir William nodded jovially at Georgiana, who jumped to her feet, looking startled and nervous.

Mr. Darcy bowed. "Delighted to make your acquaintance, sir."

"Indeed, sir, indeed." The man bowed deeply, obsequiously. "I am most grieved that I was from home this week and therefore did not call on you sooner to greet the new additions to my flock."

Darcy stared at him in amazement. "I was not expecting you to call, sir."

"Oh, but I always call on new arrivals to my parish, sir, always. And, given that you have taken Bayford House, why, we are close neighbours."

Darcy felt Georgiana shrink away slightly. He wasn't surprised. The clergyman gave a rather ingratiating appearance. He tried not to let his lip curl.

"Be not dismayed, sir. I have taken no offence whatsoever. But I pray you excuse me if I sit down, my leg pains me to stand." It was really quite relaxing, Mr. Hudson had no pride to lose by confessing his infirmity, and Darcy was delighted that he was not using his own name, which would mean he was forced to continue to stand and pretend no pain could prevent him doing whatever he wished.

"Of course, dear sir. Of course." The dreadful man appeared to be about to draw up a chair and converse and Mr. Darcy turned appalled eyes to his sister. But his gaze stopped at Miss Bennet's face. She nodded slightly at him, before turning to the clergyman.

"Why, Mr. Stephenson, it's so kind of you to come over to invite me to dance. There are so few gentlemen this evening, I had quite despaired of any opportunity to stand up tonight."

Mr. Stephenson looked a little dazed as Elizabeth Bennet led him away, and Darcy and Georgiana watched their saviour as she led the way to the piano.

In a very few moments, the sound of a long dance echoed out and a few couples took to the floor of the adjoining room where the carpet had been rolled back.

Darcy watched as Miss Bennet danced, her face brightly cheerful, but emotion never reaching her eyes.

Why was she doing this for them? His eyes narrowed as he watched. He felt Georgiana touching his arm.

"I'm sure she's just very kind and thoughtful,

William," she whispered. "I know you're suspicious."

He looked at her, and kept his voice very low. "We know Mr. Hudson isn't real. It wouldn't be fair to her."

She drooped slightly. "I know. It's all my fault, William. Even your leg."

He could feel the attention of other people. "We had better leave this conversation for later." Even though he was sure they wouldn't be overheard, they must stay in the parts they were playing.

"I think we will be able to go soon, Georgie. I can quite truthfully say my leg is paining me."

She looked anxiously at him. "Is it? I am sorry." She watched Elizabeth for a moment and glanced back at him. "May I ask Elizabeth to call on me at Bayford House? I should like to have her as a friend."

"Of course." He knew she needed a friend. Miss Bennet was quiet and reasonably refined, compared to some of the people here, even if he knew her background must be dreadful.

But she was thoughtful, and kind. And he couldn't take his eyes from her face. He stifled his groan. He hoped that he could find somewhere to go when she called — at least until he'd talked some sense into his errant mind.

CHAPTER 8

*E*lizabeth ended the dance with great relief. Catching Charlotte's eye and receiving the tiny nod of acceptance, she deposited Mr. Stephenson with her friend, mouthing the words *thank you* behind his back.

She took a deep breath and went to her mother. "Mama, may I introduce you to Mr. Hudson and Miss Hudson? She is very shy and I would like her to meet you before I invite her to Longbourn." It would be much better for Georgie to get only a few minutes of Mrs. Bennet here, and be able to prepare herself for when she called.

She led her mother over to the corner where they were based. She noticed Mr. Hudson's eyes on her thoughtfully.

"Mr. Hudson, Miss Hudson, may I introduce

my mother? Mama, Mr. and Miss Hudson."

He was on his feet again. "Delighted, Madam."

Elizabeth knew he had noticed her mother sitting next to Lady Lucas. She knew he had heard the strident voice discussing the new arrivals and their lack of fortune. She knew he would think she had the worst possible mother.

She stood demurely behind her mother and caught his eye. Somehow, she knew he could see the defiance within her, the defiance mixed with shame.

But she had to introduce her mother. If he wanted to stop the friendship between her and his sister, it would be better done now, before Georgie's affections had developed further.

He should not mind, his current circumstances were probably worse than her father's. But he was high-born. She didn't know quite how she knew, but she did.

He straightened. "Mrs. Bennet," he said. "My sister has asked me whether your daughter might call on her at Bayford House. Might we say tomorrow?"

Elizabeth wondered what the expression on her mother's face was.

"Well, that's up to Lizzy, I suppose." She obviously had no designs on him for one of her daughters and she peered suspiciously at his leg. "It will be better when you are able to dance. We are very short of eligible men for the girls to practice their dancing."

"Mama ..." Elizabeth shouldn't have been surprised at her mother's ability to embarrass her. She steered her mother away as soon as she could, before returning to them as they prepared to leave, accompanied by Jane.

"Might I introduce my elder sister, Miss Jane Bennet? I thought you'd be happier having met someone else from my family before you call upon us, Georgie." She turned to her sister.

"Jane, this is Mr. Hudson and his sister, Miss Georgia Hudson."

She smiled possessively as her sister curtsied. She wanted him to know she had family she could be proud of.

"Delighted to meet you, sir. And Miss Hudson." Jane smiled warmly at the girl in front of her. "I'm sure you'll soon make many friends here in Meryton."

Mrs. Bennet's hectoring tones could be heard across the room, and Jane cast a look of resignation at Elizabeth.

"I must go, Lizzy."

She turned to the others. "If you will please excuse me?"

CHAPTER 9

*H*e turned his attention to Miss Bennet. "Would you do my sister the honour of calling tomorrow?" Mr. Darcy was more anxious than he cared to admit that she might not wish to call.

"Of course! I would like that." Miss Bennet's eyes crinkled delightfully at the corners as she smiled genuinely at Georgiana. He wished she was looking at him.

He turned away and reached for his stick. He must stop this. The real Mr. Hudson might develop designs on such a young lady, but she certainly did not have the right breeding or background for Mr. Darcy to even consider.

He could hear her talking to Georgiana.

"I wonder, Georgie, if you have any experience of drawing and painting? I have been fairly restless recently, and I was thinking I might like to attempt some sketching. But I do not seem to have any talent and need to be shown where I am going amiss."

"Oh, yes! I enjoy sketching."

He watched a shadow cross his sister's face.

"But I do not know quite where my pencils are at the moment."

He was pleased when Miss Bennet came to her rescue. "If you do not mind, I could bring some pencils. My middle sister fancies herself an artist, and I am sure she would allow me to borrow them."

"Then that is all arranged." Mr. Darcy wanted to get away. Being in Miss Bennet's company was far too disturbing for a settled mind.

He found the footstool had been moved out of his way so that he did not have to take care to avoid it. He was touched by her simple actions, done without artifice or fanfare.

He knew no one else who seemed to care about trying to make his life easier, no one who would have considered how she could help make his wound less painful.

He had to admit that even Georgiana had not thought about asking for a footstool for him, although he instantly excused her by thinking she would have left such an action to the servants.

Surely that was as it should be? But he had a little warm feeling inside that he couldn't remember before. Someone seemed to care about him. And not for his money or his estates.

You must not become involved, he berated himself. *She will only be hurt when you leave this all behind and return to your real life.*

He nodded curtly at her, she must not think well of him. He saw the warmth in her eyes change to hurt, and he could not bear it.

"We shall both look forward to seeing you, Miss Bennet. But now, we must go."

"Of course." She looked puzzled now, as if she could not make him out, but she walked alongside Georgiana to the door.

"I asked Sir William to arrange for your coach to be brought to the door," she said. "You will not have to stand for long."

There she was again, he thought. Making things easier for him that no one else would have considered.

But she stopped at the door. "It has been most enjoyable, Georgia, renewing our acquaintance. I will look forward to calling in the morning." She curtsied to Georgiana, and then to him.

"Goodnight, sir." She barely waited for them

to return their farewells, and then she turned and was lost in the crowd.

He would not allow himself to gaze after her, and put his mind to navigating the steps down to the chaise and Mr. Thomas waiting with the driver.

Georgiana was tired, he could see that, but she was still cheerful.

"I am so happy it is over, William. But I think Elizabeth helped a lot to make it easier for me. Do you not agree?"

"I do." He nodded and watched as the horse drew them slowly home in the fading light.

He wondered how she would get home. Surely they wouldn't walk? He didn't even know how far it was to Longbourn.

THE NEXT MORNING DAWNED FAIR, and he and Georgiana were up and breakfasting quite early despite their evening out. There was only the one dining room and he missed having a breakfast room that faced southeast to the rising sun.

He hoped they were early enough. He wasn't sure what time a young lady would visit another in the countryside, and he certainly could not ask the servants.

Still, his breakfast was becoming more acceptable to him, with coffee, and the morning newspaper to peruse.

He glanced over at Georgiana. She seemed tolerably cheerful and composed.

As for himself, he was chagrined that he would need to be out of sight when she called and for the time she spent with his sister.

Because she was calling on Georgiana, not himself. She could not do that in any case, could she? Or was it different in the country?

No, of course she could not do that. Sir William Lucas had called on him and waited for his return visit before the proprieties had been upheld. And Mr. Bennet too, had called on him. Although Miss Elizabeth Bennet coming here before he had returned the call on her father — he frowned slightly. No one had seemed to think that was amiss. No, country manners were not so very different to the town.

He smiled at his newspaper, remembering his friend Bingley. He was looking for an estate to rent in the country. But his charming smile and amiable manners would make him much approved of wherever he settled. His smile widened. Bingley's fortune would help, too, especially among the ladies — and their mothers. He doubted Bingley would have had a moment to himself, had he been at the gathering last night.

"You seem amused, William. Is there an item of news you would share?" Georgiana was smiling as if his own mood were infectious.

"What? Oh, no. I was thinking how Mr. Bingley would fare if he was here." Mr. Darcy looked over the newspaper at her. She giggled.

"I think every mother would be fighting over him for their daughter's advantage."

He smiled. "Indeed. I think you're right." He folded up the newspaper for later. He would need something to occupy his time when he sat in the library while Miss Bennet was spending time with Georgiana.

He reached to refill his coffee cup.

"Perhaps when you stop for tea, you might permit me to join you and Miss Bennet for a short while?" he couldn't prevent the words, and was as surprised as Georgiana seemed.

"Of course, if you should wish it, William."

"Thank you." He wondered what she thought of his request. But at least it meant he could pass a few words with Miss Bennet. His lips tightened. He should not be so pleased about that.

They saw Mrs. James hurry through to the front door. "I have just seen Miss Bennet walking across the field, sir!"

He put down his cup. "Walking?"

"Yes, sir." Mrs. James laughed. "Miss Elizabeth Bennet walks everywhere! She knows every path and field — much better even than the farmers who work the land." She hurried to the front door.

Mr. Darcy looked at the table with distaste. "We should not receive her like this."

"She is very early," Georgiana seemed amused. "Perhaps she would like to join us."

"Perhaps." But he was not that comfortable about it.

CHAPTER 10

*E*lizabeth acknowledged Mrs. James as she opened the front door. She did not know her well, but enough to recognise her.

"Please come in, Miss Bennet."

"Thank you."

She followed the housekeeper through the hall. She'd never been to Bayford House before. It had been owned by a pair of elderly sisters, and the last of them had died only a few months before. Their nephew must be delighted the house had let so quickly.

She realised she had arrived too early when she was led through to the dining room.

"Oh, I am so sorry! Would you like me to come back later?"

"Not at all." Mr. Hudson acknowledged her gravely. "Please join us." He indicated a seat next to Georgia and looked over at Mrs. James.

"Please bring fresh tea for Miss Bennet."

Elizabeth sank into a chair next to Georgia, deciding that the formality in this house really wasn't quite appropriate for this area and determining not to be cowed by it.

"Good morning, Georgie!" She indicated the sheets of drawing paper and her small pocket bag. "I've brought all the sketching materials I could find." She gave her hostess a sidelong glance.

"I'm very hopeful that I will surprise my sisters with my new-found accomplishments very soon!"

The girl looked startled. "I hope I can help you."

Elizabeth laughed. "Do not be anxious, Georgie. You will soon get to know me and find that I am an inveterate tease."

She was rewarded as the girl relaxed a little and gave her a small smile in return.

The rustle of the newspaper told her that Mr. Hudson had returned to reading and she relaxed a little. She did hope, though, that he would disappear after breakfast and allow her and Georgie time to get to know one another.

If her call was to remain stiffly formal, she wasn't sure whether she'd want to return.

She turned to the girl. "What sort of things are you used to drawing? Do you paint flowers from the garden, or sketch from paintings?"

Georgie looked animated. "I have done both, Elizabeth." She looked thoughtful. "But I cannot believe that your governess or schoolteacher did not teach you the elements of form and structure."

"Oh, Georgie!" Elizabeth laughed. "I have never been to school and Mama only got us a tutor for a short while, until we knew our letters and were beginning to read." She felt a little ashamed of her family.

"Mama was not concerned with teaching us much, but my sister Jane — you met her last night — is excellent at needlework, so she has taught me that. And I like music, so I was able to teach myself to play and sing."

But the newspaper had stopped rustling, which meant that Mr. Hudson was paying far too much attention to the conversation. She drank the rest of her tea down hastily.

"Perhaps we can take the pencils into the garden, Georgie. I would love to see how you approach the drawing of flowers in real life."

They both curtsied to Mr. Hudson as they left the room, and his grave glance unsettled Elizabeth enough to make her much relieved as they left the house.

Wandering around the garden, she pointed out a little wild area at the corner. "Shall we choose some wild flowers to examine, Georgie?"

As they made their way over, she wondered at the conversation they had just had. Georgia had implied she had had a governess and been to school. Both of those were expensive luxuries for a woman.

Mr. and Mrs. Bennet had not deemed either necessary for their daughters. And Elizabeth was sorry about it. She would have loved the opportunity to learn about new things and far-flung places that she might never see.

And Lydia and Kitty might have more than bonnets and dresses, gentlemen and soldiers in their heads. She shook her head, suddenly sad.

Georgia glanced at her. "Are you not happy being here, Elizabeth?"

"Oh, Georgie, no! Please do not think that." Elizabeth hastened to reassure her. "I was just sad that my family did not think it worth paying for an education for their daughters." She made a face. "I know it is expensive." She tucked her arm in Georgia's.

"Your brother clearly feels a good education is

worth paying for, even if the money is hard to find. You have a very devoted brother, Georgie."

"Oh, yes! I know that, Elizabeth, and I am so grateful to him. You cannot believe how much he has sacrificed for me. Even now, he is still thinking only of me."

"You are very fortunate." Elizabeth was surprised by the girl's fervent tone. She decided to lighten her visit.

"Now, let's see if we can find some flowers that you think a beginner might be able to draw without it looking too dreadful."

Georgia laughed and they began searching through the flowerbeds. "Look. These yellow ones. They look a bit like daisies. I can show you how to shape and shade the petals today."

"All right," Elizabeth agreed. "It sounds like a good idea."

Georgia looked around with a furrowed brow. "But it might be better to go back to the sitting room. There is a table in the window and you will be more comfortable while you are concentrating."

Elizabeth saw her glance over.

"My brother will be in the library by now, Elizabeth. Although I expect he will join us when it is time for morning tea."

She had to be aware this young woman was

more astute than she had surmised. Elizabeth reached to pick a few of the flowers. "I'm very happy to be wherever you think will be best."

In the sitting room, they sat by the window, and both sketched the flowers in various places on the paper.

"Look, it's like this, Elizabeth." Georgia deftly drew a few lines. "See, a twisted petal shows the reality of the flower. You don't want perfection in every one of the flowers you draw, or people will think you are tracing from a book."

Elizabeth bent over the paper. "Like this?" she bit her lip as she drew the lines.

"Yes, that's good." Georgia was watching. "But maybe try and be a bit lighter, more flowing? I'm sure when you write, you can flow the letters as you make the words." She seized a pencil.

"It's easier to learn it right at the beginning."

She began criss-crossing the paper with flowing lines. "Yes, just like that."

They both looked up, startled, as Mrs. James knocked and came in carrying a tray of pastries, followed by the scullery maid with a tray of tea.

"Thank you." Georgia was absent-minded and when Elizabeth looked back at the paper, a few beautifully formed daisies had sprung to life.

"How did you do those? They're beautiful!"

Georgie laughed. "You've done the same. Now

just see if you can tell what I've added to finish the sketch."

Elizabeth bent carefully over the drawing, looking at the lines of shading that had suddenly brought the flowers to life.

"Go on, then," Georgia urged her. "You shade yours, too."

$\mathcal{M}$r. Darcy watched from the doorway, amused by their close attention as Miss Bennet carefully drew a few lines.

"They don't look like yours, Georgie." She frowned and compared them.

He was really pleased that, for the first time since they had arrived here, Georgiana looked happy and cheerful. It would be worth enduring his own discomfort at the presence of this girl if she could entertain his sister so well.

He cleared his throat and both of them looked around, startled.

"May I join you for tea, Georgia?" He was going to anyway. He had spent the last few hours wondering what they had been talking about, wishing he knew more of the girl whose wit and intelligence belied her unsuitable background.

"Of course, William!" Georgiana straightened up and Miss Bennet followed her lead in a brief curtsey.

As they sat over their refreshments, he watched his sister. Already she seemed to have increasing poise and confidence as she poured the tea and Miss Bennet offered him the plate of pastries.

"So, do you feel you are improving in your artistic skills?" he tried to make polite conversation, knowing how poor he was at finding the right words when amongst those he did not know well.

Her eyebrow lifted slightly. But she smiled politely. "I am not sure that all Georgie's talent will make that possible, sir. But I have certainly enjoyed myself, and I hope Georgie has found the occupation diverting."

"Oh, I have!" His sister was eager to show her enjoyment. She turned to her new friend.

"You must not take my brother's words too seriously." She gave him a sidelong glance.

"He is very protective of me."

"Indeed." Miss Bennet sat back and regarded him. Her smile was mischievous. "I think Mr. Hudson perhaps wonders what we have been conversing about."

He cursed under his breath as he felt his face suffuse with colour. How could this young woman get under his skin so?

"If it will relieve your mind, sir, we hardly discussed you at all." She laughed lightly, and he instantly wondered how he could arrange to hear it again.

"I am relieved to hear it." He forced a smile and hastily drank his tea. Perhaps he had been wrong to join them. He must go back to his library, even if the selection of books was so dreadful as to make for poor entertainment.

"Although — *hardly*?"

She laughed again, more openly this time. "We will not always tell you the content of our deliberations, sir. But this time I will ease your mind. I merely said to your sister how rare it is to find a gentleman who thinks so highly of the importance of a good education for girls, no matter how much it costs him. It showed how devoted you are to your sister."

"My mind is much relieved." He bowed. "I am much flattered." He felt rather guilty. It had not cost him anything really, to pay for Georgiana's education. He would never miss that amount of money, he had far more than he needed.

"You are right in that I am devoted to my

sister." That much at least was true, and he smiled indulgently over at Georgiana, who flushed a becoming pink and looked down.

Miss Bennet looked from him to his sister and seemed to decide that a change of tone was needed.

"I am happy to see you have a piano here, Georgie. Is there any music that was left here? If not, I will have to find some at home. I enjoy playing duets."

Georgiana jumped to her feet. "I think there is some old music in the chest beside the piano — but it is not in tune."

There was that lilting laugh again. "That will then prove a challenge for us to find a new way of playing together."

He could not stay. His mind was too much taken up with this young lady. Mr. Darcy put his cup down and rose to his feet.

"You will please excuse me. Thank you for allowing me to join you for some refreshment."

They looked over at him. "Will the noise disturb you if we attempt some music?" Miss Bennet seemed concerned.

"Not at all." He bowed gravely. "If it did, I would take my book and sit in the garden."

"I hope your injury would not be too painful if you had to do that." There she was again, showing more consideration than he was used to receiving. A warm feeling in his chest drew his attention.

"Not at all, Miss Bennet." He bowed at them gravely and escaped to the library.

Selecting a book at random, he flung himself down in the big leather chair beside the darkened fireplace.

How could he do this? He had much better keep his distance from Miss Bennet. Her laugh echoed in his mind. He smiled, that laugh could bewitch him if he wasn't careful. He frowned, she had not been laughing at him, had she?

He thought back. No, he was sure she hadn't. He felt a strange moisture at the back of his eyes. She seemed to take such care over his well-being. Care such as he had not known since his mother had died.

He blinked furiously. He must be going soft in the head. He levered himself to his feet and limped to the window, scowling.

What would she think of him if he let her think there was some hope of him and then she found out where he was really from?

No. He turned back to the chair. She would never forgive him, and it was right that she should not.

He dropped heavily into the chair. What was

he thinking of? She was entrancing to be sure, but her background was totally unfit to ever be mistress of Pemberley.

He bit his lip. But she wasn't trying to inveigle her way into his affections to become mistress of Pemberley. He knew ladies like that, he could tell their attentions from a mile away.

No, Miss Bennet would know the settled opinion in the neighbourhood, that Mr. Hudson did not have an estate worthy of pursuing for their daughters. Miss Bennet was merely being kind because she was a kind and thoughtful person.

And that made her a danger to his peace of mind. He looked at the book he had selected in disgust. Why was he wasting his time with it?

He dropped it on the side table. He did not want to write any letters that were not utterly necessary, but he was frustrated that he knew nothing of what was going on back in London and Ramsgate about how the gangs that threatened Georgiana were being hunted down.

The sound of the small, battered piano intruded into his mind. The sound was muted, as the door was thick, but enough penetrated under it to make it obvious even to him that the lack of tuning made the tune unpleasant to hear.

Miss Elizabeth Bennet's laugh drifted through the music and the music changed to a racing lilt that threaded through his mind and made his heart race.

He sat forwards and faced the closed door, listening to the tune as he'd never listened before. He knew it wasn't Georgiana playing. Her technique was more skilled, but less exuberant. Miss Bennet may not have had any formal tuition, but her sheer love of music shone through the notes and made him smile.

As she stopped playing, he sat back in the chair and stared into the distance. He wondered if he could send Mr. Thomas to find someone to tune the piano. Surely other families worked out a way to afford it?

He could not expect Georgiana to keep up with her studies and her practice with a piano so abominably looked-after.

He heard the front door close and surmised that they had gone out into the gardens to walk a while. He sighed and got up, going to the small writing desk. If he wrote to Colonel Fitzwilliam, he could send the letter north to Pemberley first, instructing that it be sent to Matlock House from there. Then it would not be traced back to Hertfordshire.

He smiled. He wondered if he was imputing too much skill and opportunity to the gangs who wanted his sister. But he dare not take the risk.

He hoped to God that he would soon be able to hear the news that they were safe, that he and Georgiana would soon be able to return to their lives in London.

But his heart was unaccountably heavy. He wondered if he would be able to leave Miss Bennet with quite the equanimity he would hope for and expect.

A fleeting thought crossed his mind. Would Miss Bennet be sorry they had left the country? If she did, would it be for Georgiana alone, or might there be a regret at not ... No, he must not think of her in this way.

CHAPTER 12

*E*lizabeth trod lightly through the fields, glancing up at the sky. Today she thought it might rain, but the weather had been kind to her so far as she slowly wore a pathway in the grass from Longbourn to Bayford.

For two weeks now she had spent at least part of each day in the company of Georgie Hudson and she was no closer to coming to understand the reason why this odd family had come to be in the country.

She smiled. The girl was good company and Elizabeth was growing very fond of her.

Her shyness was gradually easing, and Elizabeth had eventually prevailed upon her enough to entreat her brother to allow her to visit Longbourn.

Mr. Hudson was uncommonly reluctant to allow his sister out of his sight and his opposition to this had made Georgie hesitant to importune him further.

Elizabeth had thought it absurd, and been quite determined to wear them down with her suggestions of things they could do.

Finally, she had brought an invitation to dine at Longbourn, and the sight of Mr. Hudson, serious and polite, but very out of place at their table had almost reduced her to a fit of mirth.

But she had relented and after dinner had seen them to their carriage with a suggestion that she come to Bayford House the next day with some small twigs of blossoms from the late-flowering cherry trees at Longbourn.

Georgie had looked at her with almost pathetic relief and her brother's face had suddenly relaxed too.

Elizabeth puzzled over it as she walked, the twigs held loosely in her hand. She was certain in her own mind that they were well-born and had lived a privileged life. While she didn't know what had led them to this new life here, she was pleased at their welcome of her, that they had not seemed too proud to speak to her.

They had even seemed to try to copy her ways, breakfasting earlier each day so that Georgie was ready for her visits, and Mr. Hudson solemnly enquiring after her father's farm business.

But they never talked of their past, never said what part of the country they had come from, never mentioned how Mr. Hudson had come across his injury, even when the topic was pertinent, as when the apothecary had appeared at Bayford House to tend it.

At least he seemed to be better. He no longer used his cane to lean on so heavily, and he sometimes could be seen pacing around the garden.

He seemed to her to be a caged being, waiting; just waiting.

She wondered what he was waiting for, and what would happen when it did.

She jumped the final stile and smiled. Perhaps he thought he would suddenly become wealthy again. She wondered that if he did, would he still look at her in that grave and serious way that made her heart give a little jump whenever she saw it?

Don't be silly, I'm friends with Georgie. I'm helping her overcome her reticence because I like her. It's nothing to do whether her brother is handsome, or makes my heart race when he looks at me.

She shook her thoughts away. She didn't want him to guess how she felt, in fact, she didn't want to acknowledge even to herself how she felt. She hadn't even confided in Jane. And that showed just how important he was becoming to her.

She swung into the road and hurried the few yards down it to turn in at the gate.

Mrs. James met her with her usual smile. "Good morning, Miss Bennet. Miss Hudson is waiting for you in the sitting room."

"Thank you." Elizabeth was welcome now to go straight through to join her friend.

"Hello, Georgie!" She swung through to the sitting room and saw her friend's face light up when she saw her.

"Dearest Lizzy, you are so good to call each day. I do not deserve it."

Elizabeth sat down at the table beside her.

"Why do you think you don't deserve it?" She wondered why Georgie was so shy. Certainly, coming from a life of privilege, she must have been protected from those who would have shunned her.

"I ... don't know," Georgie stammered. "But you have been so kind, coming here, rather than expecting me to take my turn at coming to you."

Elizabeth laughed. "I know my home perhaps a little too noisy for you, and Lydia can be very loud."

"You see? You are so thoughtful, not expecting me to fit in." Georgie looked down at the twigs

Elizabeth had placed on the table. "It seems to me, that as the newcomer, I should have done the fitting-in."

Elizabeth reached for the sketching materials. "I know that you are very shy, and I don't want you to feel uncomfortable." She examined a twig. "I think I might try and draw this one today." She looked over at her friend. "You have been very long-suffering with my attempts at drawing, and I am grateful for your patience."

The moment passed, and the two ladies worked industriously until the tea arrived, and following it, Mr. Hudson.

This routine had been settled now. He would bow gravely, and ask after Elizabeth's family. Then he would sit by the fire and listen to their conversation, only occasionally making a comment or asking a question.

Elizabeth wasn't very comfortable with it, but she could see the way Georgie idolised her brother and she was always interested to see how they behaved together.

She sipped her tea. "I wondered, sir, if you had received a call from Sir William Lucas?"

He glanced up from pretending to read his book. She knew he pretended, because the pages never turned.

He carefully closed it and placed it on the

small table beside him. "I did, Miss Bennet. He called yesterday afternoon."

She smiled. "I thought he would wish to ensure you knew how very welcome you would be at the assembly tomorrow."

His face was impassive, but Elizabeth was sure she could see the distaste behind his eyes.

"You are correct again, madam."

She smiled into her teacup. "I considered he was most likely to enquire over your injury and your ability to dance, given the scarcity of gentlemen."

Georgie gave a muffled laugh, but Elizabeth kept her attention steadily on him. A stray thought intruded — what would it be like to dance with him, to be the object of his attention? She shivered a little, and realised he was regarding her curiously.

She made sure her expression was guileless and bland and gave him a small smile.

"Indeed, he seemed very glad that my injury is much improved." Mr. Hudson's tone dripped with irony, and Elizabeth had to smother a laugh.

"I fear you will be expected to dance the night away, sir."

He grimaced and nodded ruefully, and Elizabeth felt curiously honoured that she was permitted to see how he really felt.

"I would wish to apologise in advance for the attentions and persistence of my fellow townspeople, sir." She took another sip of her tea, regarding him over the rim of the cup.

He stretched out his legs. "I was in some hope that my lack of fortune would render me less likely of pursuit." He sounded a little resentful.

"Indeed, you might be right, Mr. Hudson." Elizabeth's heart beat fast. Was she about to find out what had happened to him?

"But I think being a popular dance partner during one assembly is very different to being pursued by all the mothers of unmarried girls in the town."

His mouth quirked in acknowledgement, but he thought carefully before answering.

"And is your mother desirous of your visits here bearing fruit in that direction?"

Elizabeth felt her face grow warm. "I do not think so, sir. You must have heard that Longbourn is entailed away from the female line. So Mama is setting her sights on rich men to secure the family."

She watched his lips tighten. But he did not speak further, and she swallowed her irritation.

Despite sharing her own family difficulties, it did not seem that she would learn the history of the Hudsons.

CHAPTER 13

*G*eorgia broke the slightly uncomfortable silence. "Elizabeth, would you agree to look at the gown I would like to wear to the assembly? We could go up to my bedchamber."

Elizabeth smiled at her, grateful for the intervention. "Of course I will. Now?"

As she followed the girl upstairs, Elizabeth wondered what would transpire over the next few weeks. Her frequent visits to Bayford House were now quite in the manner of a habit. However, although she was there to call on Georgia, Mr. Hudson was always there. Unsmiling, grave, invariably polite and proper; she could feel his attention always on her, even if he appeared to be reading.

The situation could not go on as it was. But what was she to do? Her father would never give his consent to a gentleman who had not the means to support her.

She shook her head. She mustn't think of it. Mr. Hudson had never been anything but perfectly proper, it was her own thoughts that had taken this turn and she must not countenance it.

"I was thinking I'd like to wear this blue gown, Elizabeth. I haven't worn it for such a very long time."

Elizabeth pulled her thoughts back to the present moment and stared at the gown Georgia was holding up.

"It's very beautiful, isn't it?" Her heart sank as she wondered how to stop her friend wearing it.

"Let's sit down." She drew the girl away and sat beside her on the edge of the bed.

"You know you can't really wear it, don't you?" she spoke as gently as she could, but the younger girl's eyes still filled with tears.

"Oh, Elizabeth!" Georgia clasped her friend's hand. "I'm sorry. I knew that, I suppose. But I hoped you'd say it would be all right."

"Why do you want to wear it, anyway, Georgie? I can't think you want the attention."

"No." The girl sniffed. "Well, maybe I want to

look beautiful. But really it is because it makes me feel special."

"Georgia, look at me." Elizabeth turned to face her friend. "You are special, very special. I've wondered for a long time why you are so shy, so sure that you do not deserve any special favours?"

The girl dropped her head. "I cannot tell you, Elizabeth."

"Is it that you do not want to tell me, or that you are not permitted to?"

Georgia looked up, a wavering smile beginning to break through. "I think a little of both, Elizabeth. I think you've been very patient with us."

Elizabeth jumped to her feet. "Well, let's choose a gown you can wear to the assembly, and then we can take a turn around the garden."

She went to the closet with the blue silk gown draped across her arm. The sheer luxury feel of it made her long to have a gown like that. She would feel like royalty if she wore one. She carefully hung it at the back. She wasn't likely to ever find out how it felt to wear a silken gown, so she must pull herself together.

"Elizabeth, I want to hang it at the front. I like it there." Georgie was beside her, reaching for it.

"It's your closet, Georgie. But do you think it is wise to do that?"

The girl looked puzzled. "Why should I not?"

"I can think of two very good reasons." Elizabeth smiled. "Let me challenge you to think of one." She reached for a simpler gown, hanging behind.

"This is a really pretty one. Why not wear this?"

The girl glanced at it. "I will wear that if you say so, Elizabeth. But I cannot think why I should not hang my blue gown at the front of the closet."

"I will explain when we are in the garden, I think." Elizabeth decided, and they descended the stairs, Elizabeth hoping that Mr. Hudson would not notice his sister's reddened eyes.

Fortunately, he was still in the house, and they sat on the seat under the apple tree. "I've two concerns, really, Georgie." Elizabeth stared at the dappled shade overhead. "If you look at that gown every time you open your closet, then you might never accept the reality of your life now." She smiled sympathetically at her. "It's a hard lesson, perhaps."

"But perhaps one I should hear," Georgia said quietly. She looked up.

"And what was the other reason?"

Elizabeth looked carefully at her. "You will have to excuse me if I am talking out of turn, Georgie. But have you ever thought that the servants might gossip about what they see? And if you are hiding here, you need not draw attention to things that might seem out of place."

She put her hand on the girl's arm. "Do not be distressed. I am sure everything is all right, and I am just imagining things and being overdramatic."

Georgia's head dropped. "No, you are more right than you know. But I know we can trust you."

"Of course you can. I will always be your friend, Georgie, you must know that."

As they stood and began to continue their walk around the gardens, Elizabeth saw Mr. Hudson walking out to join them.

Her heart gave another little jolt and she knew that one day soon she would have to confront her partiality and begin to curtail her visits here.

Nothing could come of her feelings. She had never had the slightest indication that he regarded her with anything other than a friend of her sister. And if his eyes did rest upon her very often, it was surely because they had so few callers to the house.

"So you have made the important decision on which gown to wear for the assembly, have you, my dear sister?"

Georgia glanced at Elizabeth, then turned to her brother. "Yes, William."

A tiny frown appeared between his brows as he looked protectively at his sister, and he glanced at Elizabeth.

He didn't say anything, though, and Elizabeth took her leave after a few more minutes.

"I am afraid that my mother will detain me at home tomorrow with the preparations for the family at the assembly. But I will see you there, and perhaps we might find another corner to sit in to begin with." She turned to Georgia. "But I very much hope we can talk to my sister Jane and my friend Charlotte. They have been looking forward to getting to know you."

"Well," the girl said doubtfully. "I suppose if you are there, I could try."

"I will be there and you will succeed. "Elizabeth laughed. "They are kindness itself and I will be very happy when we can all go together for walks and picnics."

She turned to Mr. Hudson. "Good day, sir. I will see you tomorrow at the assembly rooms."

He bowed gravely. "I look forward to it, Miss Bennet."

She curtsied back, thinking it was perfectly obvious that he did not look forward to it at all.

She wondered that he had not politely asked if

he could engage her for a dance, given that she was practically the only lady he knew well enough to ask.

But as she swung along the lane, she thought that he might not wish to leave Georgia alone by them both being on the dance floor together.

Yes, that was certainly the reason, and her steps were lighter as she hurried home. She must arrange that Jane sit with Georgia. Not for anything would she wish Mr. Hudson to find a reason not to dance with her. She would be most offended. She laughed to herself. No, it would never do.

CHAPTER 14

*M*r. Darcy muttered under his breath as he pulled his boots on. He hadn't known how much he had relied on servants to make his life easier before.

Apparently it wasn't the thing to afford an indoor manservant at his level of income and Mr. Thomas had even been concerned at the need for a driver and groom when he purchased the chaise.

Darcy sighed as he checked in the glass that his cravat was tied properly and he was properly attired. He wished almost that he dare appear looking rather dishevelled and the worse for wear.

Surely then he would find ladies finding a prior engagement than agree to dance.

But he wished to dance with Miss Elizabeth Bennet. He really wished to dance each dance with her. Even the touch of her hand on his was something he longed for.

But it would not be possible. How could he guard Georgiana properly, if he was dancing and she was sitting alone, without even her friend?

He wasn't sure what was going to happen and he had a real urge not to attend. If only he knew how infernally long they were going to have to stay here at Bayford House. Then he would know whether he could afford to cause offence or if he must continue to be careful.

He walked to the window and stared out into the dusk. The view was becoming familiar, but it still felt like a prison and he could see no end in sight.

He scowled. The newspaper that morning had another of the advertisements in it. The Hudson Shipping Company notifying shareholders that the naval situation was unchanged.

They hadn't changed in the weeks he'd been watching. He turned back to pick up his hat and stick. At least he'd managed to arrange this notif-ication with Colonel Fitzwilliam. Otherwise he would be wondering how he would know when the situation had resolved.

But without any intimation of change, he must maintain his appearance of being here for the longer term.

But he hated it. Every day he hated that he was bored, achieving nothing. He hated that Georgiana was living a life below her class, learning things that she should not know, not be troubled with.

But he stopped short of saying he hated her friendship with Elizabeth Bennet. He could not say that.

He smiled slightly. Miss Bennet was the one bright moment that lit each day for him. It had taken him a long time to admit it to himself, and he still didn't know what to do about it.

As a man without fortune, Mr. Hudson was not a good match for her, and no lady would expect such a gentleman to propose to her.

But, of course, he wasn't Mr. Hudson. However, Mr. Darcy could not propose to her either. She might be a kind, thoughtful, beautifully mannered lady; but her background … he shuddered. Mrs. Bennet at Lucas Lodge. Mrs. Bennet, entertaining them at Longbourn. Mrs. Bennet, loud and vulgar.

The only bright moment at those times were meeting Elizabeth Bennet's gaze and knowing she was equally as ashamed of her mother as he was embarrassed.

He wondered what she would think when she found out that he was living a lie.

It was time to go. He didn't want to think what she would think of him. But he must not think about her. He was here to protect Georgiana, that was all.

He descended the stairs. She had been right about the gown. When Georgiana had told him yesterday of Elizabeth's fears about the servant's gossip, he had been perturbed. She was right to be concerned, and a sense of dread had begun to settle around him.

Why had he not thought to warn his sister? Did he need to take action? But they had a good situation here, and would surely be hard to find?

She was waiting for him downstairs, dressed in the simple cotton dress Elizabeth had picked out for her.

"You look very nice." He forced the words out. She looked extremely anxious and sad. He smiled reassuringly at her. "Do not be concerned. Miss Bennet will be there, and you will feel better."

She looked up at him and forced a smile. "I am sorry, William. It is all my fault, all of it."

"It is not to be discussed, Georgia. And I do not feel as you do." He turned away.

"And just think, you would not have discovered your talent of teaching drawing." He must make her cheerful somehow. He could not. He wished Elizabeth Bennet was here with her. She would help her.

And perhaps he must reconsider her unsuitable background. If she could be such a help to Georgiana here, she would be of just as much benefit to her back at Pemberley. And at Pemberley, her family would not be close by.

He made a rueful face. He was trying to justify a way of having her at Pemberley.

He offered his sister his arm. She was almost back to the nervous person she had been when they first arrived here and he cursed the need to put her under this extra pressure. She did not need it, and she had been becoming so much more confident until now.

But there was nothing to be done. He set his jaw. Nothing at all, but to go and endure as best they could.

And he would see Miss Elizabeth Bennet. This morning had felt wrong without her presence, and he had wandered restlessly around the gardens.

He sighed.

Georgiana's hand tightened on his arm. "I will do my best, William. Do not be uneasy on my behalf."

"Thank you, Georgia." He led her out to the chaise, and assisted her up into her seat.

He turned to Mr. Thomas, who was standing

beside him ready to fold the step, and lowered his voice.

"Stay close and ready, Mr. Thomas. I am uneasy today." He glanced around the drive.

"Yes, sir. We will be ready."

"Good man." Darcy was relieved. He wondered what he was so worried about. An assembly was deplorable, but there was nothing to be considered dangerous in attending it.

And Elizabeth Bennet would be there. He tried not to think about how much he was looking forward to seeing her.

CHAPTER 15

*T*hey were not early and the music from the trio of rough and ready musicians floated out from the open windows. The street was crowded and he felt the hairs on the back of his neck rise as he hurried Georgiana inside. He looked around for Miss Bennet and his heart lightened as she came towards them.

"Mr. Hudson." She curtsied. "Georgie."

They both greeted her with relief.

"I have asked Jane to keep us a place over there." Their saviour pointed to the back of the assembly room, and they followed her, only stopping to greet Sir William and Lady Lucas. Finally, they got to the corner and Elizabeth reintroduced them to her sister, the very pretty, well-mannered

107

young lady that Darcy remembered from visiting Longbourn.

"Good evening sir." Miss Bennet curtsied. "I hope you are both well?"

"Very well, thank you. And your family are all well?"

They stood and made inane light conversation together for a few minutes, before Mr. Darcy suddenly realised his opportunity.

He turned toward his sister. "Georgie, I wonder if you feel able to remain here with Miss Bennet, so I may have the honour of requesting a dance with Miss Elizabeth Bennet?"

He sensed the sharply indrawn breath of Elizabeth Bennet beside him, but he wanted first of all to be sure that the elder Bennet girl knew to stay with Georgiana.

His sister smiled at him. "Of course I will, William. Miss Bennet and I will find much to converse about."

He bowed slightly, and turned to Miss Elizabeth Bennet. Her eyebrows lifted slightly, and a tiny smile played around her mouth.

"Without the honour of surprise, Mr. Hudson, I might demand a very formal request."

He smiled back. "I regret I cannot offer a complete surprise, Miss Bennet. But I can hardly claim that you might have been surprised by such an offer."

"Indeed not." She let him lead her out to take their place in line.

He stood facing her as they waited for the dance to begin. She was most breathtakingly beautiful to him, and he wondered when that had happened. He recalled he hadn't noticed her appearance particularly when he had first met her, save to notice her fine eyes.

But tonight her face seemed luminously lovely, her colour heightened and her expression animated and warm.

With a start, he noticed he was late to bow as the music began. They stepped together.

"Your mind is far away, sir," she noted with a wry smile.

"I was thinking that you look very lovely this evening, Miss Bennet. And that I am fortunate your sister can remain with mine while I have this honour which I had not anticipated being able to request."

Her colour heightened a little more and he berated himself. She would think he was giving an idle compliment, not being in a position to make her an offer.

"Thank you." Her voice was quiet, not offended. They danced in an easy silence for a few moments. He thought he could get very used to her company, very used to her quiet good humour, punctuated by her sharp wit and lively ripostes. He smiled, and her eyebrows went up.

"I amuse you? Without speaking?"

He lowered his head to hers, not even thinking ahead what he was going to say, when a movement out of the corner of his eye caught his attention.

He stiffened. By the door, a man was in dispute with Sir William, trying to enter the assembly rooms.

Darcy instantly turned his back, stooped a little to reduce his height and began to limp, drawing Elizabeth Bennet back towards where Georgiana was.

"Mr. Hudson? Is your injury paining you?" Miss Bennet looked up at him as she hurried beside him.

The man was not a gentleman, and even in gentleman's clothes, ill-worn, looking incongruous, Darcy was not about to forget that face last seen as he was being set upon at Ramsgate.

"I fear so, Miss Bennet." He must act. She must not know the true facts or she might be in danger, too.

Georgiana was no longer where she had been.

The shock of it nearly made his heart stop. Oh, why had they come? He looked around wildly.

"It is all right, sir. She is there, with Jane." Elizabeth pointed out his sister, standing speaking to the rest of the Bennet family a few paces from the corner. He breathed a sigh of relief.

"Miss Bennet, may I presume to ask one thing of you?"

At her nod, he continued.

"Please, could you make your way to the door and find my steward, Mr. Thomas? Ask him to have the chaise ready instantly for us. Thank you." He continued to move, apparently hesitantly, towards Georgiana, keeping his head bent to hide his height more.

He hoped he hadn't been seen by the ruffian before he had turned away, but he knew his genial host was very likely to bring him straight over to him.

He held on to his mask of unconcern and made his way to the Bennets and Georgiana.

He bowed to them. "I am most sorry not to be able to talk this evening and pray you will forgive me. Georgia, we must leave. *At once*." He gave her a steady stare, hoping she would not ask any difficult questions.

She did not. "I'm sorry your injury is paining you." She took his arm.

"Thank you, Mrs. Bennet, Miss Bennet. Please excuse us."

He guided her swiftly to the edge of the room, behind a group of local people, but when she turned to the front of the room, he shook his head.

"No, we cannot go that way."

"But my hat and coat!"

"No. There is a side door here, open for some air. We will use that." He knew Mr. Thomas would have seen what was going on. His chaise would be there, if Miss Elizabeth Bennet had done her task.

He did not doubt that she had, he trusted her implicitly.

But how the devil had the Ramsgate gang discovered them?

He glanced around, seeing Sir William gazing around the room for him, looking puzzled. He could not see the other man.

He urged Georgiana through the door while they were hidden by others, and he ducked through behind her.

His mind began to plan what he would say to Miss Elizabeth. She deserved more than he would be able to articulate to her tonight, and his heart was heavy. Would she ever be able to forgive him?

The chaise was there. He uttered a prayer of

thanks and assisted Georgiana hastily into it. Miss Bennet appeared from around the front. She didn't stop, but whispered in passing. "I will distract them." And hurried up into the side door.

He frowned at her retreating back. What did she know?

Mr. Thomas was beside him. "I think she saw several men outside when she came to find me, sir."

He wanted a chance to speak to her, and he hesitated. But there was not a moment to lose.

"All right, Mr. Thomas. We cannot risk going back to Bayford. London. By the back lanes if you can."

He wondered if she really would be able to prevent their absence being remarked upon for long enough to delay their pursuit.

Even five minutes would mean their pursuers might think they had returned to Bayford House and would waste time checking there.

Mr. Thomas turned around from his seat beside the driver.

"Would you wish to hire a larger coach at the first post, sir? Or the second?"

"The second." Darcy didn't hesitate.

"Are we not going back to Bayford House?" Georgiana suddenly seemed to understand what was happening.

"No, we are not." Darcy turned and looked at her. "I don't think you saw them, Georgiana, but the men from Ramsgate have discovered us. We must try to get to London before they can take you."

Her hand covered her mouth and he saw the fear in her eyes. He smiled at her.

"Please do not be anxious, Georgiana. I will never let them take you." *While I am alive.* He wouldn't let that thought occur to her. He reached into the storage box and pulled out a blanket, draping it around her shoulders.

He glanced at the sky, wondering just how far they could go before it became too dangerous to carry on. He leaned forward.

"Mr. Thomas!"

"Yes, sir?"

"We will not get to London before dark, but I expect they will try to catch up with us. Tell the driver to turn towards Epping. They will not expect us to go that way."

"Very good, sir."

"You have planned this for a long time, I think." Georgiana's voice held only the tiniest trace of a wobble. He was very proud of her.

She took a deep breath and her eyes were huge in her face.

"Please, William, please don't be angry with

me ... but do you think ... Mr. Wickham was there?"

He took a deep breath. He didn't want to be angry with her, her only fault was her youth and innocence. But the name was bile in his throat.

"No, I did not see him. My worry is that now they would force you to marry any one of them to get your fortune." He saw her face whiten, but he needed her to trust him, to do as he said without question.

"And will I ever see Elizabeth again?" Her voice was very small.

His heart gave a little jump. "I don't know, Georgiana. She might be very angry at my lies." But his heart sank at the thought.

"May I write to her?"

He took her hand. "Please, Georgiana, let us just get to a place where I can keep you safe. I will tell you when you may write to her."

"All right." Her voice was only a whisper.

CHAPTER 16

*E*lizabeth woke early the next morning after a restless night, her head throbbing. It was still only just dawn, but she knew she would not sleep any more, so she slipped out of bed.

She would go to Bayford House at her usual time after breakfast, but until then, she would go for a walk on the hill behind Longbourn and try and get clear in her mind what had happened last night.

As she shut the front door quietly behind her, she stopped to take a few deep breaths of the dew-laden air. Why had they left without saying goodbye?

Why had the rough-looking man been so insistent on waiting for Mr. Hudson?

She thought with some satisfaction that she'd

kept him waiting for nigh on forty minutes, assuring him that Miss Hudson would not leave without her coat and hat.

But how she could prevent him knowing where they lived, she didn't know.

Her steps speeded up. She was concerned the man and his friends would go to Bayford House and Mr. Hudson and Georgie might be in danger.

She needed to go and find out. Even if they were still abed, the servants would be about. She hurried on. She could still be home in time for breakfast.

She had another half a mile or so to walk and she found herself almost running at times. Who were they really?

She knew she had had suspicions about why they had come to this part of the country. But perhaps they weren't even who she thought they were.

As she drew near the lane, she slowed down, dreading seeing the rough man from last night, dreading still more that her friends might be in trouble.

She forced herself to walk on and turned in the drive, breathing a sigh of relief at the normal appearance of the house in the early sunlight. She went round to the side windows, not wanting to knock on the door and disturb Mr. Hudson before breakfast.

She saw Mrs. James walking through the hall, and tapped on the window glass. Soon she was inside and understood from the housekeeper that the chaise had not come back last night following the assembly. No one at the house had seen anything of them.

"I wanted to ask Mr. Thomas if we should ask the magistrate what has happened, but he went with the chaise, so he is not here, either." Mrs. James' face was creased with worry.

Elizabeth sat thinking. She was worried too. But one thing she was certain of, was that Georgie and her brother had left the assembly rooms at least half an hour before the uncouth man had. And surely he would have come here to check whether they were home before chasing them to — where?

"Mrs. James, did any men come last night to speak to Mr. Hudson? Late, but before you would have expected him home?"

"Well, yes. There was a man at the door, but I just said they were at the assembly and I wasn't expecting them back until later. I told him to call back tomorrow — well, that's today." She looked at Elizabeth.

"What should I tell him?"

Elizabeth wondered if the woman had discovered anything about her employer. "Do you know if they might have left a note? Any intimation of the address they had come from?"

"No, Miss Elizabeth." The woman shook her head. "We clean all the rooms each day, of course. I would have seen a note this morning." She rubbed her hand across her face.

"I suppose a magistrate might wish to look through Mr. Hudson's papers if he doesn't come back. But we would have to wait a few days, I suppose."

"Yes." Elizabeth stood up. "Perhaps I will speak to my father. He will know what is to be done."

"Thank you, Miss Elizabeth." Mrs. James seemed much relieved. "I will continue as I would each day and expect them to arrive home soon."

Elizabeth nodded as if in agreement, but she didn't think they would return.

As she made her way home, she wondered where they were now. She wondered if they were thinking of her, if she would ever hear from them and find out what had happened.

Her heart sank at the thought that maybe they'd been caught by whoever was searching for them. If they had been hurt — or worse — she might never know.

She felt rather ill, and her steps were heavy as she approached Longbourn. It was still an hour before the family would be about and she could speak to her father. She wanted very much to know how she could enquire after them, when she had not the remotest idea what their names really were or where in the country they came from.

Breakfast seemed endless, listening to her mother and the younger girls all talking about the dance.

"And your Mr. Hudson, Lizzy. What was he thinking of, to go off so suddenly like that? Right in the middle of your dance!" Mrs. Bennet waved her fork at Elizabeth.

"Well, you must never go there again! It was most rude of him. It just shows he deserves to have no fortune."

Elizabeth waited for her anger to abate, but she didn't have to reply. Jane intervened.

"Mama, that is not correct. Anyone can see that he would not be rude to Lizzy. Could you not see his injury was paining him?"

"Well, he must have been feigning pain. He walked all right when he came here for dinner."

"Yes, but Mama, dancing is much more stressful, you know that." Elizabeth wasn't going to take any criticism of Mr. Hudson, however she felt about him.

"Lizzy, you are not to see them again! I forbid it." Her mother's voice rose shrilly. "He is without fortune, he cannot marry you. He is just using your friendship for his sister. He must find a woman of fortune."

"Yes, Mama." Elizabeth pretended acquiescence. If the Hudsons did return, she would still visit, her mother would forget. But she was more certain than before in her own mind that they were gone forever.

Mr. Bennet put down his knife and fork and wiped his mouth with the napkin. He pushed his chair away from the table.

"Lizzy, come through to my book room, if you please."

"Yes, Father." Elizabeth followed him through the hall.

He sat behind his desk. "I am sorry your mother was so direct this morning, Lizzy. Can you tell me what happened at the assembly?"

Elizabeth pushed back the irritation that he never attended these events if he could help it. If he had been there, he might have assisted her.

She sighed. "Yes, Father." She told him what she had seen and how she had acted. Then she stood and went to the window.

"I walked over to Bayford House early this morning. I was concerned for them. The stranger was — not pleasant." She turned to face him. "I spoke to the housekeeper. They did not go there from the assembly, Papa." She went over to stand close to her father. "I admit I am anxious for them."

Mr. Bennet looked thoughtful. He took off his eyeglasses and polished them with his handkerchief, thinking. He sighed.

"Sit down, Lizzy."

CHAPTER 17

*E*lizabeth sat down in the chair opposite him. She really hoped he would be able to help her, although she could not imagine what form that help might take.

"We have a dilemma here, to be sure," her father mused. "You must recall I have only met the man a few times, but you know him and his sister much better. So let us see what we can discover."

He looked up at her. "We will take only the facts we know. We will have to call him Mr. Hudson for now, as that is the name we know him by."

Elizabeth leaned forward. "Do you think that is not his real name, Father?"

"Certainly." Mr. Bennet's eyebrows went up. "Do you?"

"I admit I have always wondered if that is the case."

He smiled. "I am sure no one else suspects it. You and I notice more than many, I think, the little things that others consider unimportant."

He leaned back, frowning. "I am not asking questions now to be difficult, but to try and gain a better picture."

"I understand, Papa." Elizabeth was just happy that he was going to help her.

"Do you think they really are brother and sister?"

"I do." Elizabeth thought back. "There is not much likeness, but they have never given me any suspicions that they are not." She hesitated. "I have the impression that he is hiding her from something."

"Do you? That is interesting." Mr. Bennet closed his eyes, a habit of his when he was concentrating.

Elizabeth waited for the next question. But she did not anticipate what came next.

Her father's eyes snapped open and he leaned forward and stared into her eyes. "And what is Mr. Hudson to you, Lizzy? Do you have feelings for him?"

She opened her mouth to issue a hot denial, but shut it again to think. She shook her head, sadly.

"I don't know, Papa. I just do not know. I think I do, but I have always known that things were not as they seemed and tried not to allow myself to hope."

Her father grimaced. "Thank you for being honest with me. And have you talked to Jane about him?"

Elizabeth shook her head. "No, I have not. I did not want to raise any questions in anyone's mind that things were not as they seemed."

"That is sensible, my dear." He rubbed his hand absent-mindedly along the spine of the book currently on his desk. He thought of something else.

"Do you believe his lack of fortune?"

Elizabeth made a face of distaste. She knew how much Mr. Hudson would hate the thought of her discussing him with her father. She bit her lip. Mr. Hudson was no longer here. *I don't think I will ever see him again.* But she needed help to find out what had happened.

"I do not know, Papa. They live as simply as would be the case if they had little fortune. I have never seen any indication that they had more, except I do not think they would afford a chaise."

He tipped his head, nodding. "Continue."

She thought. "But I have always thought this situation was a new one to them. They must certainly have been very wealthy in the recent past."

"I agree, Lizzy. Their whole manner tells of their breeding and upbringing as part of the very wealthy."

"So why were they here?" Elizabeth shook her head helplessly. "I thought they perhaps had lost it all, but they did not really make any serious attempt to belong here, not more than they felt they should if they were to be believed." She shook her head in frustration at her disordered words. "I mean that …"

"I understand what you were attempting to say, Lizzy." Mr. Bennet held up his hand.

He put his elbows on the desk before him, gazing at his steepled hands.

"Do you think, Lizzy, that they come from a newly rich background, or an old wealthy family?"

She looked at him, puzzled. "An old wealthy family, I would think. But why …?"

He waved a finger at her. "This is of course, all supposition, Lizzy, but do you not think that Miss Georgia Hudson — if that is her name — might not then have a fortune settled upon her on the occasion of her marriage?"

Elizabeth jumped to her feet. "Of course! He must have been hiding her from someone he does not approve of!" She turned to him.

"And then he turned up last night and Mr. Hudson decided she might not be safe."

He smiled. "Perhaps. But it is not certain. We must not spread our thoughts around."

"Of course we must not. But Papa! I am certain you are right. You are so discerning, I would never have considered that." She kissed the top of his head.

He jerked away, embarrassed. "Get away with you, Lizzy." He indicated the chair again.

"But we still need to find out what has happened to them. I will think about what can be done."

"Thank you, Papa. I do not know what I would have done without having you here to assist me."

He smiled a little sadly. "I do not know whether we will get very much further in our enquiries, but at least we have surmised enough to perhaps satisfy our curiosity." He patted her hand.

"But, Lizzy. Miss Hudson was fond of you. You might get a letter if nothing has befallen them. However, you must be prepared for the fact that her brother may forbid her to write to you. You will have to try and forget them, although I know you had become extremely fond of her."

She knew he spoke the truth, and wondered if she'd ever stop wondering if they were safe. But as she made her way from her father's library to her bedchamber, it was Mr. Hudson's face that intruded into her mind, not Georgie's.

It was his face, the way he looked gravely at her when he enquired after her health each morning.

It was his tall, lean figure, as handsome when he was limping with his cane as when he was striding out round the garden.

She shook her head. She would never see him again. She wondered why she wasn't more angry with him, that he had allowed her to think she might even be of a similar family to her, able to even think about … knowing him better.

But a poor man was as far out of her reach as a truly wealthy man. He had never been available to her.

But his eyes had burned into her and she wanted to keep the memory of him.

She collected her hat and jacket from her closet. She would walk over to Bayford House one more time and see if they had returned and everything was all right again.

She hesitated, would their pursuers want to

take her, find out what she knew? Perhaps it was foolish to go alone.

She shook her head at her silly fancy. She knew nothing useful for them, and she pushed away the thought that they didn't know that.

She had to go and find out. If Georgie and her brother were back, she wouldn't wish them to feel she was angry with them.

CHAPTER 18

*F*inally they were home. Mr. Darcy hurried up the steps of Darcy House, Georgiana on his arm. They had not come here for the first three days since leaving Bayford, but it had been the right thing to do, going direct to Bingley in Grosvenor Street. Although always welcome, they had never previously stayed, because it was not too far from Darcy's own establishment. But Bingley had ridden over to call Fitzwilliam for him and the Colonel had ridden back immediately with him.

Both his own home and Matlock House had acquired a few men who loitered outside, and Cousin Richard had consulted with the Earl of Sandwich. Now those men had been detained and the House had tabled questions about the gangs.

It seemed that Darcy's misadventure in Ramsgate had begun a general clean-up of a menace that had been gathering attention for some time.

And only now it was safe to go home, although Darcy knew he could never relax his guard while Georgiana was such a prize.

He'd hoped he could allow her freedom to grow up unworried by her future, give her the chance to meet people and find someone she could love, who would treat her well.

But the gold-diggers were circling. She must marry young. He could not keep her safe and give her the freedom to grow up as he wished her to.

He knew she still felt herself in love with the man Wickham, whose very name was now hateful to him.

Still, it appeared Wickham had paid the price of his indolence and arrogance. Not only had he amassed huge debts, those debts were in the hands of men who would never allow him to get away without paying for them.

Wickham's last chance had been to elope with Georgiana and it had only been her letter to Darcy that had brought him there in time to remove her. He shook his head. And only the presence of the Earl of Sandwich that had saved him from a terrible fate. And now …

"Fitzwilliam?" Georgiana's hand tightened in

his arm. "What are you thinking so angrily about?"

He forced his mind away from his news. She was not ready to hear it.

"It is nothing. I am sorry, I will concentrate better on the fact that we are now home. Let us take tea in the drawing room." He nodded at the footman, who departed to arrange for tea to be served.

He led her through to the gracious, elegant room. This was much better.

Bayford House had suited his purpose for those weeks, but living there had been almost intolerable. He'd felt caged — impotent to do anything that could extract him from his duty.

Only the presence of Miss Elizabeth Bennet had given focus and interest to each day. He felt his spirits lift as he thought of her.

"I think Elizabeth would like to see our real home." Georgiana was thinking of her, too.

"I hope she will not be very angry with us for lying to her as to our names and circumstances." Darcy was not sure at all that would be the case.

"But she must be very worried about us. It is nigh on four days since we left without saying goodbye." Georgiana seemed as anxious as she thought her friend was, and he searched his mind to reassure her.

"As soon as I have you properly safe, you can write to her."

"Thank you, Fitzwilliam, I will wait for you to tell me I may, but how long is it likely to be?"

He regarded her carefully. No, he could not tell her yet.

"We will travel on to Pemberley tomorrow. Cousin Richard has permission from the Brigadier that the local militia will protect us there for the time being. It is good training for them to secure the property." He knew his smile was strained and he made an effort to explain things to her.

"Then, perhaps, you might like to invite her to visit there. She would be a companion for you for the rest of the summer."

He tried to imagine how she would receive the letter, what she would think of Pemberley.

"Oh, I would be very happy with that!" Georgiana only just managed to prevent herself clapping like a small child, and he watched her indulgently.

FINALLY, it was time to change for dinner. He washed and changed, then took a few moments to sit in the chair by the window, overlooking the peaceful gardens. There was little of the bustling noise from the great London street at this time of night.

He had time and solitude now to think of the news he had heard. Wickham was dead. Dead at the hands of one of his creditors. He had arrogantly assumed he would win a duel and would escape his debts to run up more. So he had paid the ultimate price.

Darcy grimaced. He was sad for the loss of his childhood friend, and sad for his father's sake, who had loved the father so much he had raised the son almost as his own. And it had ended like this.

But he was content. The world was a better place without Wickham in it, and certainly safer for Georgiana. He wondered how Miss Elizabeth Bennet might advise him the best way to impart the news to Georgiana. He did not wish to become the enemy who had taken her away from the man in his hour of need. But perhaps he didn't know his sister and she would be secretly happy.

He just didn't know, and it was his business to know how to keep his sister happy. She had already had far too much loss in her short life. And now she might think he was keeping Elizabeth from her.

His thoughts continued as they sat over dinner although he tried to push them away.

But she was speaking. He must listen.

"I think Elizabeth would be happy to join me in my studies if I am still to have a governess." Georgiana watched him as he ate. "She is always eager to learn new things."

"Yes, I have seen that." Mr. Darcy put his knife and fork down. "You may, of course, keep a governess at Pemberley, if that is what you wish. However, you are so accomplished now, that I feel a very high quality teacher is needed." He smiled at her.

"I can send out an enquiry if you wish?"

Georgiana thought for a moment. "Yes, I think I would like you to find out if there is such a person available to us, but I can decide not to have her if the situation changes?"

"I will ask you if someone is found and then you may decide." Darcy was beginning to feel impatient to be gone to Pemberley. He was done with Bayford House, but even being here he still could not go on with his life as he would wish.

There were soldiers posted outside the house at Richard's insistence, as there were outside Matlock house too. But he still did not feel he could undertake his usual business, or make plans for the future. And he was impatient to do so.

The meal finished and Georgiana withdrew. The footman poured Darcy a glass of port and he sat idly for a few moments before he would rejoin his sister for coffee. He would not leave her alone for long.

He wondered how it would feel at Pemberley, having Elizabeth Bennet there. But he dare not think of that, not until he knew whether she would find it in her heart to forgive him for their deception and remain friends with Georgiana.

At least the journey would give him time to think. Georgiana was an ideal travelling companion, able to sit quietly with her own thoughts.

He had a great deal to think about.

And having their own coach would make for a great deal of comfort. He smiled.

CHAPTER 19

*I*t was a week since the assembly. Elizabeth walked up the hill as she did each day now, turning away from Bayford. She could hardly bear to look at the fading path in the grass she had worn away in those weeks.

She climbed fast, trying to walk away the dark thoughts that filled her mind. She and Georgie had become so fond of each other, she could not bear to think that the girl had not written to her — even if only to say she was all right.

And her thoughts of Mr. Hudson were darker still. But she could not find it in her heart to dislike him. He had never given her any indication that she meant anything to him, other than as a friend for his sister.

But she knew that wasn't true. He may not

have given her any deliberate indication, but his actions had betrayed him. The way he looked at her, his grave attention, his dark eyes as he listened to her conversations with Georgie.

She knew he had noticed her. And she had begun to harbour thoughts of what it might be like if he drew close to her, if he kissed her hand.

What if he'd said he loved her, asked for her hand in marriage?

She shook her head angrily. It would never do. He could not persuade her father that he had the means to support her.

Her father had been able to find out nothing. There had been nothing in the society pages about any of the wealthy in society missing engagements, or not seen at events.

She was quite despondent now that she would ever hear anything. Each day her father had asked her to sit with him in his book room and he had done his best to give her comfort without words, for there was nothing to say, she knew that.

She wondered what she should do, how she could now fill her days.

"Lizzy! Lizzy!" The voice was calling from far away, and she stopped and turned, trying to see who it was. It sounded like Jane, but Jane would not run after her, she was far too unused to walking far.

Elizabeth sighed, it must be that her mother was demanding once again that she be more lady-like. She began making her way down the slope towards her sister.

She smiled at the thoughts of Jane. She had been so kind to her, doing what she wanted, never commenting that Elizabeth had gone to Bayford House far too often, ignoring her older friends.

And now she was paying the price. Dear Charlotte was kind and she had called a few times, but there was some reticence between them now, and Elizabeth knew she must work hard to win her friendship back.

As she drew closer to Jane, she saw that her sister was waving something — a letter? She began running. It might be. It must be. What else could it be?

She drew close to Jane a few moments later, managing to check her headlong dash down the slope.

"I knew you'd want to know it had come, Lizzy." Jane was beaming. "I'm so happy it is here."

"Thank you, Jane. Thank you so much!" Elizabeth took the letter from Jane, her hand shaking. "They must be safe, I am so happy to know it."

Jane embraced her sister. "I knew how anxious you were, and now you may read it and enjoy

HARRIET KNOWLES

hearing their news." She patted her sister's shoulder. "You can tell me about it later."

She turned and began making her way back to Longbourn.

Elizabeth watched her for a few moments. Then she looked round. She knew of a grassy knoll not far away, where she could sit and read in comfort.

As she walked, she looked at the letter. Several sheets of paper, and a large seal in red wax. She looked closer. The letter P formed the seal and she wondered what it stood for.

Soon she was sitting alone and she broke the seal and began reading eagerly.

> *My dearest friend,*
> *I hope you are able to forgive me — and*
>   *my brother — for our deceptions once*
>   *you know the truth about our stay at*
>   *Bayford.*
> *It should have been the worst time of my*
>   *life, but you made it the best and I*
>   *was sorry to leave, especially in the*
>   *way we had to.*
> *I have been so worried about you, and*
>   *that you must be concerned for us too,*
>   *but my brother was not able to give*

*me permission to write to you until
just now.*

*So I am writing at once and I will send
this letter by express so that it reaches
you just as soon as it possibly can.*

*Elizabeth, you have been such a good
friend to me and you deserve so much
better than we were able to give you at
Bayford House.*

*But you are most astute and I know that
you knew we had a secret.*

*It was all my fault, but I was in love
with a childhood friend and we were
to elope to Scotland. I was uneasy
about doing so in secrecy from my
brother, who is my guardian as our
parents are dead. When I told him
about it, he came immediately to
save me.*

*I appears now that my friend was in very
great debt to some evil men and it
was they who tried to prevent my
brother from rescuing me, which was
where he sustained the injury he had
when we arrived in Hertfordshire.*

*I think now that perhaps he did not love me,
that all he wanted was the fortune that*

is settled on me for my marriage. And now the gang who were plotting for him to have me are now trying to take me to make me marry one of them. Fitzwilliam says that once they have control of my fortune I would not have a happy life and I am sure he is right.

We had to leave the assembly in such a hurry because he saw one of the gang who attacked us at Ramsgate. We spent a few nights in London and then travelled with some militia here to Derbyshire, where there is a guard around the estate until all the gang have been detained and I am safer.

I cannot write much more, although there is so much to say, but I am writing to beg that you visit me here and we can then talk much more freely.

Fitzwilliam has said that I may invite you to stay for as long as you would like to and he would be pleased if you agree, because he has to go away soon and he hopes that you would be good company for me.

I do hope that you will be able to come and Fitzwilliam has agreed to send the coach for you, with two maids to

*accompany you here. He says that if
you do not wish to come, or your
father does not consent, then you can
just send the coach back.
It is leaving in the next hour or two and
will arrive probably the day after this
letter.
I hope so very much that you will come
and that you can forgive us for the
terrible concern we must have caused
you. I do not know what I will do if
you are not soon here with me.
Your affectionate friend,
Georgie — Georgiana Darcy
Pemberley, Bakewell, Derbyshire.*

Elizabeth sat amazed after she had finished the letter. She turned back to the beginning and read it again, her lips curved up in a long-absent smile at the obvious haste with which it had been written.

Her father had been right. There was a fortune settled on Georgiana, and her brother was trying to protect her.

She shuddered at the thought of the uncouth man at the assembly dragging Georgie away to marry him. No, she forgave Mr. Hudson — no, he was not Mr. Hudson, he was Mr. Darcy.

Mr. Darcy. How strangely the name seemed to sit in her mind. But how it fitted the man she knew.

And Pemberley. It must be a very great estate, and the family most highly connected, if he could arrange for it to be guarded by the militia for the safety of his sister.

Her heart sank. If he was so highly connected, so well-bred and wealthy, there was no chance of him even looking at her with any reason other than as a friend of his sister.

She folded the letter. She was surprised he even felt she was a suitable friend for Georgie.

He must have only been looking at her when they were here because there was no one else, not because there could be any connection between them.

People like that didn't think anything of the lower classes of people, didn't care whether they were hurt by their actions.

She ought to feel used by him. She began to walk slowly home. She could not feel used, he had always acted most properly toward her. It was her own mind that had dreamed of more.

She had to smile at herself. She had always disdained those who were wealthy, those who were protected from the worries and restrictions she knew.

But poor Georgiana was in much more danger than she herself was, and would be much restricted in what she could do to stay safe.

She wondered how soon Mr. Hudson — no, Mr. Darcy would think he should marry Georgiana to someone suitable?

Poor Georgie. She ought to go and see her. But Derbyshire was so far away. She must look at the map in Father's book room.

Would Father permit her to go? She smiled. Of course he would let her, if she wished to go.

CHAPTER 20

*M*r. Darcy paced the stone terrace outside the great drawing room. The view out over the second lake and the hills in the distance had never failed to calm him before.

But he had much on his mind. Of course he didn't wish himself back at Bayford House, back in that state of comparative poverty, but his experience there had brought home to him just how complicated his life here was.

He was waiting on another letter from his uncle. The old Earl of Matlock was blunt and forthright.

He had called while they had spent those few days in London. "You have to go, Darcy. I cannot send another."

"But I am not free to go, Uncle Henry." Mr. Darcy was quite firm.

"Nonsense! There is no one else I can send. Richard cannot go. If anything happens to David, Richard is my heir."

"Indeed. And it is none of my concern. I have Pemberley to consider. If Georgiana cannot be kept safe, and I should lose my life in France on this wild goose-chase, then it is not just her fortune, but Pemberley itself that is at risk."

His uncle had glowered at him. "You should ensure Georgiana is married forthwith. Then you will not have to concern yourself with all this hiding away. We could not find you! We had no idea where you were!"

"Those ruffians found me all right. Your men were not as good as they."

Darcy was pleased. Richard had obviously not told his uncle he knew of Darcy's whereabouts. He had been right to trust Richard, but he never would his uncle.

He continued remorselessly. "And Georgiana is only fifteen years old. She is much too young to marry. No, I really do not see that I should go to France." He turned away. "Cousin David is foolish and impetuous. No good will come of it."

His uncle had lumbered to his feet. "It is your

duty, Darcy! Your mother would wish you to protect the Fitzwilliam family and status."

"My mother wanted me to protect Georgiana! I was there for her, sir! She told me what she wanted of me."

Darcy had turned away, knowing with a sick feeling that he would eventually have to do as his uncle wanted. Or Uncle Henry would get the militia around Pemberley taken away.

It was the only way to ensure Georgiana was safe. And he must ensure she was content within the estate. For now it was her prison. If only Miss Elizabeth Bennet would come to Pemberley, that would be the best thing for his sister. And if Uncle Henry did not like the delay, then at least he would learn that Darcy could not be easily used.

He gazed at the hills, the early sunlight was exploring the crags and it was very beautiful.

If Miss Bennet had received the letter and *if* she had decided she would come, and *if* her father had consented, and *if* she was ready to leave when the coach arrived, then she might arrive as early as today.

He could hardly admit to himself how important it was to him that she came. But it was not certain and he did not know what he would do if she did not come.

He leaned on the balustrade. One thing in the

forefront of his mind after his uncle's visit to Darcy House was the reminder that Georgiana was his heir.

Those evil men who had been after her were not just after her fortune of thirty thousand pounds — if he was killed protecting her, or in France, then they would get Pemberley and the huge estates and investments that gave him his ten thousand a year as well.

She must marry. The dreadful truth sank into his mind. Hiding as they had at Bayford hadn't been the answer. Her marriage would be. As soon as she was sixteen … His heart sank. She was just a child still, and most vulnerable.

He was twenty-eight years old. He had been resisting marriage himself, thinking he had plenty of time. But he should marry and produce an heir, should take that part of the risk from Georgiana.

He grimaced, he did not relish the need. And he had never met anyone who he had thought of as remotely possible.

No, that was not true. Miss Elizabeth Bennet was in his mind constantly. He pushed away from the balustrade and nodded at his footman.

He couldn't consider marrying Miss Bennet! He could not. She was totally unsuitable in her background and her breeding. Now he was away from Bayford and back at Pemberley, he could see that. He tried to imagine Mrs. Bennet meeting his uncle — or his aunt, Lady Catherine de Bourgh — and his mind failed him.

The footman carried out coffee and placed the tray on the small table.

"Thank you." Darcy nodded at him absent-mindedly.

He wondered where Miss Elizabeth Bennet was now. Was she walking the hills around Long-bourn, having decided not to come to Derbyshire? Was his coach returning without her?

The pain in his chest made him realise how much he was relying on her travelling to Pember-ley. Surely she would come? She was a lady who loved adventure, craved change. And he was sure she cared very much for Georgiana and would wish to help her.

He sipped the scalding drink. And what did she think of him? Did she think of him as he thought of her?

He shook his head. He could no longer think of her in that way. She might not be considered suitable by others.

But he had also listened to her talk to Georgiana. She despised the wealthy, disliked how the wealthy treated the lower classes. She would hate him for his subterfuge.

CHAPTER 21

*B*ut he had to agree with her as to how the wealthy acted to others. Until Bayford, he had never considered ordinary people to be like himself, people with concerns and anxieties of their own.

Now he knew differently. He could not, would not wish to change the established social order. But his care for his servants and the estate workers would now not just be his duty, he would want to ensure their health for a better reason than just to get them back to work quickly.

Elizabeth Bennet had affected him far more deeply than he knew. She had changed his mind on many things. And she'd captivated him. Her beauty and vivacity had entranced him. He missed her more than he had wanted to admit to himself.

But he had to acknowledge to himself how he felt. It would be wrong to marry a lady who could provide him with an heir if he desired another. No, it would not be wrong, many people did that. But *he* could not.

He did desire her, he must admit it to himself, however sure he was that he must not act on that desire. Perhaps he should ...

"Good morning, Fitzwilliam." Georgiana's voice broke into his reverie and he turned and bowed to her, his smile grave. He wished he'd had longer to think about what he had only just admitted to himself, but now he must push away those thoughts and talk to his sister.

"Good morning, Georgiana. I trust you slept well?"

"I did, thank you. I always sleep well at Pemberley." She tucked her hand in his arm and they walked through to the breakfast room, where the sun sent slanting rays through the southeast-facing windows.

As they began eating, she looked at him.

"I have been wondering which bedchamber to prepare for Elizabeth. Might I ask for her to have a room near mine, rather than in the guest wing?"

His heart jumped at her use of Elizabeth's name and he waited a moment to collect himself.

"It would be perfectly suitable, Georgiana, but we should perhaps wait until we know whether she is coming."

"She will come. I know it." Georgiana's conviction was concerning. If Elizabeth didn't arrive, Georgiana's devastation would be acute. And he had to go to France, there was not time for much further delay.

It would not surprise him if Cousin David had met Madame Guillotine already, the fool! But he hoped he had not, or Uncle Henry might find it difficult to forgive Darcy for not being available the moment he asked for him.

"You are pensive, Fitzwilliam." Georgiana's voice roused him. "Are you worried about going to France?"

Mr. Darcy made a face. "I am sorry, Georgiana. It is something I must do, but I would rather remain here and ensure you are safe."

"I will be safe here, dear brother. With all these soldiers around, how could I not be?"

He smiled at her, not wishing her to be concerned. "Of course you will be safe. I would hope to know within the next few days if Miss Bennet is to join you. Then I would be more content that you will be happily occupied during the time I am away."

"Oh, I do hope she will be here soon," Georgiana said. "I want to have the room ready, with many flowers. If she does not arrive until tomorrow, I can have the flowers changed again."

"If that is what you would like to do, then of course you may do it." Darcy reached for another coffee.

"After breakfast, I am going to ride around the estate with the steward and check everything is in order." He glanced at her.

"Perhaps you might practise your playing with your governess until lunch. I will join you then."

"Yes, Fitzwilliam." Georgiana smiled demurely at him.

He gazed steadily at her. How could she marry in just a few month's time? She was just a child. He swallowed, hardly able to bear the thought of another man being responsible for her, another man perhaps ordering her to do things she might not wish to. Another man, who would expect her to run his estate competently and professionally, criticise her shortcomings and her inexperience.

His chest felt tight with anguish. Who did he know who would be kind to her? Who did he know who wasn't just after her money?

"Please do not worry about me so." Georgiana's voice held a hint of laughter. "I know you will do what is right."

He smiled mechanically. She did not know what he was thinking of, and there was no way he would concern her with it.

As he rode round the estate later with his under-steward, he considered. Why had he not taken to heart the need to marry, to father an heir? Now it was too late and this trip to France was fraught with danger, he knew that.

David was a fool. A pompous, arrogant fool. He smiled wryly. Elizabeth would laugh at David. Suddenly he knew he wanted her at his side, always. He wanted to be able to see her laugh at absurdities, wanted to hear her thoughts about his problems, wanted her as his wife, the mother of his children.

"That's enough." He didn't want to ride the rest of the estate. "You carry on and report back to me the state of the guard."

"Yes, sir." The steward touched his hat respectfully and Darcy nodded. He wished it was Mr. Thomas, but he had sent him with the coach to bring Miss Bennet here. He would be a familiar face to her, and he would protect her.

As he turned his horse and rode towards the

house, he heard the sound of his coach and four as it turned onto the long approach road.

Instantly, his heart was in his mouth. Was Elizabeth in it? Or had she sent it back empty, with a refusal?

CHAPTER 22

*T*he woman cleared her throat. "Excuse me, madam, but Pemberley is just coming into sight."

"Thank you." Elizabeth looked out of the coach window as the senior maid spoke.

As the great, gracious house appeared from behind the screen of trees, her heart beat faster.

Of course, her father had looked up the Darcy family when she'd appeared in his library, waving the letter — was it really only four days ago?

But she'd not really believed him, couldn't believe him, when he'd told her that they were one of the foremost landed families in the country.

He'd shaken his head. "I cannot believe we have entertained the Darcys unawares, Lizzy. There must be some cruel untruth here."

Elizabeth had shaken her head "I have seen Georgie's writing, Father, and this is her own hand. She would not lie to me like this."

She went around his desk, and kissed the top of his head. "But we will know for certain if this coach appears, won't we? You will be able to speak to the driver and find out whether all circumstances have been thought of."

She walked to the window. "If it all comes to pass as the letter says, will you permit me to go?"

"I will have to think about it, Lizzy." Her father's voice was heavy. "I can think of many difficulties that might mean you find yourself alone and far from home."

Elizabeth's heart dropped like a stone. "Surely you will not refuse to let me go? Georgie will be much dismayed."

"You are my daughter and thus you are my greatest concern, Lizzy." Her father sounded sterner than he had before. "You must wait while I decide what needs to be done to secure your safety if you are to travel so far alone."

Elizabeth still did not know what had transpired between her father and Mr. Thomas, Mr. Darcy's steward, whom she recognised from Bayford House. Perhaps the number of servants and the two maids sent with the coach had convinced him of her security.

But she was here now, and Pemberley was the loveliest place. She bit her lip, so she wouldn't smile in front of the maids. Pemberley was certainly very different from Bayford House.

She saw a lone horseman sitting beside the driveway. His upright figure sent a shock of recognition through her. How long had he been waiting?

As the coach rolled towards the house, the rider turned and trotted alongside her, and she saw his profile. The familiar features were strangely comforting and she felt herself relax. She was safe now.

The coach drew up beside the imposing wide steps, and she felt the springs rock as the footman jumped down to open the door and lower the step for her. She was very, very glad to have arrived.

Mr. Darcy had dismounted and he handed the reins to a groom. He approached as she descended from the coach.

"Thank you for coming to visit my sister, Miss Bennet." He bowed, grave, unsmiling, but with his intense direct gaze reminding her what she had missed these last days.

She curtsied. "I was so relieved to know you were both safe, Mr. Darcy."

She saw a brief flash of distaste cross his face. Did he expect her to call him Mr. Hudson, still?

He could hardly expect that. She smiled. Perhaps he knew he might have a few pertinent questions to answer.

But her anger at not hearing from them for so long had dissipated somewhat and, while she wanted to hear the full story, she wasn't angry.

"Elizabeth!" she heard Georgie's voice from the top of the steps and saw her running down towards her. As the girl reached her, she flung her arms round her and embraced her tightly.

"I am so happy you came, so happy!"

Mr. Darcy's cough made her hesitate. "Georgiana."

The girl dropped her hands to her sides and she stepped back. "I am sorry." She curtsied at Elizabeth.

"Thank you so much for coming to see us."

"I am very glad to be here." Elizabeth smiled at her, trying to show she didn't give a thought to any loss of manners. But Georgiana would know that, of course.

The girl tucked her hand in Elizabeth's arm. "Come and have some tea. Then there'll be time to refresh yourself before lunch."

They ascended the steps, Mr. Darcy alongside, several paces to one side, grave and serious as always.

Elizabeth stopped as they reached the top of

the steps and turned to look out over the estate. The still waters of the lake in front of the house with the hills and woods reflected in it were restful after three days' journey.

"It is so beautiful."

Georgiana was standing close. "I'm looking forward to showing you all of it." She cast a glance at the sky. "I hope the weather will be kind to us."

"I am sure it will." Mr. Darcy interjected. "Let us go in now. You may show Miss Bennet round the house and grounds after lunch." He turned back to the door, and Elizabeth and Georgiana followed him.

Elizabeth stared around in awe. Even the entrance hall was huge. Bayford House would have fitted within it completely. Twin staircases curved up each side and great portraits lined the walls.

"Are you well, Elizabeth?" Georgiana whispered. Elizabeth hadn't realised she'd stopped.

She laughed. "I am well, thank you, Georgie. I was just thinking how different it is to Bayford House." She would not shirk from the subject and she didn't think they would be expecting her to.

Mr. Darcy's rueful smile told her he was expecting some difficult questions. "I think, perhaps, Georgiana, we should have arranged for tea in the smallest sitting room."

Elizabeth smiled broadly.

"Or perhaps the gallery?" Georgiana smiled sweetly. "I think Elizabeth prefers us for what we are, not for what we have."

"That is evident." He seemed uncomfortable and gestured them through a doorway into another grand room.

CHAPTER 23

*M*r. Darcy hoped very much that he might find the occasion to speak to Miss Bennet alone. He needed to appraise her of the situation regarding Georgiana's safety.

He was sure she would not try and encourage visits to other places and situations if she was aware of it, but if she did not know, she might inadvertently cause Georgiana to take a risk in order to try and please her guest.

He watched as the two friends reacquainted themselves over tea. It was almost like being back at Bayford House, where he would sit quietly with a book and listen to them talk.

He could feel the tight tension deep within him begin to unwind. Miss Bennet was very good for him. He could acknowledge that to himself now, as he began to push aside the long-standing expectations of who he should marry, the sort of lady who would be acceptable to his family.

Miss Elizabeth Bennet was a gentleman's daughter. Despite her dreadful background and the ill-breeding of her mother, she had managed to become a well-mannered, gracious young lady. He smiled. She also had a sharp wit and was unafraid to make a comment that would make him think about the conversation.

His time at Bayford, while insupportable, had, in fact, been very good for him, and it was all because of Miss Bennet.

"I'm hoping we can do a lot of duet playing while you're here, Elizabeth," Georgiana said. "The pianoforte in the music room is more in tune than the one at Bayford House."

"We had a lot of fun there," Elizabeth mused.

"Oh, yes!" Georgiana smiled reminiscently. Darcy found himself smiling too.

"I remember much hilarity," he commented, happy to be able to contribute to the conversation. "And the pianoforte in here is pleasant to listen to, as well."

Georgiana clapped her hands. "Oh, yes! I will bring some music down this afternoon."

Mr. Darcy smiled at Elizabeth. "I am afraid you will be kept very busy, Miss Bennet."

"I am content, sir."

Shortly afterwards, Georgiana took Elizabeth upstairs to show her her bedchamber and refresh themselves for luncheon.

Mr. Darcy watched her thoughtfully as she left the room with his sister. Wondering how to get her alone, he walked out onto the terrace. Had it only been that morning he'd paced along here, not knowing whether she would come?

Now he knew, and his concern was finding time to talk with her without Georgiana being present before he had to leave. He scowled, he was most averse to leaving for France, and Miss Bennet being here was yet another reason for him to wish to stay.

One of the footmen coughed, and Darcy turned. Miss Bennet had come downstairs and entered the drawing room. He went to meet her.

"Perhaps you'd like to come out to the terrace? I can show you the grounds from there."

"Thank you."

He knew he did not have long, so as they reached the great stone balustrade, he began.

"Miss Bennet, I cannot tell you how grateful I am that you agreed to visit Pemberley. I think we might not have very long to speak before my sister joins us, so I hope you will forgive my hasty delivery."

Her delicate eyebrow arched, but her lips curved upwards and, thus encouraged, he continued on.

"I have to go away for several weeks. It is not something I wish to do, but there is much pressure on me to go. And it means that they will keep the guard around Pemberley to keep Georgiana safe." He remembered he hadn't told her about why his sister was in danger and shook his head in frustration.

"Miss Bennet, I fear I am not being very clear in my explanation."

She smiled at him. "I am listening, sir. And we will find time to speak if we need to."

He nodded. "Thank you. I have not even the right words to apologise for pretending in Hertfordshire to be what we were not. I thought it was necessary — and it was necessary, but I did not consider properly the difficulties it might cause to others."

She was staring out at the landscape. "That man who saw you at the assembly, did he want Georgiana?"

"Yes. He did and still does." Mr. Darcy put his hands on the balustrade to prevent his fists clenching. "He still wants her, and she is not safe."

"Because she has a fortune settled on her?"

He turned, and saw a ghost of a smile on her face.

"You are very astute, Miss Bennet. Yes, Georgiana does not even think about it, but she has a large amount settled, so to many men, she is a prize worth any risk."

There was a moment's silence, and Miss Bennet looked behind her, as if to check that Georgiana was not approaching.

"I think she knows why she is in danger, sir. But I do not think you will be able to protect her forever."

He grimaced. "She is only fifteen, she is much too young to marry. But ..." he too glanced round.

"Her other guardian is our cousin, Colonel Fitzwilliam. He is a good and honourable man." He hesitated.

"It is perhaps too much to ask, but might you ..." he shook his head.

"Miss Bennet, it is too much to ask, but if I do not return from France, will you — ensure Georgiana perhaps marries her cousin? It is the only way she might be safe without me."

Her face showed concern and close attention. She glanced round again. And her expression changed.

"I am glad you found us, Georgie. Oh! Perhaps I should be calling you Georgiana now." She smiled happily at her friend, and Mr. Darcy, watching, wondered at her ability to pretend nothing untoward had been discussed.

"I hadn't been called Georgie since I was a very small girl," Georgiana said as they turned to walk through to the dining room.

"Georgiana is a beautiful and elegant name," Elizabeth remarked. "It suits you very well."

She laughed as Georgiana blushed, and Mr. Darcy, walking along behind knew that, if he could only persuade Miss Bennet to become his wife, the news would be greeted with joy by his sister.

He grimaced as he thought of the rest of his family — Lady Catherine would declaim that she would never speak to him again, Uncle Henry and his Countess would be the same.

But the only family that mattered to him were Georgiana and his Cousin Richard. All the others might think what they wished.

He sighed. He could not give any intimation of his feelings until he was back from France. The danger was real, and he would not willingly have her in mourning to a man she hardly knew.

No, he must continue with the charade that

she was merely here as company for his sister while he was away.

And this afternoon, he would write to his cousin about his hopes for Georgiana if he was lost in France.

CHAPTER 24

*E*lizabeth settled in happily at Pemberley. Georgiana seemed finally to believe that she did not really harbour ill thoughts towards her because of their deception at Bayford House.

It was not in Elizabeth's nature to hold a grudge and she was enjoying the calm and tranquility of the great house in which she found herself.

Her only anxiety was the departure of Mr. Darcy, the day after she had arrived.

He had said goodbye to them and stood seriously while he allowed Georgiana to rest her head on his shoulder. Looking uncomfortable, he patted her back awkwardly.

Elizabeth had curtsied and nodded to him

before moving tactfully away to allow the girl a little privacy to say her farewell.

But Mr. Darcy had come to find her and had bowed. "I wanted to thank you again for being here for my sister. I hope not to be too many weeks away."

Elizabeth had curtsied again. "I will be of what comfort I can, sir. I wish you well in your task."

"Thank you." He'd bowed gravely, his eyes burning into hers, as if he wanted to remember every feature.

She stayed out on the terrace for some minutes after that, hoping the warmth in her face would fade before Georgiana came to find her.

But Georgiana's eyes were reddened when she saw her, and she exerted herself to listen to the girl.

"It's so dangerous," she confided in Elizabeth. "I am very anxious. He has to approach the French and try and rescue our cousin."

Elizabeth was puzzled. "Is that Colonel Fitzwilliam?"

But if he was in France, then why had Mr. Darcy told her to go to him to obtain help for Georgiana if he himself didn't come back?

"No, I'm sorry. I forgot you do not know the

family, Elizabeth. Shall we go for a walk and I will explain who the family is?"

So they had walked around the lake.

"All right," Elizabeth said, finally. "So you have another cousin who's not Colonel Fitzwilliam. But your brother's given name is Fitzwilliam."

Georgiana laughed. Elizabeth was happy to hear it.

"I know it must be confusing, Elizabeth. Let me try and explain it."

She stopped and marshalled her thoughts together. "Our uncle, Henry Fitzwilliam, is the Earl of Matlock. He had two sisters. Lady Anne was our mother, but she died when I was very young. Lady Catherine is widowed and lives in Kent with her daughter." She checked to see if Elizabeth seemed to be following her.

"Uncle Henry has two sons. The eldest, Cousin David, is his heir, obviously, and is a Viscount, styled Lord Renham. The younger brother is our Cousin Richard. He is styled Colonel, the Honourable Richard Fitzwilliam."

"Very good!" Elizabeth approved. "That's really clear, but I might need reminding of the names occasionally." She stopped and looked at the view over the lake.

"It's very beautiful here." Then she turned to

her friend. "So your mother named her son for her own family name, did she?"

Georgiana smiled. "That's right. I think she wanted to make sure her family name wasn't forgotten. Because the Darcy name seems to over-power people, I imagine."

Elizabeth nodded. "Pemberley was handed down through the Darcy line, I suppose?"

"Yes." Georgiana walked on. "I love it here, it is wild and beautiful. But it gets lonely when Fitzwilliam is in town. So he and Cousin Richard let me go to school in London last winter."

She went quiet and looked rather sad. Eliza-beth wondered if the idea which had seemed so good at the time had backfired, perhaps when someone learned about Georgiana's fortune.

She walked silently beside Georgiana who eventually heaved a heavy sigh.

"I will tell you what happened then — but not today."

"Of course," Elizabeth agreed equably. She was curious, but was happy to let the story unfold at the right time.

"So what is your Cousin David doing in France?"

"Oh, yes!" Georgiana looked animated again. "Fitzwilliam was so angry when he heard! We'd only just arrived from Bayford House and he was rushing around trying to make sure those men couldn't find us. We went to stay with friends that we never normally stay with in London, so he could check from there that Darcy House was safe." She smiled reminiscently.

"Cousin Richard came to see him there. I could hear my brother shouting from the drawing room."

"Oh, my goodness! What had your cousin done?"

"Well, Cousin David is rather — weak — I'm afraid, and my brother and cousin are always having to rescue him. This time, he decided he wanted to impress this woman he'd met, so he took her and her mother to the south of France — right where the French are fighting the Spanish." She shook her head. "Of course, we're on the side of Spain and David's got himself arrested."

"Goodness! That sounds terrible."

"Yes." Georgiana turned to her. "But it's Uncle Henry, really. He's insisting that Fitzwilliam goes out and parlays for his freedom. He won't let Cousin Richard go, in case something happens to David, because Richard would then be his heir."

"And you seemed to say that with all the shouting, your brother didn't think he should go."

Georgiana tucked her hand in Elizabeth's arm. "No, he didn't. I mean, Fitzwilliam doesn't care at all about the Earldom dying out. I think he's far more concerned about Pemberley."

"And you are far more concerned about your brother to care about any of them."

The girl looked up, her eyes brimming with tears. "Yes. Yes, I am. How can he parlay for David? What has he to offer that the French couldn't just take and then kill him?"

Elizabeth turned and took the girl into her arms. "You have to be brave, Georgiana. Very brave and very calm. That's what your brother will expect of you. There must be something that the Earl has thought of to do this parlay." She gave the girl a tight hug, and then let go, tucking her arm into hers again.

"It is a lady's duty to wait courageously when there is no news. Just waiting. I think it might almost be harder than being there and doing it, because at least you'd know what was going on."

"You're so right, Elizabeth." Georgiana stood straighter and walked a little faster. "You're so good for me. Thank you."

CHAPTER 25

The following morning, Georgiana told Elizabeth that she'd asked her governess to set up her painting materials in the room that had been her schoolroom when she was a girl.

"She's very good, Elizabeth. I've asked her to show us both how we can get a better effect on our nature drawings."

Elizabeth laughed. "You are very kind, Georgiana. You must know that you do not need to learn about such things any more. You have done this for me, and I am most grateful."

Georgiana went pink. "But it is good for me to be reminded of correct technique, as well, Elizabeth."

Georgiana's governess was a middle-aged

woman, who seemed accomplished and well-bred. As Elizabeth sketched the flowers in front of her, she wondered at the circumstances that had brought the woman to this position.

She knew that if she herself did not make a good marriage, her future was also as a governess or companion. But her own education was so deficient that she would never obtain a post like this, which required such skill.

She drew mechanically, wondering what her own future held.

"No, no, Miss Bennet! Like this!" the governess seized a pencil. "Look for the space, draw the spaces between the petals rather than trying for the actual flower."

After half an hour, Elizabeth had to admit her style was already improving. Georgiana leaned over. "I think your technique is much better, Elizabeth."

Elizabeth leaned back in the chair, regarding her drawing critically. "I think you're right." She turned to the governess.

"Thank you, Miss Jones." She caught the disapproving look before Miss Jones managed to school her face into politeness, and wondered at it.

Later, as she and Georgiana picnicked by the lake, Georgiana raised the topic.

"I wonder why Miss Jones was rather forbidding this morning?"

"Do you?" Elizabeth bit into her pastry. "I can think of several reasons, but I expect she ought to learn to hide her feelings better."

"Can you?" Georgiana twisted round to look at her. "Why do you think she was like that?"

Elizabeth smiled. "I do not blame her for her thoughts at all, Georgiana, and you must not allow the knowledge of them to affect your behaviour towards her. But she is a well-bred lady, who is highly educated. She must see me and wonder why it is she who is in reduced circumstances, forced to seek employment; whereas I am here at your invitation, living at a level to which my upbringing does not equip nor entitle me. It is entirely understandable." She dabbed at her mouth with a napkin.

"And, of course, while I am here, she is much less needed as your governess or your companion. She must feel quite out of sorts."

"I see," Georgiana breathed. "Elizabeth, you are so thoughtful and attuned to the feelings of others. I am so happy I met you. I wish I could think as you do."

Elizabeth smiled. "You must just stop and think of how you would feel if you were in the other person's position. It is not difficult, once you are in the habit of doing so."

But she did not think Georgiana would find it quite so easy. All her life she had been the one whose wishes and feelings were paramount. It would take more than merely wishing to make such a change.

And that was what had made her — and her brother — so distinctive at Bayford House. They certainly could not help it, and by playing the part that he had fallen on hard times, it did not strike quite so false as if they had pretended they were people brought up in their position.

Elizabeth wondered if Mr. Darcy had been forced to tolerate intrusive questions from other gentlemen during his time as Mr. Hudson about how his circumstances had become reduced.

She smiled to herself. She doubted very much that any response would have been forthcoming.

"I am so glad you are here with me, Elizabeth." Georgiana was constantly saying this. "You are so good at stopping me from moping about Fitzwilliam being away."

"Moping will do him no good whatsoever," Elizabeth said briskly. "And will merely make the days seem longer." And as she said it, she knew it was not true.

She was at Pemberley to be Georgiana's companion, she had no business wondering how Mr. Darcy was faring on his journey to France.

She had to hide her concern for him. Would they even hear if he had met with misfortune? And at that thought, her heart seemed to feel a sudden pain.

"Come, Georgiana, let us go back to the house." She got to her feet, smoothing her dress.

"Of course." Georgiana seemed to sense her need to stop the conversation and the two walked back to the house.

Elizabeth smiled ruefully to herself. She could get too used to this life, just leaving the picnic items for the servants to pick up. At home, she would be packing everything back into the hamper and carrying it home with Jane's help.

She missed Jane.

"I wonder, Georgiana, if you would permit me a half hour to write to my sister Jane? I would like to tell her what it is like here, but of course I will not mention your brother's current business."

"Of course you must write to her." Georgiana looked distressed. "I am sorry, I have been taking too much of your time, Elizabeth." She hurried to keep up with Elizabeth.

"I know, I will write to Miss Bingley while you pen your letter. I am not good about keeping up with my correspondence."

Elizabeth smiled down at her. "And who is Miss Bingley?"

"Oh, I'd forgotten I haven't told you about her. My brother has a great friend — a Mr. Bingley. I'm not exactly sure how their friendship came about, for he is some years younger than Fitzwilliam, so they would not have met at Cambridge." She shrugged. "Anyway, they are great friends. Mr. Bingley has two sisters. One is married to a Mr. Hurst and the other, Miss Caroline Bingley, is the lady I was referring to."

She suddenly went a little pink and slowed down.

Elizabeth laughed. "Georgiana, you cannot possibly not tell me what you are just now thinking about!"

"Oh, dear." Georgiana bit her lip. "Miss Bingley is very friendly, and I like to write to her occasionally, but …"

"But …?" Elizabeth prompted her, her own curiosity now piqued.

"Well, I think she very much wants to secure herself as Mrs. Darcy. And she has hopes that I might marry Mr. Bingley." She shook her head.

"He is an amiable man, but I do not find my affections are in that direction."

Her face lost its animation and she looked down. Elizabeth knew that something had happened just before they had appeared at

Bayford, but she would not ask the question. So she turned the topic.

"And is Miss Bingley able to secure the affections of your brother?" She tried to ignore the heaviness in her heart.

Georgiana giggled. "No, I cannot imagine that my brother would ever marry her." She glanced up.

"The Bingley fortune is from trade. While my brother is happy to be friendly with Mr. Bingley, I think he finds Miss Bingley tries too, too hard to act properly." She swished her hand through the flowers as they walked past the flowerbed.

"And, in any case, my aunt, Lady Catherine, is quite decided that he will marry her daughter, Miss Anne de Bourgh."

Elizabeth knew she was treading on difficult ground. She most certainly did not want Georgiana to know that her own affections were stirred by Mr. Darcy, but she wanted so much to know if she must steel her heart and leave here as soon as he returned. Fortunately, Georgiana continued, telling her what she wanted to know without having to ask the question.

"Our Cousin Anne is a sickly lady and I don't think my brother wishes to marry her. It would likely mean he has to live in Kent. Lady Catherine has a large estate there."

"Oh, so she does not have a son who will inherit?" Elizabeth tried to sound not too interested.

"No. Cousin Anne will have it all."

"It occurs to me that Miss Bingley might have ambitions for her brother in that direction, then."

Georgiana giggled again. "Lady Catherine would never entertain a man from trade, however wealthy."

"And how do you feel about it, Georgiana? If your affections were stirred by Mr. Bingley, would you mind that his fortune were from trade? Or if Mr. Darcy wished to marry Miss Bingley, would it matter that her background was trade?"

Georgiana looked serious. "It is not that her background is from trade that I do not wish her to be my sister." She looked directly at Elizabeth.

"It is that she is — uncomfortable to be around. Her words sometimes seem designed to hurt. I would not wish her to be able to hurt my brother."

"That is a reasonable thought," Elizabeth said. "But she must certainly have a good fortune."

"Oh, yes." Georgiana looked at her feet as they climbed the steps. "I wish she would take her fortune elsewhere."

Elizabeth laughed. "We ought perhaps to change the subject. We could play some duets?"

CHAPTER 26

*H*er days began to blur, one into another. Elizabeth wondered how Mr. Darcy was faring, but had to work tirelessly each day to try to keep Georgiana from fretting.

The girl was most anxious about her brother and Elizabeth was hard-put to think of new and different entertainments for them to do.

It might have been easier if they had been able to drive out and visit local places of interest, but Elizabeth quite understood why Mr. Darcy had asked them to remain within the estate while he was away.

And indeed, the grounds were so extensive that it was quite necessary to take a small phaeton to the far end of woods to explore somewhere different.

Seeing the picketed soldiers at the far end of the estate, Elizabeth wondered just how many men were quartered around Pemberley. But she knew the steward was liaising with the Captain in charge of the detail, and she was content.

After nearly ten days of their solitude, she was about ready to jump out of her skin with dread for the fate of Mr. Darcy, and with trying to pretend to Georgiana that she was not concerned.

They were taking tea one afternoon and discussing a novel that they had both read when a footman entered and bowed to Georgiana.

She looked up at him. "Yes?"

"Miss Darcy, a coach has been sighted approaching the house. It bears the coat of arms of the Earl of Matlock."

"Thank you. Please let me know when you know who it is."

The man bowed and withdrew.

Georgiana looked at Elizabeth. She was pale and anxious. "Do you think it is news? So soon?"

"I do not know, Georgiana. We must wait with what patience we can muster." Elizabeth cast around to think of something to say.

"Do you need to give instructions to prepare guest bedchambers, or will the housekeeper know to do so?"

Georgiana shook her head. "Mrs. Reynolds

will see to all that. She was housekeeper here before I was born."

Elizabeth smiled. "It makes it all very easy for you."

"I agree. Once I wanted to learn how a household is run, but I did not find the study as interesting as I thought I would."

Elizabeth glanced over at her. "I think you might feel differently when it is your own household you wish to run your way."

Georgiana laughed. "I will have to. I will not have Mrs. Reynolds then."

"No, indeed," Elizabeth responded, and the conversation ceased.

The footman returned, and bowed.

"Colonel Fitzwilliam, Miss Darcy."

"Oh, how lovely." Georgiana rose to her feet, looking pleased.

Elizabeth followed her, but waited where she was while Georgiana went forward.

Colonel Fitzwilliam was a tall, handsome gentleman of perhaps thirty years, Elizabeth surmised. He looked amiable and responsible and she could understand why Mr. Darcy would think he would be a safe husband for Georgiana.

After he'd greeted Georgiana, he turned to Elizabeth and bowed.

"Miss Bennet. I have heard a lot about you. It is very good to meet you at last."

She curtsied to him. He didn't seem to be what she had imagined the son of an Earl to be like. In fact he seemed a very agreeable gentleman.

"I am pleased to meet you, sir. Your company will be very welcome for Georgiana, who will certainly be grateful for different conversation."

She wished she could ask outright about Mr. Darcy — he must know something — but she could not seem to be too interested.

She very much hoped that Georgiana would ask. So she was grateful when the girl spoke.

"What news of my brother, Cousin Richard? Please tell me you have heard news of him."

"There is little to tell, my dear cousin. We have heard rumours that Darcy is there and has seen the local General de Corps d'Ármee, but nothing is known of what passed at their meeting."

Georgiana indicated a seat for him and they all sat down.

"I know he intends to try and parlay locally and is concerned to ensure that Paris does not find out who they actually have in their power. The revolution is not so far in the past that some would

not welcome another aristocrat to Madame
Guillotine."

Elizabeth shivered. "I hope Mr. Darcy does
not place himself at undue risk," she ventured.

"It may not be possible to avoid all risk." The
Colonel glanced at her. "But I know he is sensible
of what can and cannot be achieved, so I am
hopeful."

Elizabeth remembered what Mr. Darcy had
told her. That Colonel Fitzwilliam had not been
permitted to travel to France himself, and she felt
sympathy for him. He must surely feel some guilt
that it was his cousin who had been dispatched to
rescue the Viscount.

She glanced at Georgiana, who was staring at
her cousin, having quite forgotten her duties as
hostess.

She cleared her throat and Georgiana looked
around.

"Should you perhaps send for some fresh tea?
Colonel Fitzwilliam would perhaps welcome it
after his journey."

"It will be here soon, Elizabeth. Mrs. Reynolds
will send it without me asking."

"I understand." Elizabeth reached for her
needlework and tried to blend into the background as she listened to the pair talking.

It might be that Mr. Darcy would wish them

to marry soon, even if he came home safely. It was no life for Georgiana, having to remain at Pemberley behind guard.

Perhaps she would be able to ask the Colonel if there were any news on finding the men responsible for the attack on Mr. Darcy and the attempts to take Georgiana.

But she should not do it in front of her. She was anxious enough.

CHAPTER 27

"You are a fool, Cousin David! A fool to even think of bringing this woman to France." Mr. Darcy spun on his heel and crossed the small room.

"And to have bribed someone to send to Paris to mediate for you! Have you no sensibility of what Paris is like now? Have you no idea just how tempting you must be as a prize to denounce as a spy and throw to the remaining revolutionaries?"

He crossed the room again in a stride and loomed over the seated figure. He must intimidate this weak man, frighten him so that he was too afraid to try anything again that might sabotage their chances of getting away.

"Your job right now is not to do anything,

anything at all, unless I have said you can. Do you understand?"

His cousin looked up at him, wretched, fearful.

"Yes, Darcy. But what happened to Catherine and her mother, do you know?"

"That's her name, is it? Well, you're well out of it, man. That lady wanted the Earldom and as soon as she thought you weren't going to survive this to marry her, she abandoned the thought. The only thing I've been able to discover about her is that she and her mother are making their way back to England by selling their bodies."

"Ohhh!" His cousin dropped his head in his hands and began rocking.

Darcy observed him with astonishment, which slowly changed to pity.

"Did you really think that much of her, David?"

The man looked up at him. "She never told me I was stupid. She was nice to me."

Mr. Darcy turned away again. He pitied his cousin, of course he did. But they were still in danger and he had to get himself home, with David, just as soon as he could.

He wondered bitterly how the family could ever marry David off to someone suitable to maintain the fortune and the propriety of the name. She would need to be a strong woman with good sense. And strong women with good sense never thought David would make a suitable husband, whatever his prospects.

However, he must not think of that. His task was to get himself and David home safely, as quickly as possible.

Elizabeth. He wanted to be back at Pemberley and see Miss Elizabeth Bennet. There was a woman who would make a wonderful wife for David. But he would not permit that.

He wished to make her his wife, wished to ensure she never wanted for anything again. And even if she wouldn't have him, he would never allow her to marry a man like David.

He wondered what she was doing now, how Georgiana was coping with his absence. He hoped the guards around the estate were keeping danger at bay.

He heard echoing footsteps along the corridor, and turned to David.

"I will have to go now. I am lunching with the General. Be calm and do not do anything to alert Paris to your presence."

When the guard unlocked the door and beckoned him out, he left without looking back.

"Merci, monsieur." He followed the guard to the entrance.

"Je suis très reconnaissante pour son

assistance." He nodded his thanks. It would have helped David if he had tried a little harder to remember his French. Speaking loudly and impatiently in English had not endeared him to his captors.

Now for lunch with the General. He hoped to goodness he would accept the bribe. If he was careful enough not to make any sort of implication, he might be fortunate.

Then the journey home. He smiled to himself. David would not be happy.

THAT EVENING, David crouched behind him as he waved the shuttered lantern out from the coast. He saw the faintest glimmer of light from the moored fishing vessel in the bay, its mast outlined in the faint starlight.

"What the hell are you doing, Darcy?" David's voice was back to his usual arrogant drawl now he'd been released from his room. He was fortunate he'd been imprisoned in the garrison rather than the local jail, but then, he had never expected less.

"We're not travelling the length of France together." Mr. Darcy glanced behind him. "Do you really think an obvious aristocratic

Englishman would survive it? We're at war, remember."

"I won't go in that vessel, do you hear me?"

"Fine. I will tell your father that you relinquished your right to the title and decided to get yourself killed." Darcy turned his head and scowled at his cousin.

"And don't forget, the General has sent his Captain to make sure we leave his area. You'll be shot the moment you turn back."

His cousin stared at him, suddenly diminished again. "Is that true?"

"Of course it is. But I am not staying. I have risked enough for you, Cousin David. I have a life to live, a sister to protect and an estate to keep secure. I am taking this vessel back to England. Are you accompanying me, or not?"

David hesitated for a long moment. Mr. Darcy thought he might have to actually force him onto the boat, because he was not really going to leave without him. But then the man sagged.

"I will come. But I will be very sick."

"Just make sure you do not fall overboard then." Darcy was tired of him already. Cousin Richard would have made a fine Earl. It was a great pity he was the younger son.

The rowing boat sent from the fishing vessel grounded on the beach.

Mr. Darcy grasped his cousin's arm. "This way." He waved acknowledgement behind them to the non-existent French Captain he'd used to frighten his cousin, and they hurried towards the boat.

Four heavily-built sailors regarded them incuriously and as soon as they were seated on the thwarts, pushed off and began rowing strongly towards their ship.

As the high, raised bow loomed over them, Darcy breathed a sigh of thanks that he was clear of France. The typically Breton boat was not local to these waters, but the Captain was a good man and money had talked almost as volubly as he did.

The Captain himself helped pull them over the side, and at his signal, the sailors hurried to set the single large sail.

"Alors, Monsieur Darcy. Vous avez trouvé votre frère. C'est très bien."

He pushed him towards the companionway, and Darcy pulled David with him and went below deck.

"That's the way to the heads." He pointed out the rudimentary toilet facilities. "If you're going to be sick you'd better shove your head out there." He turned away. "Or the Captain will make you clean it up."

He did not anticipate the next few days with

any relish. But at least they were away from France. They could not sail straight for England. The Captain had explained they would join the fishing fleet as it trawled off the Channel and would then drift away to the north to beat the blockade.

"Comme vous le souhaitez, Capitaine." Darcy wasn't going to disagree. He had enough gold with him to ensure the silence of the whole crew.

He leaned back on the uncomfortable bench and wished the next days over.

CHAPTER 28

*E*lizabeth found Colonel Fitzwilliam's presence very agreeable as they waited for news. A gentleman gave the days a structure they hadn't had. Of course, with no other gentlemen around, he did not remain at the dining table long after dinner when the ladies withdrew, but the fact that they drank coffee and waited for him to join them helped in some indefinable way.

Elizabeth watched him with Georgiana, and was concerned that she failed to discern any sign of partiality on the girl's side. She would prefer her to marry for love, or at least affection.

One evening, when Georgiana was playing for them, she took the opportunity to speak to the Colonel.

"Sir, I am sorry to have the impertinence to ask this, but do you know if there is any news about the evil men who wished to take Georgiana and caused Mr. Darcy to bring her into hiding, and now needing protection?"

He looked at her thoughtfully. "I am not offended at your asking, Miss Bennet. However, I have little I can tell you. Parliament is debating certain laws to make it easier to apprehend men who do this and we are hopeful of identifying those responsible at the time."

He was watching Georgiana play, though, and his expression was sombre. Elizabeth wondered whether he knew what Mr. Darcy wished him to do if necessary and if so, how he felt about it.

Because he was a regular army officer, as well as the second son, she knew he must have but little wealth. An alliance with Georgiana would mean no monetary concerns and she was a beautiful and gentle lady who would be eager to please him.

On her side, Elizabeth could see no difficulty. Colonel Fitzwilliam was a true gentleman and Georgiana would be loved and cared for. Her fortune would become his and she would no longer be the target of evil men or gold-diggers.

She smiled at her hands, folded in her lap. All that was wanting in such a match was love.

She pondered as to whether that could grow if

the two should marry. She was sure each already respected the other, and was that not a good place to begin love between marriage partners?

Still, deep within her, a rebellion grew. Why could not a lady marry for love, even if she were wealthy? But she knew that ideal was not always possible.

She knew her own situation was also difficult. A wealthy man would wish to marry within his station, a fortune brought into the family would set younger children up with the means by which to live comfortably, because that man's estate was always committed to his heir.

No, she would never marry a wealthy man. But a man with no fortune was not in any sort of position to make her an offer. She had only one thousand pounds settled upon her.

"You seem preoccupied, Elizabeth." Georgiana's voice was close at hand and Elizabeth was startled.

"I'm most sorry, Georgiana. I cannot defend my inattention." Elizabeth forced her mind to the present.

"I think perhaps you could play for us now. A lively air will require your concentration." Georgiana's smile belied any malice and Elizabeth acknowledged it with a rueful smile.

"Excuse me, Colonel Fitzwilliam." She rose to

her feet and went to the pianoforte. Playing would do her good. She must stop pondering matters she could not change and she must enjoy the opportunity she had here.

Her fingers rippled over the keys. She was happy she had had much time to practice these last days, and she settled onto the stool and began to play.

Georgiana picked up some needlework and Colonel Fitzwilliam listened with his eyes closed. Elizabeth smiled and just played tune after tune from memory.

She hoped Georgiana would be happy, and she hoped that her security would soon be so arranged that they could go out and see the local countryside. She longed to walk in the wild hills she could see beyond the estate.

But she was so fortunate to be here, she must not lament what could not be.

OUT OF THE corner of her eye, she saw the footman move towards the door, and whisper to another just out of sight. When he turned towards the room, he held a letter in his hand.

She faltered, and Georgiana looked up, alerted.

The footman went to her. "An express letter, Miss Darcy."

"Th — thank you." The girl was pale and took the letter with a shaking hand.

Colonel Fitzwilliam leaned forward and spoke quietly, reassuringly, to Georgiana.

Elizabeth could not stay where she was and she closed the piano lid softly before moving to join her friend.

Georgiana was trembling and Elizabeth touched her arm.

"Is it your brother's hand?"

Georgiana looked at the letter. "Yes, yes, it is!" there was hope in her eyes.

Elizabeth smiled. "So if he is able to write to you, then the worst cannot have happened, can it?"

"You're right, Elizabeth." Georgiana broke the seal shakily.

She looked at the first page. Elizabeth's heart was beating so hard she was sure the others must hear it.

"He is at Chichester!" Georgiana cried out in relief.

"Three or four days away," Colonel Fitzwilliam said.

Georgiana was biting her lip. "He says he

must go to London first and take Cousin David to Matlock House."

The Colonel leaned forward. "So he has recovered him. I must say I thought it a vain hope."

Elizabeth sat and listened quietly, letting her relief wash over her. He was safe. Nothing else mattered, except that she might soon see him again.

Georgiana was reading the letter, exclaiming over parts of it, so she was not looking at her, but Elizabeth felt her face heating up when she surprised a peculiar expression on the Colonel's face as he looked at her.

She hastily looked down, hoping her colour would fade. "What else might we know, Georgiana? I expect Mr. Darcy might have had little time to write."

"You are correct, Elizabeth. He says he will tell us all that has happened when he gets to Pemberley, and that he hopes he will not be delayed long in London."

The Colonel was sitting back, relaxed in his chair. "On what day did Darcy write, Georgiana? It must have taken the express more than two days from Chichester."

Georgiana turned back to the first page. "On

Wednesday, Cousin Richard. And it is Friday evening now."

He nodded. "I wonder why he is there? It is not a seaport."

Georgiana turned over the next sheet. "He says here the ship's boat put them ashore at Selsea during the night." She looked up at her cousin. "Is that close to Chichester?"

His brow cleared. "That would be right. Of course a French boat would not wish to sail into an enemy harbour so it is unsurprising that they were put ashore by boat." He smiled.

"I am sure David will be full of complaints at the discomfort." But he did not seem disquieted at the fact, more amused.

CHAPTER 29

*A*s he turned his horse onto the path leading through the woods to his estate, Mr. Darcy spurred it on to a canter.

He'd left the coach to follow with his bags that morning and hired a horse. It meant he would arrive at Pemberley hours earlier than otherwise, and he longed to be home.

He longed to greet his sister and assure himself of her safety. He longed to be able to rest and not be on his guard all the time.

But he could freely admit to himself that he longed most of all to see Miss Elizabeth Bennet again, to remind himself what she looked like, hear her lively conversation and see her smile.

He allowed himself to imagine her accepting his approaches, joining him in conversation and perhaps even agreeing soon to become his wife. For he knew now that was what he wanted, wanted with every part of him.

He knew her background, he knew her lack of fortune, he knew how dreadful her family were. And he cared nothing for all that.

Georgiana would welcome her, and he loved her. He must have her for his own, and very soon. He had been able to tolerate the journey to France only because he knew she was here, here at his home. He could even tell himself she was waiting for him, and he wanted her always waiting for him if he had to be away, but more importantly he wanted her always at his side.

The horse slowed a little as it rounded the crest of the hill, and he drew it to a halt as Pemberley came into view through the trees.

His home. The place he loved to be more than anywhere else. A smile escaped. But it would all be spoiled for him if Elizabeth wasn't there. He knew that now.

The horse had rested enough and he urged it forward again, and cantered through the final half-mile to join the driveway, where he slowed to a trot.

He knew Georgiana would have been waiting for him for several days and he was sorry he'd been held up in London. But he needed his uncle's goodwill to maintain the guard around Pemberley, and he knew he needed to maintain it at present. Having brought David home unharmed had helped a great deal.

He wondered how long it would be before David was once more in trouble, and sighed. He did not wish ill of his cousin, but he caused everyone in the family much trouble.

He looked ahead, and saw two ladies and a uniformed officer hurrying down the steps to meet him. So Cousin Richard was here. That was very good. And Elizabeth was still here. His relief made him realise how afraid he'd been that she wouldn't be.

He stopped a few yards from them, and dismounted, handing the reins to the groom. He turned and smiled at the welcoming party. Georgiana curtsied politely, then she seemed to lose control a little and ran into his arms.

"I'm so pleased you're home, Fitzwilliam. I've been so anxious for you."

He patted her awkwardly, and she seemed to gather herself together and stepped back. He bowed to her.

"I'm very happy to be back with you, Georgiana. But I am sure you know that."

He turned to Miss Elizabeth Bennet and bowed. She curtsied back.

"I'm very happy you had a successful journey, Mr. Darcy."

Was there more happiness in her eyes than in her words, he wondered?

"I hope you have enjoyed your stay here, Miss Bennet." He smiled, "And that Georgiana was a good hostess."

"I could not have wished for better." Miss Bennet turned and smiled conspiratorially at his sister, and he was delighted at their easy friendship.

He clasped hands with his cousin. "It's good to see you, Cousin Richard. Have you been here long?"

"About two weeks. I am afraid I found Matlock House rather oppressive and presumed your consent to call here."

Darcy nodded. "You are always welcome, you know that." He lowered his voice. "We can talk after dinner."

He turned back to his sister. "I am greatly in need of tea."

Georgiana tucked her hand possessively into his arm. "I am convinced Mrs. Reynolds has already arranged it, Fitzwilliam."

They ascended the stairs together, and he knew Elizabeth was walking behind him.

HE SAT in his favourite armchair beside the great fireplace in the drawing room. The others sat nearby and he found his eyes straying to Elizabeth Bennet.

He remembered how it had been at Bayford House, how, even then, he'd been attracted to her manner, her appearance and her gaiety.

He smiled, and saw her smiling back at him, although looking a little puzzled. He pulled his mind back to the present. He would not wish to embarrass her.

He turned his attention to Georgiana, and listened as she regaled him with everything they had done while he had been away.

"You have been much occupied, my dear sister. I am happy you have not pined away."

Georgiana laughed. "I could not have done that while Elizabeth was staying with me, Fitzwilliam. But you must know that."

"Indeed, and I am very glad to hear it."

"But I do not want to talk about us, Fitzwilliam. I need to hear everything you have done while you have been gone. Was it … was it very dangerous?" Georgiana sounded almost nervous.

"You must not be concerned for me, Georgiana, my dear sister. I was able to plan for success at my task because I knew you were safe." He sipped his tea — it was good to be home. But he must tell them something.

"Do you remember, when we were quite young, a Frenchman coming to stay for a while? He was a friend of Father from when he was at Cambridge."

Georgiana looked puzzled. "I don't think so."

"Well, you were very young, I suppose. I only remember him a little." He thought back. "He was the Comte Quiberon, a French Count, I suppose. He fled France when the Revolution began, although his wife and children were not so fortunate." He saw his cousin's lips tighten, but the whole story would have to wait until after dinner.

He turned back to Georgiana. "Quiberon is on the south coast of Brittany — and the people there are very independent thinkers. They do not always agree with the rule from Paris." He leaned back. "I remembered the Comte saying to my father that a few of the local fishermen had helped him escape in their fishing vessels."

He glanced over at Richard. "I would not like these details to be discussed outside this place." And he turned his eyes on the ladies. "Or in letters, please."

At their nods, he continued. "I knew that to

traverse the whole of France would be most dangerous, so I made my way to Quiberon and found the son of one of those men who had aided the Comte. I was most fortunate that he gave me passage to the south and waited until I had recovered my cousin and then sailed directly to England with me." He sighed. "I am deeply in his debt."

There was a silence after this.

"We are all very much in his debt for enabling you to return safely." Elizabeth's voice was soft and he thought he heard warmth behind it.

"Oh, yes!" Georgiana's voice was fervent and she jumped to her feet and came and sat on the arm of his chair. "Please, dear brother, promise you will never go away like that again."

He smiled at her. "I can promise that I do not wish to, Georgiana, but whether I shall have to or not, might not be within my gift."

He glanced again at Miss Bennet. Had he caught a shadow of concern there? He pulled his gaze away.

CHAPTER 30

*E*lizabeth and Georgiana rose after dinner to leave the gentleman to their port. Elizabeth knew they would have much longer to wait tonight before the gentlemen joined them. They must have a lot to talk about.

It seemed Georgiana knew that, too. She looked resignedly at the door they'd just entered through.

"Do you think we will ever find out exactly what happened?"

Elizabeth shook her head. "I'm sorry, Georgiana. I don't think we will. It is not the place for ladies to know." She smiled at the girl conspiratorially.

"Although, as his sister, if you walk in the gardens with him, he might let slip a little more."

Georgiana laughed. "I think you are more likely to discover that than I am." She looked directly at Elizabeth.

"I can see the way he looks at you, Elizabeth. I may be young and naive, but I want to say that if I am right, I am very happy."

Elizabeth shook her head. "You cannot be right. You have seen my home, met my family. If you were Mr. and Miss Hudson still, it might be different. But not now."

She turned away. She was the older of them, it was not her place to talk about her feelings to Georgiana. But she suddenly missed Jane very much.

"Let's have our coffee while it is fresh." She looked hard at Georgiana. "I do not want you mentioning this to your brother."

Georgiana looked sad. "Of course I won't if you do not wish it. But I do think …" She shook her head.

They sat quietly over their coffee, and Elizabeth picked up her needlework. It was easier than trying to think of something to say.

"I'm sorry," Georgiana whispered after ten minutes or so. "I have spoiled everything now."

Elizabeth put down her needlework. "No, you have not, unless we both allow it to. If you wish, I can completely forget what has been said."

"Oh, could we do that?" the girl seemed relieved. "I was afraid you might say you wished to go home."

Elizabeth shook her head. "I will stay as long as you need me, Georgiana."

The door opened and they both stood. It had been less than an hour and Elizabeth was surprised. But both gentlemen were smiling as they bowed politely.

As they sat together and Georgiana poured the gentlemen their coffee, Elizabeth waited to see if she would hear any further information of Mr. Darcy's adventures in France. But he seemed disinclined to talk and soon asked the ladies if they might entertain him at the pianoforte.

Elizabeth looked at Georgiana. "I will take first turn, Georgiana. Then you may remain with your brother."

Thus the evening passed for Elizabeth in alternately playing and listening to Georgiana play. She was deeply happy that Mr. Darcy was home and safe, but the atmosphere in the drawing room was charged with more emotion than she was quite comfortable with.

"I want to thank you again for remaining here with Georgiana," he said, as they listened to his sister playing. "I can see it has made a great difference to her."

She smiled, and glanced at the girl as she played. "It has been a great pleasure, sir. She is a delightful companion and Pemberley is wonderful."

He nodded. "I love it here. It is one of the few places where I am content."

She glanced at him through her eyelashes. Did she dare? Yes.

"I wonder how you managed to stay at Bayford House so long. You must have missed Pemberley very much."

He started, but she maintained her serene expression and she watched him relax again.

"I did miss Pemberley," he said. "But I do not remember that time with satisfaction."

Her eyebrows went up. "I know you do not enjoy mixing with country people."

He grimaced slightly. "I am sorry, Miss Bennet. It was not in that sense I said that my memory of Hertfordshire is unsatisfactory. You must be aware that I regret giving a false impression of my circumstances — to you in particular."

Elizabeth felt a strangely warm feeling spread through her, and she looked down, hoping that her suddenly warm cheeks were not visible as a blush.

She was relieved when she heard the piano tune hesitate.

"I believe I am needed to turn the pages. Excuse me, sir."

At the pianoforte, Georgiana looked up at her. "May we finish with some lively duets, Elizabeth? I would love to show my brother how much I have improved."

"Of course we can. Which would you like to play?" Elizabeth sat beside her friend, glad of the opportunity to have to concentrate on the music.

They had practiced this piece so much she knew it from memory, so she was able to glance occasionally at Mr. Darcy. He sat, apparently rapt as they played, and at the end, both he and Colonel Fitzwilliam applauded warmly.

Later that evening, as her maid assisted her to get ready for bed, she wondered what the next day would bring.

Would she get the opportunity to be with them, to share time as she had at Bayford House, or would she find herself sent home? Would Colonel Fitzwilliam stay a little longer? Would the guard be removed from around Pemberley, now that Mr. Darcy was home?

Before climbing into bed, she gazed out into the darkened grounds, illuminated by the faintest of moonlight. Pemberley had become almost like home to her, and she wondered how she would fare if she had to leave it.

She shook her head. She'd always been sensible of the fact that nothing in her life was certain and she knew how to make the best of wherever she found herself.

CHAPTER 31

r. Darcy had thought he would sleep very well, his first night back in his own bedchamber at Pemberley. But he could not.

Halfway through the night he got out of bed and took a drink of water from the carafe on the table. He stood, gazing out at the faintly-lit grounds, knowing the reason he could not sleep.

She was here, here in his home. He wondered if she was asleep, or if she too, was awake.

If she was awake, would she be thinking of him? Dare he believe she held some affection for him? He knew now how important it was that he should marry, should father a child, a son who would be an heir without the crippling risks such as Georgiana now bore, a risk he had never considered before.

But he didn't want to marry unless he could make Elizabeth Bennet his wife. No one else would do.

He smiled slowly. Georgiana would be delighted, he could see that, just by having watched the two of them together.

His family would accuse her of bewitching him because of his fortune, but having met her while playing the part of Mr. Hudson, he honestly believed that she cared nothing for his wealth.

Even if she did care, and would marry him just for his fortune, he didn't care. He would still have her as his wife.

Tomorrow. Tomorrow he would walk with her in the grounds and try to regain some of the easy companionship he had felt back there in Hertford-shire. Soon, perhaps, he would be confident enough to ask her to do him the honour of consenting to become his wife.

Having made that decision, and in hope of success, he went back to bed, and slept with an easy mind.

After breakfast the following morning, the

party set out for a turn about the gardens. As they wandered along the paths, Cousin Richard offered Georgiana his arm and they gradually drew slightly ahead of Darcy and Elizabeth.

Elizabeth stepped lightly alongside him, her easy manner making the silence comfortable.

He looked around at his estate and sighed. "I am very content to be at home."

She glanced at him. "I have thought that France is a dangerous place in this time of war, and you must have been concerned for your safety and whether Georgiana would be supported in the way you would wish if anything untoward had happened."

She had the facts of the matter. Without having to explain to her, she knew his concerns. His heart warmed.

"You understand me perfectly, Miss Bennet." He was grateful to her. "Georgiana's future was — and is — a great concern to me."

She nodded thoughtfully. "I would think you have decided to make some formal arrangements now, so that if a situation arises again, you will not have the feeling of being so unprepared."

He nodded. "You are correct again. I am sorry that I must consider encouraging her to marry while she is young, but I can think of no other way to secure her safety."

"It is well thought of, sir." He knew she understood. "And Georgiana has grown and matured much even in the few weeks I have known her. I think she will understand the necessity, if she is allowed some say in the choice before her."

He nodded heavily. "That is my concern. She … has believed herself in love recently, and I would not wish to remind her too much." He shook his head.

Her voice was quiet. "I do not know a great deal of what transpired in your lives before I met you at Bayford. But when Georgiana wrote to me, inviting me here, she did explain a little of the circumstances. One thing she said was that she thought perhaps he did not really love her. I think that whatever feelings she thought she had for him have eased somewhat."

There was a long silence. He sighed. "Thank you for telling me. I have been concerned for her state of mind if I should raise the subject with her."

He looked at her, delighting that he felt he could discuss this with her, share the burden of his responsibility.

"This man was the son of my father's late steward and my father loved him. So he was a childhood friend to us. Before he turned out bad." They walked on slowly.

"But he is dead. And I have not been able to bring myself to tell Georgiana."

He heard her gasp. And stopped to turn and face her.

"Yes, I know I should have told her, but I could not bring myself to, in case I could not comfort her in her distress." He shook his head, heavily. "He died in a duel, I heard, trying to kill one of those he owed money to."

She turned and began walking again, very slowly. "You say you have heard it so." Then she looked at him, and her eyes were shiny with unshed tears.

"But do you know? Are you certain? You must not distress your sister unless the news is definite."

"Miss Bennet, I am sorry. Perhaps I should not have troubled you with the news. I would not have hurt your feelings for anything."

She shook her head. "I never met the man. I am only distressed for Georgiana, if she should feel herself still in love."

"That is what concerned me most of all." He was glad he had confided in her, having shared the news made it seem less oppressive to him.

She glanced up at him. "Do you feel it might assist if, in general conversation, I was able to ascertain her feelings for this man?"

His heart swelled, she was offering to help

him. "If you do not feel it too much of an imposition, Miss Bennet, I would be most grateful to discover as to how you feel I might approach the topic with my sister."

"They are approaching." Her voice was soft and he looked up. His cousin and sister were walking back toward them.

"Thank you for our discussion," he said hastily and quietly. He raised his voice. "Yes, the gardens are much the same as they were in my father's time, and indeed, his father's. I see no need to change what is already excellent."

"My brother is very old-fashioned." Georgiana laughed as she heard what he said. "There is nothing he would change unless it was essential."

Mr. Darcy bowed very slightly. "I see no need to change things just for the sake of it." He felt a little provoked.

"I find it hard to see how Pemberley could be improved in any way at all." Miss Bennet came to his rescue again. He felt warm, she seemed to know exactly what he needed at any moment.

"You have a strong ally in your determined resistance to change, Darcy!" His cousin laughed. "But if the ladies will excuse us, I thought we could visit the local Colonel of the militia and check on the security of the estate."

"Of course!" Georgiana let go of his arm and transferred it to Miss Bennet. "We might go inside and have tea without you." She smiled at her friend.

"We will have to promise to talk about subjects other than the gentlemen," Miss Bennet laughed.

Mr. Darcy smiled, tight-lipped. "It is a good idea, Fitzwilliam. We might return in time for some tea."

He walked away beside his cousin, refusing to allow himself to look back at Miss Bennet as she went back towards the house with Georgiana.

"So, have you made her an offer, then?" his cousin's voice disquieted him.

"What do you mean?"

"You know what I mean, Darcy. Before you went away to France you spoke to me of marriage and securing Pemberley estate. I know that you felt the responsibility should Georgiana be left to inherit was very great." He smiled.

"And now I have met Miss Bennet, and I know why your mind turned to matrimony. She is most suitable."

"Is it that obvious?" Mr. Darcy groaned.

"To me — yes." Richard answered simply, and he would not have had it any other way.

"No, I have not made her an offer, Fitzwilliam. I was speaking to her about

Wickham and how I could tell Georgiana his fate."

The Colonel's face hardened. "And what suggestion did Miss Bennet have?"

"She has offered to try to ascertain in conversation what Georgiana's feelings are now on that matter. Then I might think of how to speak about it."

"That is a good idea. And now, let us see Colonel Lessey about his business."

CHAPTER 32

*E*lizabeth felt the next few days could have been perfect, were it not for a strange reticence between her and Mr. Darcy.

She walked in the gardens with Georgiana, and sketched and played the piano with her. The governess, Miss Jones, was able to assist Elizabeth begin to learn some rudimentary French and Spanish, although she seemed reluctant to make the lessons too basic, saying Miss Darcy needed advanced language conversation.

She took an hour most days to write letters to Jane and her Aunt Gardiner in London, long letters describing what she was doing, but never mentioning Mr. Darcy.

And she sat with the party at tea, at meals and in the evenings, knowing his eyes were on her, knowing her feelings for him were such that she found it difficult to hide them.

One evening, after dinner, Georgiana was practising the piano and Elizabeth was sitting by the fire when the gentlemen came into the room. Colonel Fitzwilliam went to the pianoforte to sit beside Georgiana.

Mr. Darcy sat opposite Elizabeth. "I find these chairs much the most comfortable in the room." He smiled.

She glanced up. "They are indeed. They are so deep and welcoming that I sometimes find it hard to get out of them, such is the way they enclose me."

He laughed. "I am sorry, then, for what I had been about to say, Miss Bennet."

She looked at him in surprise. His expression was tense and he looked most uncomfortable. "But it does not matter, we can talk here just as well." He looked into the fire, as if for inspiration.

He drew breath. "It is nothing. I just thought that we had a more easy accord in company with each other when we were at Bayford House, and I have found it hard to return to that." He didn't quite mop his brow, but Elizabeth could almost sense him doing it and had to work hard to keep her expression calm.

"When circumstances change, sometimes

other things have to change too." She kept her voice quiet.

"I understand that." His gaze was steady. "But I did not want you thinking I desired it to change."

She felt herself colour and looked down. "Thank you." She wondered what she should think of his words. Did he just want not to feel uncomfortable in his own home? Or was this an opening to further understanding? She wished she knew.

"Miss Bennet, I want us to feel more comfortable and less formal with each other." Mr. Darcy was leaning forward, his voice quiet.

Georgiana played on at the pianoforte, the Colonel sitting beside her. Had the two gentlemen talked about this — about her — over the port? Elizabeth was mortified.

"Be easy, Miss Bennet." He seemed to know what she was thinking. "I am not suggesting anything more than you would wish."

She smiled rather mechanically. How would he feel if he knew what she really wished?

"Do you remember at Bayford, how we used to discuss the news of the day, or local issues, and argue our opinions?" his voice was warmer than it had been and she smiled with the pleasure of the memory.

"Indeed, sir." She knew her eyes flashed. "And what do you think about the current news?"

"Which news are you referring to, Miss Bennet?" he relaxed back into his chair, obviously relieved that the worst was over.

She would not be afraid of him. "Why, the latest news that we ladies never seem to discover. Perhaps you could enlighten me as to the salient stories?"

His lips twitched. "Ah, the old Miss Elizabeth Bennet is back." He crossed one leg over the other. "Well, the war in France seems to be spreading from Spain to Portugal as well. That self-styled Emperor, Bonaparte, has increased the tensions with Russia, and of course, as England supported the Spanish and Portuguese uprisings, the situation across the Channel remains precarious." His face creased with worry, and she had a sudden glimpse of the danger he must have endured, for a cousin he cared nothing for.

"I am very pleased you are no longer there, sir."

He nodded ruefully. "I confess to having a few bad moments while I was there."

The evening was restored. Elizabeth delighted in his conversation and the respect with which he listened to her. The fact that he was now exposed as one of the most prosperous men in the country, seemed now to be forgotten between them, and they were back to the easy camaraderie they had known before, at Bayford.

She was perfectly happy again.

THAT NIGHT, in her bedchamber, she thought about the conversation and the news she had heard. Perhaps she should write to Charlotte. Her brothers must be involved in this terrible war. But perhaps the Navy were able to keep the blockade with too much danger to the officers and crew of the ships.

She would ask Mr. Darcy in the morning. He would be able to reassure her, perhaps.

She lay in bed, smiling at the darkness. Life was very good and she was very happy he had spoken to her to improve the situation.

IT WAS VERY LATE when she was woken by a commotion outside the house. Having the bedchamber next to Georgiana, she instantly thought of the girl's safety, and slipped hastily out of bed. The great window looked out over the main entrance to the house but she saw only a single horse, saddled, and blowing hard.

There was another thunderous knock on the great doors, and then Elizabeth heard the sound of the express rider speaking to the servant. She watched as the man remounted, and spurred the worn horse to a weary canter and he rode away.

She found a shawl and sat on the window seat, wondering what news the express portended. At least Georgiana was safe. But her heart pounded at the thought that Mr. Darcy had been awakened by the express, was reading the letter and perhaps receiving bad news.

She fetched herself a drink, and sat back at the window, knowing it would be a while before she would calm enough to go to sleep again. There was the faintest dawn light in the sky, and the new moon cast a fair light as there were no clouds.

She stared at the hoof prints in the gravel drive. They would be raked out in the morning, she knew, but for now they were a testament to the unusual disturbance.

And there was more disturbance. There were men running, torches flaming over their heads, and the coach and four drew up outside the door.

The coachman sat on the box, and a couple of

grooms held the horses, stamping and snorting with the change of routine.

Elizabeth leaned closer, desperate to see what was going on. Was Mr. Darcy leaving in the dead of night? Or perhaps the letter had been from the Earl and the Colonel was going to Matlock House.

But why the haste? And what could possibly be so urgent that the journey must begin at once and not wait until the morning?

But both men were descending the stairs. Both men fully dressed and conversing quietly, grim-faced. Elizabeth strained to see. What was it all about?

It was Mr. Darcy who was leaving. He reached the coach door and the Colonel stood back a few paces. Elizabeth's heart sank. What danger might Mr. Darcy be going to?

He stood a moment, his foot on the step, and looked back at the house. His face looked almost in pain as he looked up at the windows.

Had he seen her standing there? He raised his hand, almost in salutation, before turning away and climbing into the coach. The door slammed and the coachman shook the reins. The men with torches ran ahead and the coach rolled off down the drive, taking Mr. Darcy with it.

Elizabeth clutched her hands to her shawl, she

must press hard before her heart broke. She had believed this evening might be the beginning of a new understanding. Now, all might be lost.

Perhaps he had not even acknowledged her at the window? He might have seen Georgiana in the next room.

Elizabeth turned away from the window. The room was too dark to do anything other than go back to bed, but as she thought of Mr. Darcy bumping along the darkened roads in his coach, she knew she would not sleep again that night.

But she felt cold, cold with shock. Shivering, she climbed back into bed to wait for the morning. There was nothing else to be done.

CHAPTER 33

*A*t last it was morning, and Elizabeth was waiting, sitting on the edge of her bed, when the maid brought in the jug of hot water for her to wash.

"Is Miss Darcy awake, Frances?"

The maid continued pouring the water into the bowl carefully. "Yes, Miss Bennet. I saw her maid taking hot water into her bedchamber as I came to you."

"Thank you." Elizabeth wondered how Georgiana would feel if she hadn't woken and only found out this morning that her brother was gone.

But if she had watched him go, she hadn't come to Elizabeth's room for any sort of comfort. Elizabeth hurried her toilette, and hoped to see Georgiana as she went down for breakfast.

When she entered the drawing room to wait for breakfast to be called, she saw Colonel Fitzwilliam leaning back in one of the armchairs, fast asleep. She smiled. He'd obviously not gone back to bed after seeing Mr. Darcy's coach away.

A small sound behind her made her turn. Georgiana was in the doorway, trying not to laugh at the sight of her cousin, who would no doubt be mortified when he knew that they had seen him.

Elizabeth put her finger to her lips and together the girls went through to the breakfast room.

"Let him think we have not observed him." Elizabeth forced a smile at Georgiana.

But the girl's reddened eyes told her all she needed to know.

"You saw your brother go, did you?"

Georgiana nodded. "Yes." She turned desperately to Elizabeth. "Why? What could possibly be so urgent as to make him start a journey in the middle of the night?"

Elizabeth shook her head. "I don't know, Georgiana. I cannot imagine anything that would not wait until the morning." She poured them each a cup of tea.

"We will wait for Colonel Fitzwilliam before we eat, but we can at least have a cup of tea." She handed Georgiana's cup to her.

"And I am sure your cousin will be able to tell us the news."

"Of course I can." The Colonel's voice from the doorway was as alert as always, but Elizabeth had to hide a smile at his unshaven appearance.

He rubbed his chin ruefully. "I am sorry for my dishevelled look, Georgiana, Miss Bennet. Would you allow me to have breakfast with you now, or would you prefer to delay while I attend to my appearance?"

Elizabeth looked at Georgiana, who was trying not to giggle.

"I don't mind, Cousin Richard, if Elizabeth doesn't."

Elizabeth bobbed a small curtsey. "I would rather we proceeded with breakfast, Colonel Fitzwilliam. We are both concerned about what the news could possibly be that needed Mr. Darcy to leave here in such haste during the night."

"Yes, yes!" Georgiana cried. "Please tell us at once, Cousin Richard."

He bowed politely and they all sat down, Georgiana restless in her seat. Elizabeth was able to keep still, but inside, she was as anxious as her friend.

"I am sorry you were disturbed by the noise," the Colonel said, taking food onto his plate. "But

Darcy has left you each a short note explaining why he has had to go so precipitately to London."

"Might you be able to appraise us now, so that we don't have to wait until we have the privacy to read our letters?" Georgiana expressed what Elizabeth was thinking, to her unutterable relief.

"There is, I am afraid, not much to tell. The express was from the Prince Regent at Carlton House."

Elizabeth's lip curled and the Colonel smiled wryly. "No matter what we think of him, he is the Regent, and when he summons you, you must go, or risk imprisonment or worse."

Elizabeth nodded regretfully. "And what does the Prince require from Mr. Darcy?"

"That is what we do not know." The Colonel shook his head. "I hope Darcy has time to send a note as soon as he knows, although it might come to us in an unofficial manner, if he is charged with secrecy."

Georgiana was looking completely devastated. "What will he want Fitzwilliam to do? And will it be dangerous?"

Elizabeth leaned forward. "We don't know, Georgiana. But do not distress yourself, it might be for naught."

"Miss Bennet is right, Georgiana." Colonel Fitzwilliam passed her a plate. "You must eat, or you will be ill, and you do not want to worry your brother."

Elizabeth smiled at the girl encouragingly, but she could hardly wait for the meal to end so she could read her letter. She told herself that the note would perforce be very brief, as he had left in such a hurry and had little time. But the fact that he had left her a note as well as Georgiana, made her heart race and a warm feeling suffuse her face.

"Cousin Richard, where are the notes Fitzwilliam left us?" Georgiana was not able to eat much, and thus didn't notice that Elizabeth had not made much of the meal, either.

"I have them here for you, but I suppose I cannot persuade you to eat a little more first?" Colonel Fitzwilliam looked unsurprised when both of them looked at him in amazement. "No, I didn't think so."

He smiled and produced two letters, glancing at the names written on the outside before giving them to Georgiana and Elizabeth.

Georgiana held hers to her bosom. "Please, Elizabeth, will you excuse me? I would like to read it in my bedchamber."

Elizabeth smiled her acquiescence, and the girl hurried out of the room.

She looked at Colonel Fitzwilliam, who nodded at her. "Of course."

Elizabeth hurried outside, holding her letter as if it were the most precious thing she owned. *I must not be resentful that it will be short, he will not have had much time to write.* She knew she was very fortunate to have any note, a gentleman did not write to unmarried ladies.

She found a bench in the walled garden, and surrounded by the scent of the morning roses, broke the seal.

> *Miss Elizabeth Bennet,*
> *I hope you will forgive me for writing to*
> *you, but as you will know by now, I*
> *have been summoned urgently away*
> *to an audience with the Prince*
> *Regent.*
> *I cannot but think the summons is for*
> *something untoward, and I may be*
> *away again for longer than I*
> *would like.*
> *I am berating myself for not declaring*
> *myself to you much sooner than this,*
> *but I wanted to be certain that my*
> *advances would be agreeable to you.*
> *So now you know how I feel and I*
> *must keep myself in hope until I can*
> *see you again.*
> *I know it is asking much of you, but I*

*pray that you will consent to stay
with Georgiana while I am gone. You
provide her with much solace and
comfort. I am most grateful to you for
all you have done for us.
Thank you for your time in reading this
letter,
Fitzwilliam Darcy*

Elizabeth held the letter close to her face. The sheet of paper smelled of him, an aromatic mix of leather and sandalwood. She smiled, and opened the letter to read it again.

CHAPTER 34

*M*r. Darcy scowled furiously at his uncle. "Why in heaven's name could you not keep the family quiet, Uncle Henry? Now I have to go back to France and the situation is incomparably more dangerous."

"I won't accept you speaking to me like that, Darcy." The Earl of Matlock couldn't meet his eyes, though, and Mr. Darcy knew he had the high ground.

Much good would it do him, though, and he heaved himself to his feet and went and poured himself another whisky from his uncle's decanter, knowing how it would anger him. He spun round and pointed at him.

"I need you to guarantee the security of my

sister and my estate until I say it can be removed. Do you hear me?"

His uncle shifted uncomfortably. "You cannot speak to me like this."

"But I am. And you'll take it, by God, because you know in the future I'll have to rescue Cousin David again and again, to prevent him driving the Matlock estate to ruin."

His uncle's shoulders sagged, and Darcy knew he had driven the point home quite hard enough.

"Right. So I need the following help from you to get this damned gold back and to the Prince Regent before anyone can stop us."

He wished he could take Cousin Richard — the task would be immeasurably easier and safer with him beside him. But he needed him to be at Pemberley.

Pemberley. He turned away so that Uncle Henry wouldn't see him smile. He imagined Elizabeth opening the note he'd left for her. Would she understand the meaning behind his words? He'd had to write in such haste and he had also thought he did not want to declare himself in such a manner as to make the occasion seem — ordinary.

He wanted to remember forever the day Miss Bennet would accept his offer. He hoped she would accept — surely she would accept?

And now he had been placed in an impossible position by a family whose own selfish opinions had brought him to the attention of the Prince.

He had to do this. The only way out was to succeed, and by succeeding, he would have more demands placed on him.

"I am sorry, Darcy. You must know that." Uncle Henry's voice pulled him back to the cavernous library at Matlock House.

He glared at his uncle, who looked away hastily.

"What do you need, Darcy? I will do what I can."

"No. You will do what I say you can." Darcy stood over him, and a sudden inspiration struck him. "Or the Prince might lose the gold. And then he might blame you for advising him to use me for his underhand recovery."

The Earl looked as if he had been struck and Darcy's lip curled. The whole family were servile sycophants to royalty and he despised them for it.

He was amused that they looked down on him as untitled. But the King had wanted to confer an Earldom on his father six years ago and Darcy had persuaded him otherwise. He certainly did not want to be indebted to the Royal Family. And now the son was King in all but name. Darcy despised him.

He sighed and sat down opposite his uncle. "I will need you to engage a ship and also provide me with some good servants." He thought carefully.

"I will take my own steward from Darcy House. He is trustworthy." With Mr. Thomas beside him, he would feel much better about his chances of success.

"Perhaps you have a map of the approaches around Dieppe. Or perhaps Le Havre might be better." He considered.

"It is a pity, but with the blockade, I might be better landing in Belgium and crossing the border by land." He stood up and strode across the room.

"Yes, I will go to Antwerp." He looked at his uncle. "Engage a ship for passage to Antwerp. Tell the Captain to engage for the hull to be cleaned at Antwerp. That will give him an excuse to wait for my return."

The Earl sat forward. "You have a plan?"

"Indeed." Mr. Darcy was not about to detail his plan to his uncle. If Cousin David heard of it, the whole town would know within hours.

CHAPTER 35

*E*lizabeth found the time at Pemberley now dragged more than it had before. She was anxious to see Mr. Darcy again, and more so now because she felt that his letter left something unfinished between them.

Within a few hours of having received it, she knew its message by heart, and within a day, she knew his handwriting, how his pen would have flowed over the paper.

The letter itself she tucked into her small stack of Jane's letters, knowing it would be safely hidden there, and not wishing Georgiana or the Colonel to see quite how much she treasured it.

It was a week before a message arrived for Colonel Fitzwilliam from Mr. Darcy and the days had seemed endless as she both worried about his safety and attempted to prevent Georgiana from worrying about him.

Colonel Fitzwilliam, amiable as he was, spent much time in the library and further hours speaking to the guard around Pemberley, writing endless letters and seeming to try and avoid the ladies. Elizabeth felt as if she was being driven mad by his actions.

Georgiana obviously felt that way too, and one evening at dinner, she gathered her courage together and spoke to him.

"Cousin Richard, I have decided I want to go to London." Her words seemed to fail her then, and she shrank back a little in her seat as both Elizabeth and Colonel Fitzwilliam stared at her in astonishment.

"But why would you wish to do that?" The Colonel did not seem to understand her impatience at all. "Your brother would be most concerned if he did not know you to be safe here."

Georgiana's face crumpled a little. "But I need to find out what he is doing. I need to see who's sent him wherever it is and find out how dangerous it is."

Elizabeth knew that the Colonel would be hoping she would intervene and convince Georgiana to give up the idea and stay patiently at Pemberley.

But she wasn't going to do that. She agreed perfectly with the sentiments the girl had expressed and she thought perhaps the Colonel might know something he hadn't yet vouchsafed to them. So she sat there and smiled sympathetically at Georgiana.

His eyes flickered to her and away again, uncomfortably.

He tried again. "Georgiana, you know how much effort your brother has expended to ensure you are safe here — the guard around the estate alone has cost him a great deal in favours made to the Brigadier and to your uncle."

Georgiana looked determined. "But nothing has happened, no one has turned up. I am quite safe." Her lip wobbled. "But I think Fitzwilliam is not."

Colonel Fitzwilliam leaned forward. "Georgiana, you know the danger. You were at Ramsgate when your brother was set upon. You saw the injuries he sustained when he tried to protect you."

Elizabeth saw Georgiana's face crumple, but the Colonel continued on.

"If it hadn't been for the Earl of Sandwich being close by and intervening, your brother would be dead. You would be married to one of those common men, and they would control both your fortune and Pemberley."

"I think you have perhaps said enough, sir." Elizabeth jumped to her feet and put her arms around Georgiana.

"Calm yourself, Georgiana. You know your cousin is right, don't you?"

The girl's shoulders shook but she nodded slightly, and Elizabeth smiled. "That is better. Now sit up and we will speak to Colonel Fitzwilliam about what he knows of both the work that is being done to make you safe and also what he knows about your brother's current situation."

The Colonel looked rather discomfited by Georgiana's reaction to his words, and he glanced sheepishly at Elizabeth.

"I have received a note this afternoon. I wasn't going to trouble you both with what it contains until I could vouch for its provenance."

Elizabeth could hardly believe her ears. "Do you think it to be a forgery, then, sir?

"No, I do not. But it seems to me to be such an unexpected task that the Regent has given Darcy, that I must find out if it is real."

Georgiana was staring at him, open-mouthed. Elizabeth gently touched her arm and signalled to the girl to compose herself. Then she turned again to the Colonel.

"Does the note purport to be from Mr. Darcy himself?"

He nodded. "Yes, but it has arrived in a most unorthodox way. It could have been tampered with."

Elizabeth leaned forward. "Georgiana knows her brother's hand, sir. To begin with, she could at least confirm whether she believes it is his penmanship."

"Oh, yes! Please, Cousin Richard, let me see it!" Georgiana leaned forward too, her dinner quite forgotten.

He reached into the pocket of his tailcoat and handed over a small, rather battered letter. Elizabeth felt disappointed. It could not be genuine, Mr. Darcy would never have shown such disregard for his correspondence.

Georgiana looked equally dubious as she unfolded it and read the first few lines.

"It is his writing. I know it well. It is his!"

Elizabeth jumped to her feet again and stood behind Georgiana, to read over her shoulder. The girl was right, it was in his writing. She stared hard at the small writing, trying to make it out.

Fitzwilliam,

This is a short note, which I will send unofficially to you. I do not want anybody finding out what I have been sent to do. So I hope it does not take too long to reach you.

It appears Cousin David has been unable to remain silent about my recovery of him, and the Regent has discovered I brought him back from France.

I have therefore been charged to go back to France — but not the south, this time — and recover a fortune that has been impounded by a local French commander.

I do not, however, believe what the Regent told me. I am certain Bonaparte knows what I will be about and am having to make plans to try and surprise them all.

I have no faint idea how long the whole business will take and I beg you to care for Georgiana and Miss Elizabeth Bennet to the best of your ability for my sake.

It might be best if you do not appraise the ladies of my task until we know whether it is successful. However, I

will leave it to your discretion as to
what is best for them to know.
I will write whenever I am able to do so
safely.
Fitzwilliam Darcy

Elizabeth was as certain as Georgiana that the writing was that of Mr. Darcy. Her heart had gone cold at the thought that he was to steal back a fortune from under the nose of the French Emperor.

Why, he might take months, just finding out where it was even hidden.

She saw that Georgiana had also thought of the danger her brother was in, and she stepped in to try and reassure her.

"I think, Georgiana, that we might need to remain here for the time being." She glanced at the Colonel before addressing the girl again. "Might it be a good idea to use the services of your governess to improve our own French? Then we could prevail upon your cousin to allow us to subscribe to the newspapers that cover the war."

Georgiana looked up at her gratefully. "I think it is a very good idea, Elizabeth. I am not sure Fitzwilliam will approve, but I will be happy to endure his wrath, for it will mean he is home safely."

"Bravo!" Elizabeth smiled at her. "Spoken as a true lady."

"I think if we are finished with dinner, we could withdraw." Elizabeth glanced at the Colonel. He would probably relish a few moments before joining them.

CHAPTER 36

But Elizabeth did not have long to learn more of the French language. It was two mornings later, as she tried to ignore the animosity of Miss Jones and signal to Georgiana that she should also ignore it, that the housekeeper arrived in the upstairs sitting room.

"Miss Darcy, Colonel Fitzwilliam has requested that you and Miss Bennet join him in the drawing room."

"Thank you, Mrs. Reynolds." Georgiana nodded at her, and she and Elizabeth exchanged surprised looks.

Georgiana stood up. "Thank you, Miss Jones. We will return shortly."

Elizabeth watched the governess' resentful face and wondered again what ailed her.

Following Georgiana downstairs, she turned her thoughts to the Colonel. Had he received news?

As they entered the sitting room, they saw him standing, staring out of the window. A sense of dread settled in Elizabeth.

"Cousin Richard? What has happened?" Georgiana must have felt it too. Elizabeth waited discreetly behind.

"Georgiana! Miss Bennet!" he turned and was smiling. But his smile was rather forced and Elizabeth bit her lip.

"Let's have an early cup of tea!" He tried to sound hearty.

"Have you heard bad news?" Georgiana begged him and Elizabeth was glad she didn't have to draw attention to her concern by voicing the question.

"I have no news of Darcy, Georgiana, nothing at all. But then I am not expecting it yet. He can barely be in France yet. He will not write just yet."

He smiled, a forced smile. "But I have had a letter. I am summoned home by my father." He patted Georgiana on the shoulder. "I am sorry, but I must go. I will return within a few days. And you will have Miss Bennet here with you, so you will be quite safe."

"But Fitzwilliam said you would stay here with

us!" Georgiana seemed to be very anxious, and Elizabeth thought it was high time she found out why.

"I am sorry you have to go, sir, but at least the Pemberley coach is very comfortable."

The Colonel seemed relieved at the change of tone, and beamed at Georgiana. "Indeed. The post holds little attraction."

Georgiana gave a weak giggle. "I have never ridden post." She looked at Elizabeth. "Shall we try it?"

"Definitely not!" the Colonel sounded shocked and Elizabeth laughed.

"I do not think Georgiana meant you to take it seriously." She turned to Georgiana.

"I remember you told me you came into Hertfordshire by post and that it was not very comfortable, especially as the coach was crowded."

"Oh, yes. I remember now." Georgiana looked wistful. "But you have done so much in your life, and I have been so sheltered."

"Well, I am four years older than you," Elizabeth said. "And, as you know, there are so many of us that it is hard for my parents to know where we all are at any one moment!"

Georgiana laughed. "I shall never forget my brother's face the first morning you came to call on us at Bayford House. The housekeeper came hurrying through to say she had seen you crossing the fields and Fitzwilliam said *walking?* as if it was scandalous."

Elizabeth tried to keep her face calm. "I am afraid you both had a very novel experience at Bayford."

"Oh, yes." Georgiana looked pensive. "I think it was very good for us, really." She looked up.

"Imagine if we had never met you."

Her face changed. "Cousin Richard, how did those men find us there? From Ramsgate?"

He shook his head. "We have not found that out. But that is why I am content to go to London to see my father. I will also call on the Earl of Sandwich and attempt to discover what is happening." He shifted uncomfortably in his seat.

"We cannot keep you under guard at Pemberley forever."

THEY SAT over their tea until they were called for lunch, unwilling to lose a moment of the Colonel's company before he left. It was too soon and Elizabeth tucked Georgiana's hand into her arm when they waved him off soon after their meal.

I am here with you, Georgiana. We can be

content …" she saw her face. "Well, as content as we can be."

She started off walking along the path towards the lake with Georgiana on her arm.

"So, we have possibly a week before Colonel Fitzwilliam could be back here, and several weeks before we hear about Mr. Darcy." The girl nodded silently.

"So I think we need to chart a course of action, something to do that will keep us very busy each day." Elizabeth thought that Georgiana would have too much time to think about and be anxious about her brother if she did not keep her occupied.

"But what shall we do?" Georgiana sounded despairing. "I cannot stop thinking about him."

"I know." Elizabeth patted her hand. "I feel anxious for him too. But I would be remiss if I did not make the attempt to help you to feel less anxious each day and to use our time productively."

They stopped for a moment and gazed out over the lake.

"I know what I would like to try, Elizabeth." Georgiana sounded thoughtful.

"And what is that?" Elizabeth was pleased to think that her friend was going to try and assist in her own occupations.

Georgiana smiled to herself. "I am going to choose a complicated piece of music that I cannot even begin to play yet. And when Fitzwilliam comes home, I shall play it for him and delight him."

"That's a wonderful suggestion." Elizabeth approved. "Learning music takes a lot of concentration. And I would like to ask you to help me with my drawing too."

"Yes!" Georgiana clapped her hands together. "I should like to do that." She tucked her hand back into Elizabeth's arm. "Thank you so much for your help. I do not know how I would manage here without you."

"Well, you do not have to." Elizabeth felt as close to Georgiana as if she were her sister, in fact closer to her than any of her sisters apart from Jane.

"Could we begin this afternoon?"

"Of course. We could perhaps sort through the music and find a piece that will tax you properly and also be properly impressive."

And with one accord, they turned back to the house.

CHAPTER 37

*E*lizabeth thought that she might have to keep Georgiana occupied for many weeks until Mr. Darcy came back to Pemberley.

She told herself very firmly that first night, and the subsequent one, that she must not think too much of his words in his letter to her.

If he came home safely, because it seemed his task was very dangerous, he might be much changed.

She must not hope too much. After all, she was not a suitable match for him.

She stared at her reflection in the glass and wondered what had attracted him to her. She was still wondering as she drew the covers around herself in bed, hours later.

Where was he? Was he safe? She longed to see him again and her heart was heavy that she might never see him, might never know what had happened to him.

She lay there, trying to push her fears away until the dawn crept into her room through the gap in the heavy drapes.

IT WAS NEARLY lunchtime and Elizabeth was feeling the lack of sleep during the last few nights. Georgiana, too, was looking pale and tired. But neither mentioned Mr. Darcy. His absence was too big between them to dare talk about today.

They sat quietly over their needlework, the pianoforte having defeated them both, when the footman came into the room.

"Miss Darcy, a coach and four has been sighted coming towards the estate."

Georgiana turned to Elizabeth in excitement. "Can it be him already?" her eyes were bright with hope.

Elizabeth was sorry to have to dash them.

"I'm sorry, it cannot be your brother. He has not had time to journey each way, regardless of the task. And Colonel Fitzwilliam will only just have reached London."

Georgiana drooped. "Then who can it be? Fitzwilliam does not encourage guests."

"We can only wait and see, I'm afraid, Georgiana." Elizabeth was pragmatic, and assumed that it was a local gentleman who did not know that Mr. Darcy was away from home.

Georgiana wasn't so sure. "If it is someone from London, then they might expect us to have to entertain them, at least overnight."

Elizabeth wasn't very sure about that. "If it is a gentleman, it wouldn't be very proper, would it?" She laughed.

"Perhaps we should wait and see. Your Mrs. Reynolds will know to prepare dinner and bedchambers, won't she?"

"Oh, yes. We would not need to worry about that. But if he is not family, a gentleman would not be able to stay, Elizabeth, I know that." Georgiana seemed quite interested to see who it was, and Elizabeth laid aside her needlework, unable to concentrate.

THE FOOTMAN REENTERED THE ROOM. "Lady Catherine de Bourgh, and Miss Anne de Bourgh," he announced.

Elizabeth stood up slowly, next to Georgiana.

She could feel the dismay in the girl and suddenly wished she had asked more about them when Georgiana had told her of her family.

She racked her brains. Lady Catherine was the Earl's sister, so she was Georgiana's aunt. Miss Anne de Bourgh was her daughter — who Lady Catherine wanted Mr. Darcy to marry.

Lady Catherine swept into the room, demanding all their attention with her manner, quite obscuring the two ladies who entered the room behind her.

One of those was a girl about Elizabeth's own age, she judged, who looked pale and dull. The other was rather older and in drab clothing. She fussed around the younger girl and took her to sit down without asking permission.

Georgiana and Elizabeth curtsied deeply, and Elizabeth went to stand close behind Georgiana. She would not let her be overwhelmed.

"Good day, Lady Catherine." Georgiana's voice trembled a little. "I am delighted to meet you again."

The visitor looked her up and down.

"Hm. It has been a long time since your brother brought you to Kent to call on me."

"Yes, indeed it has been a long time." Georgiana didn't try and make conversation, but waited for her aunt to speak again.

Elizabeth watched carefully, wondering what the visit was about.

"And who is this person?" Lady Catherine's glance slid disparagingly down Elizabeth, standing quietly.

"Oh, yes. Lady Catherine, this is Miss Elizabeth Bennet, a friend of mine who is staying with me while my brother is away."

Lady Catherine swept over to an upright chair that commanded the room and sat down. She looked disapprovingly around.

"You do not need a friend to stay as a companion while you have a governess here. You had far better attend to your studies."

Georgiana glanced at Elizabeth despairingly. "My brother approved my invitation to Miss Bennet, and hoped that she could stay while he was gone."

"Hm." Lady Catherine could denote disgust into the smallest sound, and the room remained silent to wait for her next pronouncement.

"And how do you find your new governess?" Lady Catherine eventually said. "When the Earl told me your brother was looking for a highly accomplished governess for the final stage of your studies, I was happy to recommend Miss Jones." She was staring challengingly at Georgiana. "She is the sister of Mrs. Jenkinson," she said, nodding over at the woman who sat beside Miss de Bourgh.

"I have already had her four nieces happily placed in suitable situations."

Elizabeth found herself watching Mrs. Jenkinson, wondering if Miss Jones' antipathy to herself would be replicated in this servant, too.

Georgiana looked relieved as the servants carried in trays of tea and pastries. It would fill up the hour before lunch was called.

Lady Catherine led the conversation. Elizabeth and Georgiana were expected to sit and listen.

Answers did not seem to be required most of the time, and Elizabeth was amused to listen.

She would have enjoyed herself more if she had not been so anxious for Georgiana, who should not expect to have to entertain such a family member.

And as she listened, she discovered that Lady Catherine appeared to think she was here to take over the running of the household until Mr. Darcy was back.

"And after lunch, Miss Darcy, you should undertake an hour's study with Miss Jones. You have a responsibility to maintain discipline here. Your brother would be ashamed of you if you did not keep up your studies."

Elizabeth could not let that go unchallenged. "I do not get that impression from Mr. Darcy when I hear him speaking to Georgiana about her accomplishments, Lady Catherine."

The woman turned her attention to Elizabeth. She looked down her nose at her. "I suppose you think you are providing all the education Miss Darcy requires."

Elizabeth smiled. "Not at all, Lady Catherine. In fact Georgiana instructs me in drawing and music. She is the most accomplished young lady I have ever met."

"Then you cannot have come from a very good background yourself, Miss Bennet. All young ladies should be as accomplished."

Elizabeth looked over at Anne de Bourgh, quite deliberately. Then she looked back at Lady Catherine. "Would you introduce me to your daughter? I would like to make her acquaintance."

Lady Catherine glared at Elizabeth. "Anne is better not making the acquaintance of young women until I know their background. I have heard that you have received but little education from your family."

Georgiana gasped. "Lady Catherine, Elizabeth is my friend."

"Yes." Lady Catherine spared her the merest of glances before turning back to Elizabeth.

"Tell me, Miss Bennet, where do you live? What is your father's estate?"

Elizabeth was not at all discomposed by the visitor's rudeness. She understood that it was entirely part of that lady's thoughts of her own superior breeding.

She answered Lady Catherine composedly, quite refusing to feel ashamed of her own family, even if she had felt it when introducing them to the then Mr. Hudson.

Her smile when she thought of him at Longbourn seemed to infuriate Lady Catherine.

"I do not see what there is to smile about, Miss Bennet! It appears to me you are not at all a suitable companion to Miss Darcy. My sister would have been ashamed of her daughter having a friend from a background such as yourself."

The tirade continued all through lunch and Elizabeth was glad to escape to her bedchamber when Georgiana was sent up to do an hour with Miss Jones.

She lay on her bed, wondering how long Lady Catherine intended to stay, and whether Colonel Fitzwilliam could change things back when he returned from London.

Her frustration led to a tear trickling down her face. Poor Georgiana. How she must be feeling, seeing her friend insulted and not being able to say or do a thing about it.

CHAPTER 38

*A*n hour later, she rose and washed her face. She was certainly not going to permit Lady Catherine to get the better of her, and she would meet Georgiana after her hour's lesson and they would go for a walk in the gardens and talk as they always had.

It would help Georgiana very much if Elizabeth could show her she felt none the worse for the way this member of her family had treated her.

She went up to the sitting room she knew was being used for Georgiana's studies, drew a deep breath to knock and suddenly realised why Lady Catherine had appeared today.

Miss Jones must have been writing to her sister, who had passed on information to her employer. It meant their arrival today, so soon after the Colonel had left, had been no accident in its timing.

She knocked on the door. Would Lady Catherine try and send her away?

Georgiana looked up, pleased to see her.

"Miss Darcy has not yet finished her lesson, Miss Bennet." Miss Jones was polite but had an undefined sense of triumph.

"Then I will sit here and wait for her." Elizabeth smiled serenely and sat herself on one of the chairs by the window.

"I *am* finished." Georgiana could be firm too, and Elizabeth bit her lip so as not to laugh at Miss Jones' obvious frustration.

"What are we going to do, Elizabeth?" Georgiana closed her book and stood up.

"I thought we could walk in the gardens, Georgiana. Fresh air is so healthful."

The two friends went down the stairs once they had collected their hats and parasols.

"How have you managed this last hour, Elizabeth?" Georgiana kept her voice low.

"I have been in my bedchamber since lunch, Georgiana." Elizabeth bit her lip. "I did not think that Lady Catherine would require my company."

As they went through to the walled rose

garden, Georgiana sighed. "I think she's going to send you away, Elizabeth."

"I am sorry to agree with you, but I think she has come here with that eventuality in mind, Georgiana."

"May I come with you, Elizabeth? I could stay with you until my brother comes for me."

"Oh, Georgiana!" Elizabeth touched her arm. "I would love to be able to say yes. You know that, don't you?"

"But you aren't going to let me, are you?"

Elizabeth shook her head. "It is not that. I think that as you are only fifteen, your aunt is probably able to prevent your going. She is your closest relation within your reach."

She stopped and looked around her. "And, Georgiana, remember your security, how hard your brother has worked to keep you safe."

She met Georgiana's eyes. "If the Ramsgate gang could find you at the Meryton assembly, they will find you at Longbourn. I could not bear it if I was to blame for your loss."

Georgiana turned away from her. "I know you are right," she choked out. "But how can I stay here with her — and without you?"

"You are the mistress of Pemberley, Georgiana, while your brother is away. The staff are there to do your bidding. And you are a gentle-woman. Do not take her rudeness any more than you wish to." Elizabeth smiled.

"I think I am perhaps not very good for you, telling you this. I must be a rebel at heart. Certainly I am not well bred, so she is correct in her assessment of me."

"I don't care about that, Elizabeth!" Georgiana sounded fierce. "But I just wish I was as brave as you. I think I might be quite worn down by her within a short time."

"And is your Cousin Anne not able to befriend you?" Elizabeth was curious as to why the other girl was so quiet and dull.

Georgiana shrugged a little. "She is very sickly. I do not think I have ever really met her properly." She looked at Elizabeth out of the corner of her eye.

"My brother said he would keep me away from Rosings Park as long as he could."

"That is the name of her estate, is it?"

"Yes. It is some twenty or so miles from London, in Kent."

"Well," Elizabeth said, but as she turned she saw Lady Catherine walking hurriedly toward them.

"Georgiana, if we do not get the chance to talk again, you can always come to my bedchamber after dark. Miss Jones cannot warn Lady Catherine where you are on that occasion."

The girl nodded, staring wide-eyed at her aunt. "She frightens me with her manner towards me."

Elizabeth laughed. "I am not surprised, but be gentle and acquiescent if you wish her to be kinder towards you. An easy life is not to be disdained."

Georgiana gave a tiny smile. "But you do not concern yourself with that."

"I have not been brought up in that way." Elizabeth waited for Lady Catherine to reach them and curtsied.

"Good afternoon, Lady Catherine."

The only response she got was a regal nod as the older woman swept past her to Georgiana.

"Miss Darcy, I think you should come into the house with me. If you wish to take a walk in the gardens, then it is as well to do so with your governess, for you can converse in French or Italian and further your education."

"Perhaps I might do that sometimes, Lady Catherine," Georgiana said. "But sometimes I wish to talk to Elizabeth, and I will also wish to talk to Cousin Anne and get to know her as well."

Lady Catherine gave an audible sniff and Elizabeth and Georgiana walked demurely into the house behind her.

Georgiana leaned towards her. "What would my brother think of her being here?"

Elizabeth shook her head. "I am not certain he would be able to do much about it. He is a true gentleman."

"Oh, yes!" Georgiana smiled, then she looked sad. "But I don't think he'd be very happy."

"No, I'm sure he won't." Elizabeth walked beside Georgiana. Then she thought of something. "Georgiana? Does your aunt know about what happened at Ramsgate that requires the guard to be here?"

Georgiana shook her head. "I don't think so." She raised her eyebrows. "Does it matter?"

"I don't know. It is some weeks now and we have heard nothing." Elizabeth kept her voice low. "But I would be anxious if she were to try and send the militia away, or even take you out from the park."

"What are you two talking about? I must be part of this conversation!" Lady Catherine's hectoring tones finished their talk.

DINNER WAS STRAINED and mostly silent apart

from Lady Catherine's comments and complaints. Nothing was right, nothing was organised as she liked it.

Elizabeth sat at the foot of the table, trying as best she could to hide her resentment at Lady Catherine having seated herself in Mr. Darcy's place at the head of the table.

Since he had left, no one had sat in that seat, not even Colonel Fitzwilliam. She saw that Georgiana was indignant about it also, but Lady Catherine was indifferent.

She monopolised the conversation, allowing no one to answer, and directing a stream of criticism at Elizabeth.

Several times Elizabeth saw that Georgiana wanted to intervene, and she shook her head slightly at her. She was unmoved by such criticism, after all, the woman was nothing to her, but Georgiana would have to remain here under the same roof as Lady Catherine until that lady left here.

Elizabeth smiled gently, knowing it infuriated Lady Catherine, and thought of the letter from Mr. Darcy. How she would have loved to draw what he had said to that lady's attention, but she determined to keep it to herself, as she had previously decided.

After dinner, in the drawing room, Lady

Catherine decreed that Georgiana should play for her, and was reluctantly obeyed.

Elizabeth sat and thought of her letter, knowing that the brightness in her eyes was as vexing to Lady Catherine as her smile.

CHAPTER 39

*M*r. Darcy sat uncomfortably in the swaying cart as it lumbered along the rutted cart track, as like those in England as was the countryside around him.

"Stoop a little more, if you please, sir." Mr. Thomas leaned over to call out.

Mr. Darcy grumbled to himself. "There is no one to see."

"I agree, sir. But you would do well to get into the habit of a peasant, and it is as well to rehearse it here, where any errors will not be observed."

"Thank you for the advice, Mr. Thomas." They sat in silence for near on the next hour, Mr. Darcy almost dozing off in the bright sunlight. He had slept abominably the last week, crouched in the bottom of a fishing vessel, staying in stinking

287

hovels as he bargained with loyalists and hid in pigsties.

He spent gold aplenty on bribing those he needed to — at least it was his uncle's gold. He had forced that out of him. At night he slept alternately with Mr. Thomas, always one on guard for treachery and thieves.

He was thin, unshaven and very dirty. He glanced over at his steward. Both men looked very similar. No one seeing them now would be able to tell who was man and who was master.

"So, remind me why you consented to come with me on this venture, Mr. Thomas." Mr. Darcy decided he must stay awake.

"I seem to remember thinking you might have need of me, sir."

Darcy's smile was reluctant. "I am indeed glad to have you beside me, although I worry for your safety."

Mr. Thomas glanced sideways at him. But he had known him a long time and was able to take liberties no other man would dare to.

"I worry about my safety, too, sir."

Darcy had to laugh. "Once we are back in London, I will allow you a few weeks' rest."

"Don't know where I would go, sir."

"True enough." Darcy contemplated the dreadful old boots he was wearing. They were rather too small and pinched his feet abominably. "Pemberley seems very far away right now."

Mr. Thomas twisted round and looked ahead as the driver shook the reins to try and prevent the horse stopping to tear some vegetation from the roadside.

"I think we will be there by dusk. It might yet be not too long until we are on the way home."

Darcy grunted, and slouched further down on the bench. "All the more reason for some ruffians to slit our throats."

"Come, sir." Mr. Thomas tried to revive his master's spirits. "You recall we have other plans that should prevent that eventuality."

Mr. Darcy grunted again. "It is a good plan, and it shouldn't fail."

"You will see, we will be back in England within the week."

"Perhaps." Darcy sank into a reverie. He wished he was back at Pemberley, listening to Elizabeth and Georgiana playing the pianoforte, watching Elizabeth and Georgiana in conversation, walking in the gardens, and making the evening conversations after dinner a joy.

He glanced at his dishevelled appearance and wondered what Elizabeth would think if she could see him now. He smiled slowly, she would think it an adventure. His smile widened — she would insist on stealing a bigger pair of boots.

"There, sir!" Mr. Thomas pointed ahead. The squat buildings of the run-down farm were barely visible in the haze.

"Good man." Darcy dragged the map out of his pocket, and unfolded it. He needed to remind himself of where they had to get to the following morning.

CHAPTER 40

The next morning, Elizabeth dressed carefully. She wanted to feel invincible — quite above all the barbed comments that Lady Catherine could direct at her.

She sat at the glass as the maid brushed out her hair, wishing Jane could see her now. But her thoughts soon turned to Mr. Darcy.

She imagined him in France. He'd look just the same, handsomer than anyone else in the room.

She smiled, of course, she'd never been to France, but she knew the rooms at the Imperial Palace were sumptuously decorated. He would fit right in, having been brought up in the under-stated grandeur of Pemberley.

She tried, and failed, to imagine how Mr.

Darcy could persuade anyone to tell him where the stolen gold was hidden.

How could he possibly find out? Whoever knew where it was would surely be loyal or would steal it themselves.

She bit her lip, feeling suddenly sombre. Was he safe?

She shook her head, trying to remove her thoughts from him.

She was certain that Lady Catherine would send her home today or tomorrow and though Mr. Darcy had asked her to remain here with Georgiana, she had no evidence of that apart from his letter, which was most certainly private.

Without Colonel Fitzwilliam to insist on her remaining, she could not. Lady Catherine would pay no regard to Georgiana, if she protested, in fact, it would merely confirm to Lady Catherine that Elizabeth was a bad influence on Georgiana.

So she was sad as she walked down the stairs to the breakfast room. The whole atmosphere of Pemberley was spoiled for her, knowing Lady Catherine was here.

So she felt very much for Georgiana. It was her home and she could not know how long Mr. Darcy would be away and Lady Catherine would be here, her malign influence spreading over the estate.

Elizabeth felt very much that she should exert herself to be pleasant. Perhaps she could stay if Lady Catherine felt her to be a suitably respectful person. She didn't want to stay for herself any more, Lady Catherine was someone she would willingly leave. But Georgiana needed her, she knew that.

The girl appeared in the doorway, downcast, and Elizabeth jumped up.

"Come here and sit with me, Georgiana. We have time to talk and enjoy ourselves until your aunt comes down at least."

Georgiana smiled, but it was obviously an effort for her. "You are so good to me, Elizabeth."

"And you are, to me." Elizabeth waited as the footman handed Georgiana the plate of bread.

"You must not be downhearted, Georgiana. I have decided to be the politest, most respectful companion there is. You will see how well I can charm my way into being permitted to stay with you for a while longer."

Georgiana bit her lip. "I do not think anything can change my aunt's mind once she has decided upon a course of action. And I think she was minded to send you away before she had even met you."

"I would not be surprised at that," Elizabeth

mused. "But it will amuse me to flatter her and we shall see what is what."

"I do admire how you make the best of every situation, Elizabeth." Georgiana twisted her napkin in her lap. "I wonder how much longer we have before Lady Catherine comes downstairs."

"I would not expect her to start the day very early, Georgiana." Elizabeth thought. "And it must take some time to attire herself properly. Let us take full advantage of the time we have."

"All right," Georgiana said and faced her. "I thought last night of something and I wondered if you would know the answer." She met Elizabeth's eyes. "Lady Catherine has not come all this way from Kent for nothing. She has not been here for years. How did she know when to come? How did she know that my brother and Colonel Fitzwilliam were both gone from home? And how did she know so much about you?"

Elizabeth lowered her voice. "Can you not think of the answer, Georgiana? Your governess, Miss Jones, is not just a very accomplished gentle-woman fallen on hard times. She is here to write to her sister, and send information in that way to Lady Catherine."

Georgiana was wide-eyed. "You mean …"

"I do not know for certain *why* Lady Catherine

is doing this, but I am completely certain that she is."

She took another small mouthful of food. "But there is something else I wish to ask of you, Georgiana. If she does send me away, I am fearful that she may only send the carriage to the nearest post and leave me there. I do not have enough money to get home."

"No. No, Elizabeth." Georgiana shook her head determinedly. "I will ensure that the coach takes you all the way to Longbourn and that you take a maid with you. It would not be right to send you by the post."

"Thank you, Georgiana. I am sorry to have to ask that, but I know Mr. Darcy sent assurances with the coach that came to Longbourn that he would ensure I returned the same way. Or my father would not consent to let me come."

"It will be done." Georgiana set her lips. "I will speak to the steward and the housekeeper. It will not be possible for her to overrule me."

"Good. Then we will think no more of it." Elizabeth smiled. "Perhaps we have time to do some practice. You have chosen the piece by which you are going to impress your brother, haven't you?"

Georgiana made a rueful face. "I do not know if I want to improve any more, Elizabeth. I would like to say that Miss Jones has managed to teach me nothing while she has been here." She looked across the table. "Why does she dislike you so much?"

"I don't think it is me in particular," Elizabeth confessed. "I think she might be very resentful of the circumstances that have reduced her to seek employment."

"Well, she should be nice to me in order to keep that employment." Georgiana sounded resentful herself.

"You must be careful, Georgiana," Elizabeth said. "Your aunt may feel confident your brother might not come home and she will wish to control who gains Pemberley through you." She glanced over, troubled that she needed to appraise Georgiana of this. "And Colonel Fitzwilliam cannot help you, he is only her nephew."

"But his is my guardian, jointly with my brother!" Georgiana sounded triumphant. "So he has more say in matters of my education than Lady Catherine does."

"Yes, but he may not wish to anger your aunt." Elizabeth cautioned Georgiana again. "Come on, you have finished your breakfast, we will go and do some work on the piano to take your mind away from what we have talked about."

Georgiana rose to her feet. "Yes, I agree. But

first I will go and speak very strongly to Mrs. Reynolds about the carriage. And get her to summon the steward here to see me, as well."

Elizabeth watched her leave the room, her face tipped up defiantly. She smiled. Georgiana was certainly no longer the shy, frightened girl she had first met at Bayford House. Lady Catherine might find her less easy to manage than she supposed.

She left the breakfast table herself and went to the pianoforte in the drawing room. It was as fine as the one in the music room, and incomparably better than the small upright at Longbourn.

Her lips curved. And definitely better than the ancient instrument at Bayford House, where, despite everything, she and Georgiana had become good friends.

She relaxed as soon as her fingers touched the keys and she rippled happily into a light spring air. Each time she stretched her reach to the lower notes, she could feel the slight pressure of the sheet of paper tucked into the side of her cotton dress.

Knowing as she did that she was likely not to be able to have any secrets in this house, she had decided to keep Mr. Darcy's letter to her with her at all times. It was far too precious to lose, even though she knew it by heart.

CHAPTER 41

*E*lizabeth did not find much opportunity to charm her way into Lady Catherine's good opinion. When she heard that lady's hectoring tones from the breakfast room, she shut the piano lid with a sigh and went back through to be sociable and pleasant.

"And why have you stopped playing?" Lady Catherine demanded. "I was enjoying listening to the music and you can have no better thing to do."

Elizabeth curtsied low. "If your Ladyship would like me to continue to play for you, I will of course do so." She smiled guilelessly at her, and went back to the instrument.

After half an hour, Elizabeth needed to search

through some of the music as she could no longer
think clearly enough to play by rote.

She could hear the tones of Lady Catherine in
the other room, and, in one of the pauses, she
heard Georgiana's voice in quiet reply.

She wondered what was being said and hoped
very much that Georgiana was not upsetting her
aunt, or life might be uncomfortable for her —
especially if Elizabeth had to leave here.

And then Lady Catherine swept into the
room, Georgiana behind her.

"Miss Bennet! I have decided that you cannot
be a suitable companion for Miss Darcy. My own
…"

But Georgiana slipped past her and joined
Elizabeth.

"I am sorry," she whispered. "I have not been
able to change her mind in any way."

Elizabeth smiled at her. "We can write to each
other every day. I will be thinking of you all
the time."

"Miss Bennet! Kindly attend to me!" Lady
Catherine looked exceedingly provoked.

Elizabeth looked deliberately at Georgiana.
"Do not provoke her further. When she is gone
you may ask your brother if you and I can meet
again."

She turned to Lady Catherine, her face tipped

up. "I understand your sentiments, Lady Catherine. But I will not say that I am choosing to leave here, knowing that Mr. Darcy has asked me to stay with his sister while he is from home."

Lady Catherine drew an angry breath, but Elizabeth had not finished.

"I will, of course, leave, if you decide to overrule Mr. Darcy's decision about a guest at his own estate, but that will then be for you to settle with him."

She heard Georgiana's muffled sound, but she was certainly not minded to make life easy for Lady Catherine.

"Of course I will override his decision! It is quite obvious that since he has left, you have decided to ingratiate yourself into Miss Darcy's affections. I will not have it, and he will thank me!"

She turned away. "You may go to your bedchamber to collect your things. I have instructed your trunks be packed."

Elizabeth drew a deep breath. Mr. Darcy's letter rustled against her skin and she felt comforted.

Georgiana took her arm. "I will come upstairs with you. I do not care what she says."

"Then you should." Elizabeth kept her voice low. "Your main task now is to stay safe and make your own life as easy as possible until your brother is home."

"Miss Darcy! You should be about your studies!" Lady Catherine's voice interrupted them.

Georgiana turned to her aunt. "I do not wish to go up to my lessons until I have said goodbye to Elizabeth properly."

Lady Catherine puffed up alarmingly, but she seemed to be lost for words, and Elizabeth wondered just what Georgiana had said to her in the breakfast room.

"Write to me this evening, Georgiana, please. I need to know you are all right." Elizabeth kept her voice low as she went upstairs with Georgiana.

"And I will write to you every day. I hope you are permitted to receive them."

Georgiana's eye filled with tears. "I really would like to come with you."

Elizabeth shook her head. "We have already discussed it, Georgiana. It is impossible." She smiled at her.

"You must be very brave. I hope it will not be long."

The girl smiled tremulously. "I have ensured that the coach will take you to Longbourn, and I have arranged that your maid will go with you."

"That is very kind of you, Georgiana. You are as a sister to me, and I will think of you always."

"Don't say that," Georgiana choked. "It sounds like a final farewell."

"I am sure it will not be." Elizabeth tried to cheer her up. "After all, soon your brother will be home, and perhaps even sooner, your cousin. They, at least, know what your aunt is about."

They continued their low-voiced conversation right until Elizabeth was about to climb into the coach.

"I will write from our night-stop, Georgiana." Elizabeth touched her friend's arm, "and I will tell you all the news, which will be nothing at all." She smiled as the girl almost laughed.

"And if I do not get it, I will be able to write and give you an alternative direction, which I will arrange somehow."

"You have learned so much, Georgiana, since I first met you. I hope all goes well — and please let me know at once if you hear of your brother." Elizabeth could not stop herself asking that, although she did not want Georgiana knowing of her feelings for him.

"Of course I will. And I will write with news of all that is happening here."

And then they parted. Lady Catherine did not exert herself to come to see her away, her calculated rudeness allowing Elizabeth to speak longer to Georgiana, but still raising her anger.

Her maid was sitting opposite her, and Elizabeth smiled slightly at her, wishing herself alone. She wondered if she would ever see Georgiana or Pemberley again. Her heart pained her. What if she never saw Mr. Darcy again?

She forced herself to wave at Georgiana as the coach began to roll down the long drive.

CHAPTER 42

*E*lizabeth had been home at Longbourn for nearly three weeks. At first, she had been pleased to be home and had spent many hours appraising Jane as to what had happened at Pemberley.

The only thing she hadn't wished to share was Mr. Darcy's current whereabouts. Somehow, admitting his task seemed to magnify the danger he must be in and she shivered as she thought of what he might be going through.

"But Lizzy! Don't you think you were much too uncivil to Lady Catherine?" Jane was perturbed.

"No, I do not. Jane, you do not know how ill-mannered she was to me. Poor Georgiana was quite dismayed."

"Oh, yes!" Jane smiled. "I still find it difficult to imagine the shy and quiet Georgie Hudson is actually a Darcy!"

Elizabeth bit her lip. "She is the same quiet and unassuming friend she ever was. I admit I am most concerned, Jane. Why has she not written after that first letter? I was so sure that she would write."

"Perhaps her aunt has forbidden her. After all, you explained how you told her to obey her aunt and not behave badly."

Elizabeth stared out of the window. "No, I do not think it can be that. Georgiana will need to write to me to describe what's happening and I am quite certain that she needs someone to share her feelings with."

"But you are writing to her, are you not?"

"Oh, yes. I promised to write each day and so I am. But I confess I am worried that I have not heard from her." She turned rather desperately to her sister.

"What if something has happened to her? Or to Mr. Darcy? Will I ever know?"

"We will just have to hope so, Lizzy, for your peace of mind." Jane embraced her sister. "But perhaps we can keep you busy a few days more. Then you might get another letter inviting you back to Pemberley."

She stood up. "Now, Lizzy. You know what the answer is. You go and have a nice long walk. I will see to Mama."

"Jane, you are so good. I am sure I can never repay you." Elizabeth reached for her bonnet. "I will not be too long."

ELIZABETH REALLY ENJOYED her long walk. Having had to stay on the Pemberley estate within the ring of guards with Georgiana, she had missed her long walks over the hills and it was wonderful to be back in Hertfordshire in the familiar places of her childhood.

But her heart was heavy with dread. Something had happened to Georgiana, it must have done. And why wasn't Mr. Darcy back at home? Or had he returned and decided that he did not wish her in his life? What had Lady Catherine told him about her?

Heavy clouds thickened above her head, a harbinger of her mood, and she turned for home. She must work on turning her life back to how it had been all those months ago.

If she heard from Mr. Darcy or from Georgiana, then she would be delighted. But living each day in anxious expectation was taking a toll on all the family around her and Elizabeth did not wish to cause others unhappiness.

As she drew near to Longbourn, she heard a faint voice calling.

"Lizzy! Lizzy!" It sounded like Jane, and immediately Elizabeth recalled the last time Jane had called her from a walk with the first news after the Darcys had left Bayford House.

She began to run.

"Lizzy! Lizzy!" Jane's voice was closer and Elizabeth called back.

"Jane!"

But as she drew closer to her sister in the lane at the edge of the field, she could see no letter in her sister's hand.

"Has a letter come?" she panted. "Do you have a letter?"

"No, it is not that." Jane turned and began hurrying along the lane.

Elizabeth walked along beside her. "Is Mama wanting me?" she was bitterly disappointed.

"Oh, no, Lizzy." Jane shook her head. "I would not rouse your anticipation for that. No, a gentleman has come to call upon father." Jane clutched at Elizabeth's arm. "He asked for Miss Darcy!"

"What?" Elizabeth walked faster.

"Yes. Father took him into his book room to talk and then he came out and called for you."

Jane was puffing beside her. "So I said I would find you."

"Is the gentleman Mr. Darcy?" Elizabeth didn't know why she was asking. Jane knew Mr. Darcy — as Mr. Hudson, to be sure — and would have said it was him. But why did the gentleman want Miss Darcy? Was it one of the gang from Ramsgate? What had her father said to him? And why were they looking for Georgiana here?

They were nearly there and Jane gave Elizabeth a little push. "You run on ahead, Lizzy. I am not able to run as fast as you."

"Thank you, Jane." Elizabeth set off at a full run, only slowing to a more decorous, but still fast, walk as she turned into the Longbourn drive.

The front door was open and Kitty was watching for her. "Lizzy! Papa has said you must go straight to him in his book room."

"Thank you, Kitty. Is the gentleman still there?"

Kitty nodded, her eyes bright with excitement at the interruption to the day's routine.

"Is that Lizzy? Oh, why did she have to go out?" Her mother's voice could be heard from the sitting room. Elizabeth winced.

"Will you go and tell Mama I have gone to Father?" she asked Kitty, who agreed at once.

Elizabeth stood at the door to her father's library and took a deep breath to calm herself. If she was not sure whether the gentleman was from Ramsgate, she did not know what she was to do.

She drew another breath, and knocked at the door.

"Enter." Her father's voice.

She turned the handle and went into the room, her heart still beating fast, whether from the running or from fear, she wasn't sure.

Her father, standing by his desk. Another gentleman, rising to his feet to bow, and a feeling of utter relief — she knew him.

"Colonel Fitzwilliam!" she curtsied, with a relieved smile.

"Miss Bennet." The Colonel bowed.

"Do you bring news, sir? I have heard nothing from Georgiana and she promised faithfully to write each day."

He whitened as he looked at her. "Miss Bennet, I understand from your father that Miss Darcy is not here, but have you not heard from her at all? I had hoped you would know where she was."

Elizabeth shook her head. "She promised to write each day, sir. There was one letter here from her when I arrived, that she had written the day I was sent away from Pemberley, but I have heard nothing since. I have been very worried."

Her legs threatened to give way, and she reached behind her and lowered herself to a seat.

"Is she not at Pemberley, sir? When did she leave? Where is the coach and the servants who went with her? Please say she did not leave on foot?"

CHAPTER 43

The Colonel looked at Mr. Bennet. "May I sit down, sir, and talk to Miss Elizabeth?"

Mr. Bennet nodded, his face drawn as he looked at his daughter. He went over to the high-backed chair in the window seat and sat down, facing away from them.

Elizabeth was pleased at his attempt to give them some privacy. She looked at the Colonel.

He grimaced slightly. "Miss Bennet, I must apologise very much for what you must have endured at the hands of my aunt. Darcy and I had not even considered that she might appear at Pemberley. If we had, I would never have gone to London." He shook his head.

"I cannot understand how she knew that neither I nor Darcy was there."

"I may be able to assist you there, sir." Elizabeth said quietly.

He looked at her enquiringly. "I would be interested to hear your views, Miss Bennet."

"Georgiana's new governess, Miss Jones, is the sister of Mrs. Jenkinson, Miss Anne de Bourgh's companion. Lady Catherine arranged her appointment." Elizabeth made a face. "She very much disapproved of me, thinking I was a bad influence on Georgiana."

"Did she say that?" he sounded disbelieving.

"No, sir. But she made it obvious. Georgiana found her attitude very difficult."

"Why did she not say anything to me?" he wiped his hand over his brow. "And why would Lady Catherine wish to know what is going on at Pemberley?"

Elizabeth raised an eyebrow and he laughed. "Yes, I think I know exactly why. But Darcy will never marry Cousin Anne, whatever her hopes might be." The smile left his face.

"But that does not help us. You tell me that you were *sent away from Pemberley*. Do you know why that was?"

"I do. Lady Catherine said that I was of an unsuitable family to be a companion to Georgiana. She said that Georgiana had much better attend to her studies and Miss Jones was a very suitable governess and companion." She drew a deep breath.

"But where is Georgiana, sir? Are we perhaps wasting too much time on this discussion?"

He shook his head, looking despairing. "I do not know. I arrived back at Pemberley to find Lady Catherine had dispensed with the guard around Pemberley the same day she had sent you away." He scowled.

"She did not, of course, know about the danger to Georgiana from Ramsgate, but I do not think she was thinking of anything other than her own plans for Darcy."

"Oh, that is why Georgiana would have felt free to leave!" Elizabeth suddenly remembered.

"She did ask if she could come with me and stay here until you or her brother came for her. But I said I could not keep her safe as they had been discovered here when at Bayford, and I also said that Mr. Darcy had gone to great lengths to ensure her safety with the guard outside Pemberley. She agreed she should remain in that safe place. But I suppose with it gone, she might have decided she was now free of that promise." She bit her lip, thinking.

"But why would you think she has come here

and not travelled to Matlock House to try and find you? She would choose that, surely, as being a place where she might hear news of her brother at the earliest possibility."

Colonel Fitzwilliam shook his head. "She left me a note at Pemberley. Lady Catherine had of course opened it, but she had at least not destroyed it in a fit of pique." He grimaced. "It told me nothing, I suppose Georgiana thought that our aunt would read it. But she did say she was going to come to Longbourn as she has very happy memories of her time in Hertfordshire."

"And is the coach still missing?"

He nodded. "Yes. The coach, two coachmen and two maids. Nothing has been seen of them and none have made contact with Pemberley or Darcy House staff."

Elizabeth sat dismayed. Such news seemed to say that the coach and staff had been lost by accident or that they had been waylaid by the gang. If such was the case, then Georgiana was lost too, either by accident or she had been taken to Scotland. And they were too late to save her.

Her voice was indistinct and she had to start her words again. "So she has been gone nearly three weeks?"

He looked down, wiping his brow. "It is a terrible thought. She is very young to be alone."

"They will have taken her to Scotland." Elizabeth felt defeated. "It is too late."

"I pray not." The Colonel shook his head. "I would have expected a triumphant letter or call from the man who would be her husband, demanding her fortune, if that had been the case." He got to his feet and strode about the room.

"No, I believe she must have met with an accident. And I am despairing that it must be a serious one for all the staff to be lost, too."

Elizabeth jumped to her feet, too. "Surely we must search for her! There must be indications of any accident."

"Indeed. I intend to do so immediately." The Colonel turned heavily to her. "I started some of the staff and the steward on the search from Pemberley, and rode on here in the hope that she was here, or that you would know where she was. But now I will start out and search the road back to Pemberley." He turned to Mr. Bennet.

Mr. Bennet, might I beg your assistance to furnish me with pen and paper, so that I might write to Darcy in London, such letter to await his return?"

"Of course, Colonel."

Elizabeth watched as her father indicated his desk with a wave of his hand, and felt a small irritation that he did not rise politely to furnish his guest with the requested items. But she did not refer to it. She wanted his permission to go too.

"Papa, may I join the search? Georgiana might have need of me when we find her."

Colonel Fitzwilliam looked startled. "I am sorry, Miss Bennet. I cannot think it would be considered suitable."

Mr. Bennet shook his head. "No, Lizzy. The Colonel is right. You cannot travel with a gentleman who is not related to you."

Elizabeth was prepared to entreat him further when Colonel Fitzwilliam interrupted her.

"Miss Bennet, might I beg you to remain here? It is still possible that you might receive a letter from Georgiana, or even that she might yet arrive here."

He looked at her. "I will leave directions and your father may write to me, conveying any news you might receive that will assist me in the search for her."

Elizabeth felt her shoulders droop. She had known, really, that it would not be possible for her to go with the Colonel, but she couldn't imagine waiting at Longbourn, not knowing what was happening.

"Yes, Lizzy will do that, Colonel," her father said.

"You will, won't you, Lizzy?" He looked at her sternly. "And as soon as the Colonel has finished his letter, you will go to Meryton and send it express."

"Yes, Papa." Elizabeth knew it was useless to protest further.

CHAPTER 44

*M*r. Darcy was glad to mount a horse at last. Three days it had taken aboard the rotten little ship to avoid the French blockade and enter the Thames estuary and his legs still felt the rolling deck beneath him.

Why any sensible man would wish to take a commission in the Navy, he would never know. The ordinary sailors were often unfortunates dragged aboard by the pressgangs, but he felt for the poor young men sent to sea by their wealthy families.

He shook his head. It was all very well when one of them rose through the ranks to become an Admiral, but how many were killed or maimed before that could happen in this endless war?

But he was back in England now. Mr. Thomas

was with him, riding in the cart that held a good selection of battered trunks and bags. They'd been loaded by sweating sailors under orders from their Captain, highly delighted by the payoff he had got from Darcy.

Mr. Darcy rode his horse behind the cart, determined to ensure that it received no more than the usual casual glances from passers-by, or that there were any groups abroad that seemed to be out of the ordinary.

But they had returned to England in a different vessel than that his family would have expected, and he was certain that no one knew of the time or place of their return.

His appearance was certainly such as would not be possible to appear before the Regent, but neither was it at all advisable to return to Darcy House with a cart full of gold when many must know what he had been about.

No. He was going direct to Carlton House. If the Regent was offended by his appearance, then so be it. He had no wish to be summoned again to Court, in fact, the absence of such summons and the resulting tasks would be a great relief to him.

Once the gold was back in the hands of the Regent and his servants, he would be much relieved. And then he could think of Elizabeth Bennet with positive hope now he was safe. He smiled. And Georgiana would be very happy to have her for a sister-in-law.

The cart slowed, and turned into the gateway of Carlton House.

"Halt!" the guard on the gate was obviously suspicious of the dirty men and battered cart before him.

Darcy rode forwards. "Quick, man! Send for the Captain of the Guard, and extra men. At once!" he let his voice crackle with authority and the guardhouse erupted into activity.

As a young ensign strode into view, a petulant expression on his face, Mr. Darcy reached for his pocketbook.

He extracted the sheet with the signature of the Regent and his instructions. He handed it to the ensign, letting himself look thoroughly bored.

Keeping his bored look, he enjoyed the youth's sudden attention.

The ensign saluted sharply and handed back the sheet.

"Sir!"

"Fetch your Colonel at once, please." Mr. Darcy caught the eye of Mr. Thomas as he glanced at the cart. His steward was as impassive as he was himself, but he could sense his amusement.

Mr. Thomas was a good man, as was the

Pemberley steward, and he could now understand his father's dependence on Mr. Wickham senior. It was as well neither of them had seen what became of the son.

He saw a Colonel hurrying from the house, and dismounted.

The man bowed to him. "Colonel Williams, sir. And you?"

"Darcy. Fitzwilliam Darcy, of Pemberley." He lowered his voice. "I have the recovered gold here in this cart. You will need to place a guard on it, with a trusted officer." He glanced around.

"I am not sure if the Regent will wish to see me in my current attire, but I do not intend to stay in London long. Please have him notified that I am here."

"Yes, sir. Do you have your token?"

Mr. Darcy handed over the sheet again and the Colonel perused it carefully. Then he turned to the ensign waiting behind him.

"Close and bar the gate. Call the rearguard. Set a close guard around this cart. At once!"

The young man saluted. "Yes, sir!"

Within moments the Colonel was back. "Come this way, sir, if you please."

Darcy nodded at his steward. "Wait here for me."

Fortunately the delay was not too onerous, and

only a couple of hours later Mr. Darcy arrived at his London home. Leaving Mr. Thomas to pay off the cab, he hurried up the steps. There would be several letters from Georgiana, and he would get news of Miss Bennet from those.

He handed the dreadful hat and coat to his housekeeper.

"These can be disposed of, Mrs. Stephens," he said with a shudder. "And tell my valet I want a bath at once."

She curtsied. "At once, sir."

He turned into his library. It was very good to be home. And tomorrow he would set off for Pemberley. Cousin Richard would hopefully be able to tell him of any news from the Earl of Sandwich.

He leafed through the pile of post, frowning. Nothing from Georgiana. One letter from Richard with a seal he didn't recognise. Where was he?

He slit the letter open, and read with increasing horror.

"Call Mrs. Stephens!" he barked at the footman. He glanced at the clock. Nearly four, it was getting late.

When the housekeeper hurried into the room, he was pacing up and down.

"Get my valet to hurry with the bath and

clean clothes! Call away fresh horses for me and Mr. Thomas, and get him in to see me at once!"

"Yes, sir." Mrs. Stephens hurried from the room and Mr. Darcy turned back to his letter.

He had to get to Longbourn and see Miss Elizabeth Bennet, had to find out what had really happened. Most of all, he needed her help to find Georgiana.

His heart dropped like a stone as he thought of what might have befallen his little sister. It was as well his aunt was not in front of him at this moment or he would have forgotten his manners.

Mr. Thomas hurried into the room and waited for him to speak.

"I am sorry to interrupt your evening, Mr. Thomas." Mr. Darcy was well aware he had told the man he was grateful for his help and had offered him a short holiday. But that was when he thought he'd be in Derbyshire and there would be little to do in London.

"But I have had news that Miss Darcy is missing." He saw the man's features change to shock.

"It appears she ran away from Pemberley and tried to get to Longbourn to join Miss Elizabeth Bennet. But she never arrived. The whole party; coach, servants, and Miss Darcy have not been seen. For more than three weeks." He folded the letter.

"I am going to have a bath and set off to Longbourn within the hour. I would like you to come with me. You know the area quite well as you were with us at Bayford House." He nodded at him.

"Get ready and have something to eat. We will leave before five."

"Yes, sir. I am very sorry." Mr. Thomas bowed and hurried from the room. Mr. Darcy gazed after him, then turned and took the stairs two at a time. He needed that bath, but he didn't have time for it to be the long soak he wanted to ease out the ache in his back.

Georgiana. Where was she? Was she safe? Would he find her? He knew he needed Elizabeth Bennet to help him. With her by his side, he might be able to sustain himself for what he knew was going to be a long, desperate time.

CHAPTER 45

*E*lizabeth sat over her book, the candle as close to the page as possible. The long summer evenings of daylight were beginning to pass again, and she was already dreading the winter.

Colonel Fitzwilliam had been most kind, and had written to her father twice since he had left. But he had no good news and his progress was slow.

She threw the book down in disgust. She had read the same page several times and was no closer to knowing what it was about.

And soon it would be time to go to bed and she would toss and turn in anxiety for another night.

She was equally fearful now for Georgiana, added to her longer-standing dread for Mr. Darcy.

Where was he? She remembered him as she had last seen him, climbing into the coach in the middle of the night, and gazing up at the windows of Pemberley, where she watched from her bedchamber.

The sound of hooves scattering gravel on the drive made all of them look up. Elizabeth glanced at the clock again. Near half after eight. Her heart jumped, surely it was news? No one else would call at this time of night. It must be an express post.

She sat, trying to control her trembling. It would not do to run out to the hall. But no one came to the sitting room. The letter would be to her father.

She got up and joined Kitty at the window. Two horses, being held by — she blinked and looked again — Mr. Thomas. Mr. Darcy's steward from Bayford House. It must be news, and she almost ran outside to speak to him. But her mother was glaring at her — she knew nothing and cared less of the dramas that had unfolded.

Mr. Thomas would have accompanied Mr. Darcy, not Colonel Fitzwilliam. So he was here, at Longbourn, and her sense of relief overwhelmed her.

She felt resentful that she had to stay and wait for her father to call her into his book room. But after a few minutes, she realised that if he had asked for her directly, her mother and sisters would have sat with her and inhibited their conversation.

The door opened and her father looked in. "Lizzy, come with me, please."

"Yes, Papa." Elizabeth's heart was pounding as she hurried after him.

Mr. Darcy was standing in her father's library, grave and unsmiling. He was thinner, very much thinner. There were lines of exhaustion on his face. But he smiled as he saw her. He bowed to her.

"Miss Elizabeth Bennet."

"Mr. Darcy." She curtsied. The formality made her smile as she recalled his letter to her.

> *I am berating myself for not declaring myself to you much sooner than this, but I wanted to be certain that my advances would be agreeable to you. So now you know how I feel and I must keep myself in hope until I can see you again.*

Now he was here. But Georgiana was missing. Things could never be the same.

"I am grateful to your father for allowing me to speak to you, Miss Bennet, and also for permitting me to see the letters he has received from Colonel Fitzwilliam." He shook his head. "I am overcome by the fact that there is no news of my sister."

Elizabeth felt his acute anguish. He had done so much to try and keep her safe. And she would still be safe had he not been summoned by the Prince Regent, leaving them to the control of Lady Catherine.

"I am dismayed by the fact there is no news, Mr. Darcy." She shook her head and looked at him. "But I am very pleased to see you back from abroad. It seemed so dangerous and I was fearful for your safety."

He smiled tightly. "I landed back in England only at noon, Miss Bennet. But reporting to the Regent took a number of hours, so I only received the news from my cousin at four."

"And you came straight here." Warmth spread through her.

He bowed. "Indeed." His gaze was steady and direct. He had not changed.

"What shall you do, sir?"

He glanced at the darkening sky. "Mr. Thomas

and I will stay at the inn at Meryton tonight. Although Bayford House is still rented, it is not ready for us, and it will not be fair to the housekeeper to arrive unexpectedly." He bowed to Mr. Bennet. "With your permission, sir, I would like to call on Miss Bennet again tomorrow before deciding the best course of action."

Her father nodded. "You will always be welcome here, Mr. Darcy."

"Thank you." He bowed, and then turned to Elizabeth. She shook her head.

"I will walk out to your horse with you, Mr. Darcy."

As they walked slowly out to the horses, she sighed.

"I feel desolated, sir, that I cannot help more. I would dearly wish to come with you on your search. I feel sure that I might be of great assistance to Georgiana when we find her."

He stood beside the horse before mounting, looking at her. His expression was unreadable.

"And I would have found your presence a great comfort, Miss Bennet. But I would not wish to compromise your position in any way."

She nodded sadly. "I understand. But I confess, sir, that I do not like it at all."

He looked down at her. "One moment."

She waited quietly, while he seemed to

consider something, then he turned to her, his back to Mr. Thomas.

"Miss Bennet, you smiled at me this evening, and seemed to be happy that I was back in England."

"I am indeed happy at that." She wondered what he was meaning.

"And you received my note from Colonel Fitzwilliam when I had to leave Pemberley?"

"Yes, sir." Her face grew warm.

"And you were not angry at what I wrote about …" He seemed to not be able to think how to complete the sentence.

Elizabeth felt her heart tighten within her. "No, I was not angry," she said softly.

His sudden indrawn breath was like a sigh.

"I have been able to think of little else while I was in France." His voice held a hint of laughter. "I was glad you could not see me in my peasant disguise or you certainly would not have me."

She rippled into laughter. "Perhaps you misjudge me, Mr. Darcy."

"Perhaps." He became serious again. "I know a young lady wishes a romantic proposal and plans for a family wedding with everyone around." His eyes seemed to burn through the darkness.

"But if I were to delay half a day and obtain a

licence, we might marry here and then we could begin the search together."

"Oh!" Elizabeth's hands covered her mouth. "You would do that for me?"

"It would be for me too, Miss Bennet. I cannot tell you how much I have missed you." He shook his head.

"I am so sorry that I delayed. If you had done me the honour of accepting me if I had offered before I went away, then Lady Catherine could never have sent you away."

Elizabeth wished she could touch him. "But, sir, I could not have remained there in that case. An engaged lady could not stay in the gentleman's home, even with his sister as chaperone."

"That is true, I suppose." He looked as if he did not know what to do. "But would you wish for a more traditional arrangement? It might seem strange for our first married days to be spent searching the roads for my sister."

"Mr. Darcy, you have offered me a chance to accompany you. You have offered me the chance to become your wife. I will accept whatever you decide."

He bent his head. "I am honoured and over-whelmed. After all I did at the beginning, pretending to be someone I wasn't, then leaving without apology. And yet you have forgiven me." He shook his head. "Dearest Elizabeth."

She was glad it was too dark for him to see her blush.

He stepped away after a moment more, and looked at the sky. "It is light enough to ride soon after four. I will start direct for London then. I could not use the time more usefully. Then I can be at Lambeth Palace to see the Archbishop at the earliest moment." He looked at her.

"I took the liberty of speaking to your father before you joined us. I hope you do not mind. I will be back during the afternoon, and I would prefer to wait here for another letter from Cousin Richard before we commence our search. As your father did not receive one yesterday, I hope there will be another tomorrow."

"You will be tired with riding, sir. And you are only just back from France. I would not like to fear an accident."

"Your concern and thoughtfulness to me has always warmed me, Miss Elizabeth. But I will be able to rest in the coach I will return with. We will need it. Now I must go." He bowed and she watched as the two men mounted and walked off as the darkness deepened.

CHAPTER 46

*I*nstead of a sleepless night of anxiety, Elizabeth had a wakeful night full of thankfulness that Mr. Darcy was safe, and hugging to herself the secret of her engagement.

She could not quite explain to herself just why she had not told Jane during the evening, unless it was to keep it all a special secret between him and herself.

Her father had not said anything to her when she had gone back into the house, but she had seen him look thoughtfully at her when she said goodnight.

But Georgiana was much in her thoughts. She prayed they would find her very soon and that nothing terrible had happened.

She did not know how Mr. Darcy would bear

the torment if all his work to keep Georgiana safe had been in vain and her heart broke at the thought of his anguish.

She thought of him, lying in bed at the inn in Meryton. He must be so tired, there had been exhaustion in every line of his face. But she could not imagine he would sleep, now he had learned that Georgiana was missing.

She turned over and tried to get her pillow more comfortable. She would be married very, very soon. She could not imagine that he would wish to waste more than a day of searching, so perhaps the ceremony would even be the next day. Was that possible with a special licence? She presumed it would be, or Mr. Darcy would not spend the morning obtaining it.

Eventually she slept lightly, her dreams of a tall, dark man looking at her with warmth in his eyes. How could he have chosen her? His family would be enraged.

Early the next morning, she rose and dressed, not feeling at all herself. She must tell Jane, it would not do for her to find out at the same time as the rest of the family.

She slipped along the hall and tapped on Jane's bedroom door.

Jane's voice sounded sleepy and Elizabeth turned the handle and went in.

"I am sorry to disturb your sleep, dear Jane. But I have some news to tell you and I can only think of telling you now."

Jane sat up on the edge of her bed and drew her shawl around her. "I could tell there was something you did not wish to talk about last night." She looked calmly at Elizabeth. "But you will have all day to tell me once Mr. Darcy has joined Colonel Fitzwilliam for the search."

"No, that is what I want to tell you about, Jane." Elizabeth leaned forward. "I am going with Mr. Darcy to look for Georgiana."

Jane looked very shocked and Elizabeth hugged herself in glee. "It is all right, Jane. There will be no impropriety. Mr. Darcy at this moment is on his way back to London and will obtain a special licence from the Archbishop." She enjoyed watching the emotions crossing her sister's face.

"Marrying Mr. Darcy! I cannot believe it! Today! Oh, Elizabeth, how can you be sure this is the right thing to do?"

"Jane. I have known him for many months now, both as Mr. Hudson and Mr. Darcy. You know that, and you know him too."

"Well, yes, I do. But he has such high breeding that surely you will find it very difficult to stay so formal?"

Elizabeth smiled, hugging Jane's pillow to her.

"No, Jane. I think he found it very hard at first to be Mr. Hudson. But he became much more amiable over those weeks and he is generosity itself to me."

"I am glad. But it all seems so rushed. People will talk and think ill of you because of it."

"You will not think ill of me, I hope, Jane?"

"Of course not!"

"Then that is all I care about. Let the others think ill of me if they will." She leaned forward.

"I think Mr. Darcy will not wish to delay beginning the search unnecessarily. So it might prove the marriage will be later today. Will you stand up with me and be beside me, Jane? It will make my day complete, to stand between the two people I care most about in the world."

"You really love him?"

"I do."

"Then I will stand up with you and wish you all the happiness in the world, my dearest sister. But I will miss you so very much."

Elizabeth embraced her. "Once we have found Georgiana and all is well, then I hope you will come and spend a lot of time with us at Pemberley, Jane."

Jane pulled back a little, looking troubled. "And what if you do not find her, or it is bad news?"

Elizabeth closed her eyes. She did not wish to think of it, not even for a minute.

"I will not admit to it, Jane. But, if it should come to pass, then he will need me even more. He is a most devoted brother."

Jane nodded slowly. "I will hope very much that your search will be successful, Lizzy." She smiled her gentle, serene smile.

"Lydia will be disappointed. I think she always wanted to be the first to marry, because she is the youngest."

Elizabeth laughed. "Well, I think she will not envy me, because he is not an officer. But he suits me very well." She stood up. "Very well indeed. I love him so very much, Jane. I still cannot quite believe he has made an offer to me."

"I will get ready quickly, Lizzy, and then I will help you choose what you should take with you when you leave here."

CHAPTER 47

M̄r. Darcy and Mr. Thomas rode into the yard at Darcy House in London just after seven. It was a good road and the horses had made good time at first.

Then, when they had slowed, Darcy had eased back to a walk and gestured Mr. Thomas alongside him.

"I am grateful for your loyal assistance, Mr. Thomas."

"I am pleased I am able to help, sir."

"We will go to Darcy House first and get things ready. The biggest coach and four. Then I will ride around to Matlock House and see the Earl. It might be that he has heard from Colonel Fitzwilliam."

"Yes, sir."

"I would like to be at Lambeth Palace by nine, or soon after — with the coach — and be ready to return directly to Longbourn as soon as I have the licence." He shook his head.

"No, after the Archbishop I must go to my lawyer and arrange the settlement on Miss Elizabeth. That is most important. Then we will go to Longbourn and I very much hope that there will be a new letter there from the Colonel and we can soon begin the search."

Mr. Thomas was silent, riding almost beside him. "I beg your pardon, sir, but how might I assist you to make the ceremony memorable for Miss Elizabeth Bennet?"

Mr. Darcy was silent for a moment. "I do not know, Mr. Thomas. It troubles me somewhat." He smiled grimly. "But since you have raised the matter, I expect you have a suggestion to make."

He listened carefully to the steward. It was a good plan and he nodded.

"It is well thought of, and I will see to it when I see the lawyer."

He looked around. "Well, the horses are rested somewhat. We will make more speed now." He spurred the horse to a trot and his steward dropped back a little, respectfully.

$\sim$

"You took long enough, Darcy." The Earl was not happy, and Mr. Darcy stood leaning against the fireplace. He ignored his uncle's tone.

"It was not an easy task. If you thought it could be done more speedily, then perhaps you could have sent Cousin David."

His uncle grunted. "That fool. Perhaps I should have left him in France to get killed."

Darcy spun round in anger. "So why did you send me to bring him home if you feel that way? That whole sorry business and this trip would not have happened if it had not been for you!"

"You cannot talk to me like that, Darcy!" the Earl blustered. "I outrank you, sir!"

Well, not quite, not now. Darcy chuckled to himself. He would not tell his uncle. He would not tell anyone just yet. Let them find out in the London Gazette - oh and his marriage also. He was not inclined to be forthcoming just yet.

He smiled. He imagined Lady Catherine's fury which would be worth much. But he had accepted mainly for Elizabeth. It would be worth the disadvantage and he would soon get used to it.

He turned his mind with an effort. "I am not here to discuss my task for the Regent, except to say it is done. Nor am I here to discuss Cousin David. I merely wish to enquire if you have any news from Cousin Richard, or of Georgiana?"

"No." The Earl sounded petulant. "What was the child thinking of, running off alone like that? You should have brought her up better."

Darcy pushed away from the mantel. He drew a deep breath. He must not let his anger overwhelm him.

"That is uncalled for, sir! She would be safe now, had it not been for Lady Catherine's interference. And your own heir seems not to have benefitted from his upbringing." He could not resist that last barb as he strode from the room, and out of the house.

AT LAMBETH PALACE, he paced around the waiting room, unused to being kept waiting long, but eventually he was beckoned through to the dean's office and relieved of his five pounds before the man would go any further. He was grimly amused.

But the questions were thorough and he was relieved to have with him the letter of consent from Mr. Bennet. He explained the reason why he intended to marry and the dean put down his pen.

"It is a good tale, sir. Usually it is to flatter the mother of the bride so that she can boast of the riches of her new son-in-law!"

Darcy smiled at him. "I think it will not escape that lady's pleasure, sir."

The dean laughed, and completed filling in the licence.

"Very well, sir. If you would kindly wait here, I will ask the Archbishop to sign it."

"Thank you." Once he was alone, he glanced at the clock. Time was passing and he still had much to do before he could be back with Elizabeth. He wondered how her family had received the news of today's ceremony, and his lips twitched. He would wager that Mr. Bennet would arrange things as secretly as possible, to surprise Mrs. Bennet as late as possible.

The dean returned with the licence and dried the signature on it. "Please check it carefully, sir."

Mr. Darcy did so, and then handed it back. The dean affixed the ribbon and applied the great wax seal. Rolling it up, he handed it over to Mr. Darcy.

"Thank you."

"Here, you might also need the father's consent letter if he is not present."

"Oh, yes. Thank you." Darcy bowed his thanks and the dean showed him to the door.

Back in the coach, Mr. Darcy stowed the licence and the letter away carefully. His main objective was accomplished and he felt profound satisfaction.

He could take the woman he loved as his wife and he felt supremely content with that. If only Georgiana was not lost, he would have nothing else he could wish for.

Through the streets that were now much busier, and on to his lawyer. He strode up the steps and was greeted deferentially by the secretary.

"Good morning, Mr. Darcy. It is a pleasure to see you. How might we be of assistance?" The man bowed low.

"I need to see Mr. Mordaunt urgently." Mr. Darcy placed his hat and cane on the table and tugged his sleeve down.

"Indeed, sir. If you could wait one moment, I will tell him you're here."

Darcy walked to the window. Three hours — if they were fortunate with the changes at each post. His coachmen were good and they could change horses and be on their way again within fifteen minutes perhaps.

"If you would come this way, Mr. Darcy." The secretary was back.

"Thank you." Mr. Darcy picked up his hat and cane and walked through the door held by the servant.

His lawyer was waiting for him, rather more

portly now than he had been when he had first visited with his father many years ago.

"Good morning, Mr. Darcy. How may I be of assistance to you? Let me send for some coffee. If I may say so, you are looking very tired."

"Coffee would be most agreeable, thank you." Mr. Darcy put his hat and cane down again. "I have several things I wish you to arrange, and they are quite urgent. I also wish to remove some items from the security box you hold here."

"Of course." Mr. Mordaunt sat behind the desk and pulled a ledger toward him. He looked up expectantly.

"The first matter is that of my forthcoming marriage." He had to stop then and accept the man's deferential congratulations.

"It is very good news Mr. Darcy. You will wish to arrange the settlement on the lady?"

"Yes. That is what I am here for today. I want it done at once, now."

"To be valid from the date of your marriage, I presume?"

Which is today." Mr. Darcy watched the man's surprise with some amusement. Let him think what he liked.

"I have been in France on the orders of the Prince Regent. I only returned yesterday and have found that my sister is missing. I need the lady beside me as I search and therefore we must bring forward our union."

"I see, sir. I am most sorry to hear about your sister."

"Yes." Mr. Darcy stopped a scowl. It was not Mordaunt's fault.

"I have just been to Lambeth Palace and obtained a licence. We will marry this afternoon and can then travel together." He looked out of the window. "I wish to take some of the diamonds from the strongbox and my mother's ring. It will make the occasion a little more memorable for her." He turned back to the lawyer.

"And the other thing. You must send the details to the London Gazette for tomorrow's edition." He smiled thinly and gave Elizabeth's name and her father's details as the man wrote busily in the ledger.

Only a few more moments and he could be on his way to Longbourn. He longed to place his ring on Elizabeth's finger, make her his.

But the fate of Georgiana intruded into every thought of happiness with Elizabeth. He must find her, he must. Elizabeth would be very distressed if anything had happened to her. And he did not know how he would ever forgive himself for not keeping her safe.

CHAPTER 48

*E*lizabeth had spent time with Jane in her bedchamber, placing the gowns she wished to take with her on the bed, with a few other things. She did not know quite what she would need, but was sure that they would stop at a different inn each night.

She shivered to herself with nerves. She would be closer to him much sooner than she might ever had anticipated.

She sat on the edge of the bed beside her clothes, and drew out the letter he had written those weeks ago at Pemberley.

> *I am berating myself for not declaring*
> *myself to you much sooner than this,*
> *but I wanted to be certain that my*

*advances would be agreeable to you.
So now you know how I feel and I
must keep myself in hope until I can
see you again.*

She smiled at the words, and read them again.

"Lizzy! Lizzy! Come down here this instant!" Her mother's voice broke the spell and Elizabeth lifted the letter to her face and smelled it again. It barely held his scent any more, but there was the faintest trace of him there.

"Coming, Mama!" She got up and tucked the letter carefully between the leaves of her book, before slipping downstairs to her mother.

Her younger sisters were all clustered around her mother, who was staring at her in half-disbelief and half scorn.

"Your father told me to arrange a special luncheon — a very special luncheon. I thought … Well, never mind what I thought, but he has just told me that Mr. Darcy is returning and you are marrying this afternoon! How could you, Lizzy? How could you?"

Elizabeth lifted her chin. "It is certainly not what you think it is, Mama. And I am vexed that you would think it of me." She turned her back on her mother and knocked on the door of her father's library.

"Come in," he called and she turned the handle.

"Don't you dare walk away from me like that!" Mrs. Bennet's voice rose in anger, and Elizabeth turned back to her.

"I do not wish to be spoken to as you did, Mama. I am offended." She went into her father's room.

"Come and sit down, Lizzy." Her father got up and shut the door and the sound of her mother's frustration was muted.

"I am sorry, Lizzy, but you should not upbraid your mother like this, even though I understand it is an anxious time for you."

"I am sorry, Papa. I do not like to disappoint you."

He smiled uneasily. "You must understand that marrying in such haste will lead to gossip."

"I understand, Papa, and I am sorry at any embarrassment caused to you."

He waved it away. "I am sure it will soon be forgotten. But I hope you can assist your mother to have a little more enjoyment of the day."

Elizabeth smiled wryly. "If you tell her he has ten thousand a year, she will be in transports of delight, I am sure."

He chuckled. "I think you should be the one to tell her that." He sat down in the chair next to her.

"Now, Lizzy, I have called on the vicar, and he has asked if you wish to be married here at Longbourn or at the church. The special licence will allow him to accede to either request."

Elizabeth bit her lip while she considered. If the wedding was at Longbourn, would there be even more talk? But if it was at the church, it might delay them getting away to look for Georgiana.

"I would like it to be here at Longbourn, Papa, if you do not mind. I think Mr. Darcy will be anxious to get away to join the search for Georgiana."

He nodded. "I will see to it. But I am sorry that it has to be this way. Your good name in this town may be lost forever."

"I will be sorry if my friends think ill of me, but I cannot sit and wait here much longer, Father. What could possibly have become of Georgiana? What could have happened?" She blinked back the tears.

"And Mr. Darcy will need me so much. He is a most devoted brother."

Her father nodded. "That was evident when they were here, masquerading as the Hudsons. I just hope he will be as devoted a husband to you."

"I am sure he will, Papa. And thank you for arranging everything."

Elizabeth drew a deep breath. She must go and try and pacify her mother, for her father's sake.

She went through to the sitting room where the whole family were having tea. The clock showed eleven. Surely he must be on his way by now?

Her heart beat fast. Soon they would be married. And he was willing to take on much more trouble with his family than she would ever suffer. She thought of Lady Catherine and almost smiled. She would be enraged indeed.

Her mother ignored her and Elizabeth sat beside Jane. "I thank you, Jane, for assisting me to prepare my things ready to pack. I am sure Mr. Darcy will be anxious to join the search for Georgiana." She glanced at her mother's turned head and looked back at Jane.

"It was very generous of him to delay another day in order to prevent compromising my position and also allow me to assist in the search."

Her mother sniffed.

Elizabeth smiled. "And, Jane, you must come to Pemberley very soon. It is the most enormous estate and a beautiful mansion. You know, he has ten thousand a year." She winked at Jane, who smiled serenely.

"Ten thousand a year? A grand estate?" Mrs.

Bennet could not help herself.

"Yes, Mama. The family will be secure."

"Oh, my dear girl! You are such a clever girl to have such a man. None of us knew a thing while we thought he was Mr. Hudson. You are a clever thing." Mrs. Bennet was beside herself with joy, forgetting completely the mood she had been in before.

"But, you must get him to delay it a week! Then we can have a grand affair and the whole town can be there and see your marriage."

"No, Mama. I am sorry, but we would not wish to delay. We must go this very day, and Mr. Darcy would not consent to a delay. He would begin the search alone. There might then be no wedding."

"Oh, well, whatever must be, then." Her mother sat back. "Ten thousand a year! A great estate!"

The sound of hooves on the drive sent her hurrying to the window. But it was a single horseman. Her heart leaped into her throat. A letter!

She sat back down, trying to be patient. Was it from Colonel Fitzwilliam? She hoped so, Mr. Darcy would be glad of the news.

It was only a few minutes later that her father called her through. "Come and read Colonel Fitzwilliam's letter, Lizzy. He has news."

CHAPTER 49

"*W*hat?" Elizabeth leaped to her feet and hurried after him. He indicated a chair and waited until she was seated before giving her the letter.

> *Mr. Bennet,*
> *Thank you again for being willing to*
>   *receive my letters and pass the*
>   *information to Miss Elizabeth*
>   *Bennet.*
> *I am hopeful that soon Mr. Darcy will be*
>   *back in England. I am sure he will*
>   *come to Longbourn because of the*
>   *letter I left him at Darcy House. So*
>   *he will hear the news from you.*
> *I have searched much of the road between*

357

> *Longbourn and Pemberley and as you*
> *know, have met with little success.*
> *However, today I reached the town of*
> *Enderby, near Leicester. I have*
> *found her!*
> *Dear Miss Bennet; and Darcy, when you*
> *see this, be assured, she is not severely*
> *harmed.*

Elizabeth closed her eyes in her relief. Georgiana was found. She was not too unwell. She smiled, Mr. Darcy would be so happy, and her own heart was filled with joy. She turned back to the letter.

> *I have seen her and she was very pleased*
> *to see me. It appears the coach met*
> *with an accident in quite a storm and*
> *she and the servants were rescued by*
> *a local landowner and gentleman, a*
> *Mr. Peake.*
> *Georgiana has been cared for very well by*
> *Mr. Peake's sister and the local*
> *apothecary. The servants are also*
> *accommodated there until Georgiana*
> *says what is to be done about them.*
> *I am sure you will be amused, Miss*
> *Bennet, when I tell you that*

Georgiana had refused to tell her rescuers who she was because she feared being taken back to Pemberley and Lady Catherine.

So Mr. and Miss Peake had been unable to alert any member of the family as they did not know who to inform.

The servants have been very loyal and also refused to give away her secret, because of course, they understood that she was otherwise in danger.

I have been welcomed to stay at Havenfield Hall until Darcy comes to us, or until Georgiana's injury — to her leg — is improved enough to enable me to recover her to Pemberley.

I am writing this to you so you may inform Mr. Darcy, if you see him before he sees my next letter to him at Darcy House.

I am so happy that you now know Georgiana is safe, and she sends her most heartfelt apologies for causing you such concern.

Richard Fitzwilliam.

Elizabeth folded the letter slowly, still feeling

the relief stealing over her at knowing her friend was safe.

"Well, Lizzy." Her father's voice interrupted her thoughts. "What do you think will happen now? Mr. Darcy may wish to postpone any wedding and go straight to this place in Leicestershire."

"Yes, he might." Elizabeth knew she would be bitterly disappointed if that were to happen.

"And how would you feel if that is to be the case?"

She forced a smile. "I will have to wait and see, Papa, won't I?"

The sound of a coach drawing up outside made her heart flutter and she bit her lip. He was here.

SHE ROSE TO HER FEET. "May I take this letter out to meet Mr. Darcy, Papa?"

At her father's nod, she hurried out to the hall and down the step. The large coach gleamed and the coachman lowered the step and opened the door.

Her heart almost stopped as she saw Mr. Darcy — her future husband — step out of the coach, a formal smile directed at her. But his gaze was drawn to the letter in her hand and he went white.

She hurried closer. "It is good news, sir!" It might not be right to call out before she had greeted him, and she dipped into a curtsey.

He took a step towards her, his eyes blazing. "Thank you for telling me, Miss Elizabeth." He bent over her hand and kissed it and the touch of his lips on her hand sent a searing jolt through her heart.

"We have only just received it, sir. And Colonel Fitzwilliam said he was also writing to Darcy House in case you went there first."

He shook his head, smiling. "I left there quite early to do my tasks and then came straight here." He already looked younger and less tired.

She smiled in relief at seeing him and held out the letter. "Here, sir, it will be quicker if you read it."

"Thank you." She stood beside him as he unfolded the sheet and read rapidly.

After a moment, he sighed. "Enderby!" and continued to read.

It seemed many minutes later before he folded the letter and gave it back to her.

"Thank you. I cannot tell you how much happier I feel now." His eyes danced. "I think you must also be much relieved."

"I am indeed." She smiled, waiting for him to say she obviously no longer needed to come with him.

A tiny frown line appeared between his eyes as he looked at her. "Might you take a turn about the garden with me, Miss Elizabeth?"

She turned with him and they walked towards the seat under the trees.

"The need for haste is now much eased," he remarked. "I am very happy that I can now enjoy the ceremony without the crushing anxiety that I might be rushing you too much."

The sudden relief of his words made her light-headed, and she was very glad to be able to sit down on the bench.

He perched on the edge of the seat next to her.

"Elizabeth? I may call you Elizabeth?"

She nodded, silently.

"I have the special licence right here. I intended to marry you this afternoon. Are you still in agreement with that, now we know Georgiana is safe? Would you prefer to wait a few weeks, and I will come back for you?"

Her heart ached. "Is that what you would want to do, sir?"

"No, it is not what I would wish to do, but I am aware there might be some degree of gossip or ill-regard toward you which you might be less inclined to accept now we know that Georgiana is safe."

"I have discussed that with my father," Elizabeth commented. "My own opinion is that those who would think ill of me are not worth calling my friends."

His smile was warm and concerned. "But you have friends here with whom you would surely wish to keep in touch?"

"I am gratified at your concern, sir, but my sister Jane is standing by me and her views will prevail." She looked directly into his eyes. "But I would like you to feel you can say what you really wish for, yourself. I would not like to do anything which you do not agree with, just because you do not feel you can say so."

His rich chuckle warmed her right through. "Right from the beginning, Miss Elizabeth, at Bayford House, I could see how thoughtful and kind you were — quite naturally." He rose to his feet.

"If you would not mind the occasion of your marriage appearing hurried and without extra ceremony, then I would wish to marry you at once." He laughed. "We will spend our first night together at some anonymous inn between here and Enderby."

"I look forward to it." Her voice was low and he turned to her.

"And I also." His voice sent a shiver of excitement through her.

He extended his hand. "Let us go into the house. As we have to stop a night before we can get there, we have several hours before we need to leave Longbourn." He smiled. "Let's go and get married."

He stopped a moment when they reached the coach and collected a small box, and then nodded to the coachman, who drove round to the stables. Then they walked on into the house, side by side. She hesitated and he looked down.

"Please don't mind what my mother says," she whispered.

"Not at all," he whispered back and his fingers brushed hers comfortingly.

CHAPTER 50

*H*e stood beside her in her father's library. He knew it quite well and Mr. Bennet sat in his chair. He was watching his daughter and so was Mr. Darcy.

He turned to her. "I have a small gift for you to mark the occasion, Miss Elizabeth."

"Oh!" her little gasp was endearing and he wanted to run his finger along the lips that formed the sound. He bit back his groan. He had not long to wait and now there was no longer a gnawing anxiety to spoil his love.

He reached for the box. The rolled licence was on top and the smaller box was beneath it. He opened it, and the diamonds glittered beneath his fingers.

Her gasp was music to his ears. He looked at

365

her father. "May I?" and when Mr. Bennet nodded, he lifted the delicate necklace and gave it to her.

She looked up at him, her eyes brimming. "You are too good to me."

"It is but a small token for today. After we are wed, all I have is yours." He watched as she unclasped the necklace and held it up. He moved behind her and fixed the clasp, trying hard not to touch her. Her scent wafted around him, heady with promise.

She turned, and he saw the emerald, surrounded by the glittering diamonds, nestling … He dragged his eyes away.

"I believe …" Mr. Bennet cleared his throat. "I believe we should go through to join the family. The vicar should not be long."

As Mr. Bennet moved ahead of them, Mr. Darcy felt her fingers brush against his and looked down.

"Thank you," she whispered. "Thank you for your trust in me. I'll never let you down."

He let his finger grasp hers, just for a second. "Dearest Elizabeth."

THE CEREMONY WAS short but Mr. Darcy found it

very moving. More so, perhaps, because her family was close around them and their responses were like a promise. Placing his mother's ring on her finger felt like the most momentous action of his life.

Once it was done, he permitted himself to relax and allow Mrs. Bennet to fawn obsequiously over him, all the while watching his wife as she spoke to her family and reassured them that she would write very soon.

IT WAS an hour later than he had planned when he assisted his wife into the coach, but he still hoped to make good time. All their goodbyes had been said and Elizabeth leaned out of the window to wave.

He watched her indulgently, knowing that she had changed him very much. The act he had played as Mr. Hudson had seemed to him to be a dreadful necessity. But then he had learned so much from Miss Bennet and he could find much of Mr. Hudson still within him.

He smiled. Mrs. Darcy. He was proud of his wife.

She had turned to watch him and was looking quizzical.

"May I ask what you are thinking about, Mr. Darcy?"

"Why, I ..." he paused. Then he smiled and shook his head. "It does not matter, dear Elizabeth. What does matter is when you feel you might call me by my given name. I wish to hear you say it."

She went a delightful rosy colour and his heart swelled with love.

"Fitzwilliam," she said softly. "I must admit it feels very strange to be alone with a gentleman who is not my father."

"I'm sure it does, Elizabeth. But please be assured I will never harm or misuse you."

"I know you won't." There was a hint of laughter in her voice. "Or I would not have married you."

He felt a little anxious. "Would you have preferred me to remain Mr. Hudson, or are you pleased I am Mr. Darcy?"

She considered carefully, and he suddenly wondered if he should have warned her about the changes that were coming.

"You are you, sir. I would not wish you different, whatever role you play."

That was not quite what he had asked, but it would do.

"I am hoping got get as far as Woburn today,

and we will find somewhere comfortable to stay. With your consent, I would like to start again quite early tomorrow, so that we can arrive at Havenfield Hall at a reasonable time."

"Of course." She laughed. "Although I hope when you say early, you do not mean at half past four again, like you did today."

He suddenly realised how much he had packed into such a short time. "Of course, it was only yesterday I landed back in England." He shook his head. "A great deal has happened in that time." He smiled ruefully. "And before that, it was three days in a rotten little ship trying to avoid the blockade and get home."

She reached out towards him, then drew her hand back as if she felt she should not. "You must be very tired, sir."

He reached for her hand. He had ached for her touch for long enough. "Fitzwilliam."

She made an annoyed sound. "Oh, yes. I'm sorry."

"Don't be. Everything is new for both of us." He drew her closer and placed his arm around her shoulder. Her presence was ineffably comforting, and he sighed and relaxed.

～

He STIRRED when the coach began to slow down, and realised he'd gone to sleep. "I'm so sorry, Elizabeth. You should have woken me."

"No, I can see how tired you are, Fitzwilliam." Her smile was gentle. "I don't think we're there yet, it's just to change the horses."

He glanced out of the window. "You're right. Would you like to get out, or shall we move on?"

"Let's move on so we can get as far as possible before dark." She was looking out of the window with lively interest.

"Of course. Thank you."

Dusk WAS DRAWING in as they drew into the inn at Woburn, and Mr. Darcy was very pleased to get there. Elizabeth had exclaimed as they'd passed the Abbey.

"I had thought it to be bigger."

"It is very big, but I think having been to Pemberley, it makes the Abbey seem smaller."

She laughed. "I suppose so. But Pemberley will still seem very big all over again when I see it."

He helped her out of the coach while a servant ran in to engage the best possible room and the private parlour. Then they strolled for a short while along by a small stream to a large pond.

They leaned over a gate and he waited while she looked over the still water. He watched her, the tendril of hair escaping down the side of her throat, her eyes distant as she thought. She was most beautiful to him.

Then she sighed and turned to him. "Don't look anxious. I was just thinking how different my life is going to be now and remembering how I had protested to Jane about how I could not see any way to change my life — it was only the day before you came to Bayford House."

He smiled. "And overturned your life."

"Yes."

CHAPTER 51

*E*lizabeth ate little dinner. It had been easy to marry him, the man she loved. But now night was coming. They were at an inn, and had but a single bedchamber. She had not shared a bed since she was five years old and used to crawl into Jane's bed for comfort when she had a bad dream.

He was looking at her, and she felt a tightness within her. She loved that warm, concerned look.

"Eat a little more, Elizabeth. We have a long day ahead of us tomorrow."

She felt shy and could feel her face getting warm. "I was not thinking about tomorrow."

His lips twitched. "Elizabeth, I do not wish you to be uneasy about anything. If you want to

HARRIET KNOWLES

wait until we are safely back at Pemberley and you can be properly prepared, then I will wait."

"I think I will be just as anxious." She looked at him. "I think I would like you to make the decision, Fitzwilliam."

"As you say." His gaze was thoughtful. "Just remember I love you very dearly, Elizabeth."

She wanted to reassure him, remove the anxious look in his eyes.

"And I feel the same." She shivered. "When I knew how dangerous your journey to France was, I thought I might never see you again."

His hand squeezed hers, but she wanted to tell him how she had felt.

"And then, when Lady Catherine sent me away, I thought I would never know whether you were home safely or not."

She blinked back the tears, it had been a bad time. She pushed it away and smiled. "And now I am here beside you."

"Forever."

"Yes, forever."

He leaned forward and she felt a shiver of desire.

"I'm so sorry you had to go through that — and that Lady Catherine made Georgiana feel she wanted to leave Pemberley and find you."

374

She smiled. "I hope Georgiana will be pleased we have married."

"I think there is little doubt about that," he said comfortably.

Elizabeth laughed. "But perhaps she will be dismayed that we did not wait until she could stand up with me for the occasion."

"Well, we will see. I am just very content that she is safe and that my cousin is with her. It means I am able to enjoy this day with you without being fearful for her or feeling guilty that I am happy."

He was happy. She felt a weight seem to lift from her. She was still not sure that he would not regret marrying so far beneath his social standing, but he knew her family, she had hidden nothing from him.

His eyes pierced her thoughts. "I think I know what you are thinking about, Elizabeth. If you have finished eating, let us retire for the night and I will show you how much I care for you."

She swallowed, and nodded. As they left the room, the innkeeper bowed.

"Is everything satisfactory, Mr. and Mrs. Darcy?"

"Quite, thank you." Her husband nodded and they made their way upstairs. At the door to their bedchamber, he paused.

"I am not sure I like you travelling without a

maid. We will rectify that once we are home." He looked around. "I will wait on that window-seat there for a few moments so that you may have some privacy."

"Thank you. I will not need long." Elizabeth pushed open the door and went into the room. A single large bed dominated the room, and her trunk was placed on a chair within easy reach. She looked around. Her husband's trunk was on the other side of the room.

She was soon done with her toilette, hurrying rather through the more personal aspects, so she was ready, standing gazing out of the window, when he knocked on the door and came into the room.

She was wearing a shawl around her shoulders over her simple night shift and she saw his eyes darken as he looked at her.

It was a small room and he was beside her in a few steps.

He drew her into his arms. "My lovely Elizabeth."

She gazed up at him. How could she have been so fortunate? His embrace was comforting and she felt more secure than she had for a long time.

"Never let me go, Fitzwilliam."

"Never." His voice was husky and she smelled

the scent of him, and relished that soon it would be more familiar to her than any other.

His finger under her chin tipped her face up to his and her heart raced.

SHE WOKE in the night to find herself curled up in his embrace, warm and secure. As she stirred, his arm tightened around her and she heard his sleepy murmur.

He needed to rest and so she kept still, loving the feeling of him relaxed against her, his body lean and strong.

He had been so gentle, so considerate of her feelings, and she wondered how she had never known how powerful the feeling of real love could be. She could never bear to part from him again, could never risk losing him.

She was afraid of the strength of her feelings. She had always been so proud of her independent mind and thinking. Would she lose that?

"Don't be afraid, Elizabeth." His voice was thick with sleep. "What are you afraid of?"

"How did you know I was afraid? You were asleep."

"Your breathing changed." He nuzzled his face into her neck. "Why were you feeling afraid?"

"Oh, it was just a silly thought."

"Tell me," he urged her.

"I just … well, I just thought that I could never bear it if I lost you now, or if you had to go away again, how afraid I'd be for you." She shivered at the memory, and his arms pulled her closer.

"Elizabeth, my love, I will always be with you. Whenever I have to be away, I will come back to you as quickly as I can. I promise."

"I know. I'm just being silly."

He kissed her neck. "I will never think you are silly."

She lay, quietly content in his arms, as the dawn stole across the sky. Her life was complete, and today they would continue together and go and find Georgiana. Colonel Fitzwilliam would be there too, and she looked forward to seeing his face when told of their marriage.

She heard her husband's breathing deepen as he slipped back into sleep. He must be so very tired, and yet he'd shown no impatience, no pride, no irritation with her mother. He was truly a man to love.

CHAPTER 52

She was glad they had booked the private parlour for breakfast, because the inn was busy at that early hour, with servants and their masters shouting impatiently across the yard.

Her husband held her chair for her and nodded at the innkeeper.

As they ate, he watched her. "It will seem a long day in the coach, I am afraid. But as we are starting early, I hope to be able to stop for lunch in Swinford. There is a good inn I know.

"I am hopeful we might arrive at Havenfield Hall during the afternoon. I would not wish to impose on Mr. Peake too late in the evening."

"Oh, yes." She thought a moment. "I think we

stopped at Swinford when your coach took me to Pemberley."

He smiled. "Ah yes. It would have. The innkeeper knows me and always provides good service."

"But it is all quite new to me," she said. "Apart from that one journey, I have never been so far north."

"That is interesting to know, Elizabeth." Mr. Darcy looked across the table. "In that instance, as soon as family and business concerns permit, I will take you to Scotland. I know you love the wild hills around Pemberley, and Scotland is even more beautiful."

Elizabeth knew her eyes were shining as she looked at him.

"That sounds wonderful, Fitzwilliam. I will look forward to it very much."

"But now, we need to begin our journey to Havenfield Hall." A few lines creased his brow. "I hope Mr. Peake is a gentleman."

Elizabeth knew what was concerning him. "I am sure your cousin will have ensured Georgiana is safe."

She looked over at him. "But I have finished eating. Would you like to begin our journey?"

He bowed slightly. "If you are ready, Elizabeth."

The morning was rather difficult. Elizabeth could think of nothing to say to relieve Mr. Darcy's mind. She wondered if he was feeling that he should have travelled alone, on horseback, and therefore reached Enderby yesterday.

He took her hand. "We do not always have to speak. I remember at Bayford House, there were many companionable silences." His thumb traced over the back of her hand.

"We have the rest of our lives together. There is time enough to say what needs to be said." He leaned forward and dropped a kiss on her forehead.

"I love that I may be close to you now and no one will part us."

Elizabeth relaxed and leaned against him, enjoying his comfortable nearness.

The comfortable movement of the coach was soporific and soon she dozed.

"ELIZABETH. ELIZABETH!"

She stirred when his hand lifted hers to his lips and looked up. There was laughter in his eyes.

"I do not feel so bad now about sleeping in the coach yesterday!"

"I thought I needed to make you feel better,"

she teased him, and he shook his head.

"I do not believe you, but as a newly-married couple, I suppose I am not yet permitted to say that."

"Indeed not." Elizabeth shook out her skirt. "Did you wake me because we have arrived?"

"Yes, Swinford is the next village. I must confess to feeling hungry."

"I am also," she confessed. "I am not usually hungry when I travel — although that is not often, of course."

"You must tell me about your family, Elizabeth. I confess I am a little confused from only hearing the conversations around your dinner table."

Elizabeth laughed. "I know with all the sisters talking together, it must seem very confusing." She became serious. "I think Georgiana was very brave to visit us."

His eyebrow rose. "And I was not?"

She looked him full in the eye. "Your courage is of a higher order, sir. You do not need to fear a simple dinner with a country family."

He laughed. "You have no idea, Elizabeth, how difficult it is to follow the easy familiarity you have with your sisters."

"I was concerned when you met them that you would think my family deplorable."

He looked serious. "It pains me to admit it, Elizabeth, but I confess my pride when I first arrived in Bayford made me feel everyone in the country was beneath my notice." He shook his head. "I am ashamed to admit it, but my honesty will not allow me to hide what I now see as terrible faults."

She turned to him. "I think that took some courage too, Fitzwilliam." She smiled. "I knew it already, but I am glad you have told me."

"How did you know it already?" he looked shocked, but the coach was slowing, and he made a wordless sound of annoyance.

She laughed. "Let us enjoy our lunch and we can talk again in the coach this afternoon." She looked out. "But if there is a little time, I would enjoy the chance of a short walk."

He got out of the coach and turned to assist her out. He grimaced slightly as he straightened up. "I think that is a good idea."

He turned to his servant. "Arrange for lunch to be served in twenty minutes. Mrs. Darcy and I will take a short walk to gain our appetite."

She laced her hand into his arm. "I enjoy hearing you refer to me as Mrs. Darcy."

They began to stroll along the roadside until they came to a path through the fields.

"We cannot be overheard here," he said to

her. "So how did you know I was proud and contemptuous? You never acted as if you knew."

"Of course not. You were newcomers. I believed you had been high-born and were in reduced circumstances. As such, you were to be pitied and not confronted."

He winced and she felt for him. "I'm sorry, sir. I should not have been so blunt."

"It is well, Elizabeth. My steward suggested we play the part of those in reduced circumstances as being easier to portray than those who had always been at the income we were playing."

"I think it was a wise suggestion, if you will permit me saying so. But again, it must have taken some courage to play the part. You must have known you would be much talked about."

He looked out over the fields. "The only way I could bear the thought was that I would never need to see anyone from Hertfordshire again." He chuckled. "And then you came into our lives and turned my thoughts aback."

She felt a swooping sensation. He had been affected by her. "You cannot know how sad I felt that I was placing my affections on a man who would never gain my father's consent, for he had not the fortune to support me."

"It felt intolerable to be playing such a part, to be deceiving you — especially when I thought I would not easily be able to forget you when I needed to leave Mr. Hudson behind." He shrugged. "And then events overtook us and you helped us get away without knowing the nature of the danger from which we were escaping."

"And is that danger past, Fitzwilliam? I have not heard you say much about it since you returned."

He shook his head. "I do not know, but I hope Cousin Richard will be able to tell me whether all is well or not." He sighed heavily. "But even if those men have been apprehended, the same risks will arise in the minds of others. Georgiana will never be truly safe until she is married." He stopped and looked at her. "Come, let us return to the inn. We must eat and then be on our way."

"But you will not force Georgiana into marrying someone she does not hold in affectionate regard?" Elizabeth was determined that it must not happen.

"No, I will endeavour to find someone of whom she is fond. But she is very young to know her own mind. If it were safe, I would much prefer to wait until she is full twenty years old or more." He sounded defeated. "But I cannot guarantee her safety until then."

"Do not be downhearted, Fitzwilliam. I am sure things will work out for the best."

CHAPTER 53

The afternoon coach ride passed quickly. Now they seemed to have much to talk about and Mr. Darcy enjoyed telling his wife about the estate of which she was now mistress.

Her eyes sparkled with enjoyment and she showed a keen interest in the whole estate and the staff who ran it.

"And I liked Mrs. Reynolds very much. I thought when I was there that she is an excellent housekeeper."

He loved the way she bit her lip when she was thinking.

"I just hope that she will accept me."

"I know she will." He wanted to erase all anxiety from her mind.

He watched as she hesitated and then seemed to make up her mind to speak.

"One thing I think is important. It may not have been in the letter to you from the Colonel, and is about Georgiana's governess."

"What about her? I asked the Earl to arrange it. Is she not adequate?"

Elizabeth looked at him. "She was placed by Lady Catherine. I believe it was she who wrote to her sister at Rosings who then told Lady Catherine what was happening at Pemberley. It is how Lady Catherine knew as soon as you and Colonel Fitzwilliam were gone from home."

She took another breath, seeming not to care that his expression was tightening. "She was extremely rude — I do not mind that she despised me, but she was not respectful to Georgiana."

She saw his face darken with anger.

"Thank you for telling me. I will ensure she is removed from Pemberley forthwith and I will deal with my aunt."

He stared out of the coach window with jaw clenched. All this trouble for Elizabeth and Georgiana because of Lady Catherine's dream of uniting him with her daughter. He was grimly amused at the thought of her discovering about his marriage.

But it had nearly cost Georgiana her life — or

worse. And Elizabeth. She had not deserved her treatment at the hands of that lady, and he smiled as he realised that his aunt would soon have to acknowledge his wife if she wanted anything further to do with him.

HE CHANGED the subject with an effort. "Enderby is not far from here. I confess I usually like to look up those I am going to meet in Who's Who before I am introduced. But I have never heard of Mr. Peake."

"Then I expect he will have the advantage on you, for Georgiana and your cousin will have told him all about you."

He smiled down affectionately. "Except for one important item of news." And he watched the rosy flush rise up her face.

"Please do not embarrass me when we are there." She looked a little discomfited. "I never usually blush like this."

He took pity on her. "I will endeavour to assist you to stay calm and serene, Elizabeth."

THE COACH STOPPED ONCE or twice for the

coachman to ask the way to Havenfield Hall, but it was still mid-afternoon when they turned into a large, imposing driveway, with a comfortably-sized family home situated within large grounds.

He grunted with satisfaction. There was wealth enough here. Georgiana was safe from a fortune hunter.

Servants from the house hurried out to assist them as they alighted from the coach, and a tall young man came down the steps.

Mr. Darcy bowed. "Mr. Peake?"

"Yes, sir." The man seemed confident enough.

Darcy smiled. "Mr. Fitzwilliam Darcy of Pemberley in Derbyshire. And this is my wife, Elizabeth."

She curtsied.

"Delighted," Mr. Peake murmured and bowed low. "You have received news from Colonel Fitzwilliam, then."

"I am most grateful to you, sir, for taking in my sister in her hour of need. I hope she is well."

"Come in and see for yourself, sir. You are very welcome." Mr. Peake bowed again.

He led them up the steps. Mr. Darcy had Elizabeth's arm in his and he could feel her trembling.

"Everything is well, dearest Elizabeth," he whispered and she smiled tremulously back.

"I hope Georgiana is not distressed by our marriage."

He stopped and looked at her in surprise. "Do you really think she might be?"

"I — I'm not sure. It depends how upset she was at your aunt's talk about me."

"Together. We are together and we will overcome everything. Come. I cannot wait to see that she is unharmed." Mr. Darcy led her up the rest of the steps.

Mr. Peake was waiting for them in the hall, and servants took Elizabeth's parasol and travelling jacket, and also Darcy's hat and cane.

Then they followed their host through to the drawing room.

"We have guests!" he announced cheerfully to the room, and he saw Georgiana looking up delightedly from a comfortable chair by the fire. Another young woman sitting beside her rose to curtsy, and his cousin rose from the other side of the fireplace.

"Fitzwilliam!" Georgiana sounded ecstatic. "And Elizabeth!"

Mr. Darcy bowed at her, but turned immediately to the other woman. He guessed her to be the sister that Richard had mentioned. He was right.

Mr. Peake, beside him, performed the introductions. "My sister, Miss Susannah Peake. Susannah, Mr. and Mrs. Darcy, as you must have guessed."

"Delighted to meet you, madam." Mr. Darcy bowed. "I understand I must thank you for your great care for my sister."

"Mrs. Darcy?" Georgiana cried out. "You are married? How long has that been? Oh, that I had known all my dearest wishes had come true."

CHAPTER 54

*E*lizabeth let go of his arm and crossed to Georgiana's side. She embraced her as sisters might. "How long has it been? Oh, Georgiana, it has been only one day and I hope you do not mind, or I could not have come with your brother to see you and assure myself that you were well."

"I don't mind — but I do want you to tell me everything about it and what has happened to you." Georgiana lowered her voice.

"The Peakes have been kindness itself, but I dared not write to you in case they notified my family and Lady Catherine made me go back to Pemberley with her." She sighed. "And now I can see that Fitzwilliam is safe. I am so happy."

Elizabeth looked at her carefully. "I would say you are more than happy, Georgiana." She smiled. "I think …" she stopped.

Perhaps it was something she should not yet mention. "I think I will need to tell you everything a little later, when all the pleasantries are observed."

She could hear the others in the room making conversation, but she concentrated on Georgiana. "So you seem to be well, but I understand you have injured your leg — and you did not stand when we came into the room." She anxiously surveyed the girl.

"I am all right, Elizabeth. I have been more concerned for the staff, but Mr. Peake assures me they are all recovered or recovering." Her eyes strayed to that gentleman.

"He has been so kind and attentive, and his sister is very sweet to me."

"I am pleased about that, Georgiana. But your leg?" Elizabeth was still concerned.

"It is getting better, Elizabeth. The physician says I have bruised the joint but there is nothing broken. It is just my hip and my leg threatens to give way on me when I try to stand for too long. But it is already much improved." She laughed. "For the first few days, I could not sit comfortably at all and I had to stay in bed." She sighed.

"Susannah Peake has been very attentive and she stayed with me all the time to keep me company until I was well enough to come downstairs." She looked again at Mr. Peake.

"Mr. Peake has an old bath chair of his grandmother's, and the servants carry me down each day in it so that I am entertained here."

Elizabeth nodded. She could see Georgiana glancing often at the gentleman. Her partiality was clear to her and she wondered if Colonel Fitzwilliam had noticed it.

"Please excuse me a moment, Georgiana, I must greet your cousin."

"He is your cousin too, now, Elizabeth."

"Oh, yes." Elizabeth smiled at her and rose to her feet.

Colonel Fitzwilliam was nearby and he bowed to her. "Many congratulations, Mrs. Darcy. I cannot think of a better wife for Darcy. I hope you will be very happy."

Elizabeth curtsied to him. "I thank you, sir. And I must also thank you for writing to my father so that I knew how your search was progressing. It was the happiest of moments when we got your latest letter."

Her eyes searched out her husband. He was perched on a chair near Georgiana and was speaking to her in a low voice. She saw Georgiana glance again at Mr. Peake, and observed that gentleman returning the glance.

This was going to be very interesting and she moved over to Susannah Peake. "I understand you have been very kind to Georgiana, Miss Peake. Thank you. She is very dear to me."

"Mrs. Darcy, please do not thank me. It has been a pleasure, and Georgiana is such a sweet girl. I am so happy her cousin was searching for her. I was becoming concerned that I would never persuade her to tell me who her family were."

Elizabeth smiled. "I hope you did not think all the family was distasteful to her."

"Oh, no!" Miss Peake's eyes strayed to the Colonel. "Colonel Fitzwilliam has explained what happened with their aunt. It seems a thrilling tale."

Elizabeth laughed. "I am sure it will appear so once it is all over and Georgiana is safe. But it has been very worrying."

"Oh, I do not mean to lessen the troubles you have had. I have heard that Mr. Darcy was sent to France. You must all have been very anxious for him while he was gone."

"Yes, yes, we were."

"And now you will be staying with us, will you not? Until Georgiana is well again?"

"I don't know." Elizabeth glanced at her husband. "It is most kind of you to suggest it. But Mr. Darcy may think Georgiana might be kept more safely at Pemberley." She looked at him, now deep in conversation with the other gentlemen.

"But I expect they will decide what is best."

Miss Peake nodded. "Georgiana tells me that you play and sing very well. It will be so nice to hear some music that is not my own. Georgiana is still not comfortable enough to sit at the pianoforte."

Elizabeth saw how often Miss Peake watched the Colonel and how often his eyes turned to her. Even though he had only been there a few days, his affection seemed obvious.

But she saw sadness within him. As a younger son, he was without fortune and her brother might not approve of his advances.

Elizabeth wondered what would become of it all, especially Georgiana's growing attachment to Mr. Peake. She supposed Fitzwilliam would wish to remove her to Pemberley as soon as it was possible, as she was so very young, and only recently had fancied herself in love with the man in Ramsgate.

She sighed, and her husband was suddenly

beside her. "Are you tired, Elizabeth? Come and sit down a while. Miss Peake has kindly had tea brought in."

She smiled up at him gratefully. "Thank you."

CHAPTER 55

*M*r. Darcy had never been so glad that an evening had come to an end. He waited with the other gentlemen for a short while after the ladies had retired for the night, his eyes following his wife as she walked demurely from the room with Miss Peake as they followed the servants carrying Georgiana in the bath chair.

He wondered how long it would be before Georgiana could be comfortable when seated in the coach. He wanted with every fibre of his being to be back at Pemberley, Elizabeth and Georgiana safely with him.

All the time in France he had worried whether he might ever see it again, whether Richard would marry Georgiana and keep Pemberley safely out of the hands of thieves and robbers.

But for now it was safe. And he wanted to be home. Of course, it would be most inconvenient to have an overnight stop at an inn while Georgiana was indisposed, but to do the journey in a single day might be too much for her for a while yet.

He smiled to himself. He would ask Elizabeth. She would understand. And he would be able to have her explain to him the undercurrents of emotion he felt in this place.

It was why he wanted to go to Pemberley. He felt more in control there, it was a simpler place for him.

Mr. Peake was beside him. "I hope you have a comfortable night. It seems you have achieved as much in the last few weeks as many men accomplish in a lifetime."

"Yes, I think I will find sleep a great attraction. Now I know my sister is safe and has been safe with you, I can rest. I can never repay my gratitude to you for your kindness to her."

Peake looked a little uncomfortable. "It was nothing. I am glad we were there to assist her."

As he climbed the stairs, Mr. Darcy wondered why the man had seemed uncomfortable. He thought back. Had he missed something? But he was so tired. And he wanted to be with Elizabeth, to talk to her alone. She could help him, she understood what was not said as well as what was.

In his guest bedchamber, he washed and changed. Then, he knocked quietly on the adjoining door to Elizabeth's room and went through to her.

She was standing looking out of the window into the darkness. She was wearing the same shawl over her shift. She was most beautiful to him. He crossed the room to her and took her in his arms.

"Elizabeth."

She lifted her face to him and he traced her lips with his finger. "You are so beautiful."

Her hand touched his face. "I love you so much, Fitzwilliam. But I am concerned for you. You look so tired. I think it will take many nights of restful sleep before you once again look as rested as you did when I first knew you." She laughed.

"And even then you looked under some strain."

"I confess I have not often felt calm and rested, Elizabeth. And lately, much has happened very quickly, as you know. But I am so happy you are here with me, it was worth the haste." He sighed.

"And I will be able to rest once we are back at

Pemberley and safe with Georgiana. I hope it can be very soon."

She shook her head. "I think we should not discuss that tonight. Get some rest and perhaps you and I might take a walk in the gardens tomorrow."

He frowned, was there a problem he did not know about that would prevent his plan?

"Do you not think it will be possible to go to Pemberley soon?"

"I did not say that, Fitzwilliam. But sometimes what is decided on quickly might not be for the best. For now, you need to rest."

He took her hand. "I'm so happy you are with me."

SHE HAD BEEN RIGHT. The next morning he awoke refreshed, his wife in his arms, and he knew some peace as he lay there quietly while she slept.

The scent of lavender rose up around him. He would never smell it again without thinking of her.

He let his mind idly return to the conversation over the port when the ladies had withdrawn after dinner.

Mr. Francis Peake was not as young as he

HIDDEN IN PLAIN SIGHT

looked, being twenty-four years of age. His breeding was impeccable, having come from a long line of landed gentry here in Leicestershire. His estate farms were predominantly sheep, although some of his land was quarried for local stone. His mother was descended from the Reeve family, and so of ancient lineage.

But he hadn't presumed upon his ancestry. He seemed a pleasant, well-mannered gentleman, and Mr. Darcy was pleased to know him.

However, he was perplexed when his cousin seemed to agree with Peake that they should not attempt to remove Georgiana too soon to Pemberley. He did not understand it, being certain that they should not continue to presume upon their hospitality much longer.

But he had not pressed the matter, knowing his weariness might make him forget some important issue.

And now he was rested. The bed was comfortable and his wife was beside him. Perhaps there was little hurry to be gone. But he could not dispel a niggling worry and he wondered what it could be.

"What is the matter? What concerns you so?" Elizabeth seemed to be awake in an instant.

"It is nothing." He brushed a tendril of hair

back from her face. "Good morning, my own Elizabeth."

She smiled. "Good morning, Fitzwilliam. But I would dispute that there is nothing that concerns you. You suddenly seemed unsettled."

He chuckled. "And you sensed it in your sleep."

"Of course. You had better never attempt to keep a secret from me, Fitzwilliam, for I will certainly know about it."

"Ah, there I have a problem immediately, for there is something I have not told you and perhaps I should have before we wed."

"And now you tell me!" but she was smiling, and she rolled over to face him and nestled deeply in his arms.

"No," she commanded. "You must let me guess, first." She had a mischievous glint in her eye. "You must just first assure me that it will not mean we are parted, in fact or in our love."

"Never," he declared. "Never!"

"That is a considerable relief." She ran a finger slowly down his cheek. "Now let me guess. You have been pretending to be Mr. Darcy and you are in fact, still Mr. Hudson, and we will be forced to live close to my mother."

He hid a smile. "And is it the relative poverty,

or the closeness to your mother that would distress you?"

"Both, to be sure! Be assured, *Mister Hudson*, that I would insist you rent a house a long way from Hertfordshire."

"I shall remember that," he said gravely. "But you are wrong. It is not that which was concerning me."

"So, let me guess again." She thought for a moment, an engaging little pout on her lips. "It is something you should have told me before we wed, you say." She looked up at him through her eyelashes. "Is it something I might be troubled about?"

"It is possible," he said heavily. "I hope not, and it did not enter my thoughts, I was just so fixed on what needed to be done to be able to bring you with me on my search."

She pushed herself to sit. "Now I am concerned, Fitzwilliam. I think you should tell me now, or I will be so curious all through breakfast that I might not be able to concentrate on being a model guest."

"And that will never do," he teased.

He pushed himself to sit beside her. "I just need you to promise me that you will stay beside me always, and that you will let me love you."

She leaned against him, he felt the warmth of her body. He wrapped his arms around her.

"Well, I am embarrassed to say it, because I persuaded my father to refuse when it was originally proposed by the King." He heard her gasp, but didn't wish to stop now.

"But when the Regent saw me this week, he suggested something different. I wished to refuse and then I thought of some of my family who might disdain you — and now I have discovered how Lady Catherine treated you at Pemberley, I have been proved correct."

He turned her face to his. "You, my precious Elizabeth, will outrank them all." He smiled. "Provided that the Regent has not forgotten or changed his mind, of course. It would not surprise me, and to be honest, I would prefer it. Being plain Mr. Darcy is likely to be less onerous."

She was staring at him, her eyes wide. "Really? You are not teasing me?"

"I am not teasing you, Elizabeth. I would not do that for something so serious." He felt anxious.

"You do not dislike me for not having told you before we wed? Would you have refused me?"

She looked thoughtful. "No, I could never have refused you, no matter what secrets you hid." She glanced up at him.

"But will this make a great difference to your life?"

"It may. I hope not, but at the very least, I will be expected to take my seat in the House of Lords at least occasionally." He felt his anger rise. "I may actually be able to persuade Parliament to pass laws preventing access to a woman's fortune if she is kidnapped and forced to marry."

"That would be a worthy life's work, to make ladies like Georgiana safe." Her voice was soft. "And now we better get ready, or the maid will be disturbing us."

"Yes." He leaned over and kissed her. "Thank you for not being angered with me. And please do not let any intimation of this get out. It is still possible that nothing will happen and in any event, I should prefer to be Mr. Darcy for a few days longer."

She laughed and kissed him back. "I will not tell anyone, *Sir* Fitzwilliam."

He nearly told her, nearly corrected it. But he managed to stop himself. It still gave him pause, even now. She must come slowly to the awareness of what it meant.

And it was as they were descending the stairs to the breakfast room, that the first hint of awareness seemed to take root.

"Fitzwilliam?"

"Yes?"

"What do you mean, I will outrank them all? How would I outrank Lady Catherine, born the daughter of an Earl?"

He smiled. "Let us walk in the gardens later, Elizabeth. We cannot talk of it now."

He was still smiling as they turned into the breakfast room and greeted their hosts.

ut the morning passed in the company of Miss Peake and Georgiana. Elizabeth didn't mind, not really. But her mind puzzled over what he had and had not said.

At the urgent request of the ladies, she sat at the pianoforte and played for a long time. She was happy there, she had time to think and puzzle over what he had said, while her fingers played the familiar tunes of her childhood.

The gentlemen came into the room when the tea arrived and she saw her husband select a pastry and bring the plate and a cup of tea over to the instrument.

"If you would care to rest a while, Elizabeth, I have some refreshment for you."

She smiled at him. "Of course."

The only peerages that outranked an Earl was a Marquis or a Duke. Surely that was too much?

"Try not to look too troubled, Elizabeth." His whisper caught her attention, and she looked up. His eyes were laughing. "Or the others might think you and I have already had a disagreement."

She closed the piano lid and stood up. "I would not wish to give that impression, Mr. Darcy."

His lips twitched as he tried not to smile and they joined the rest of the party. Elizabeth exerted herself to join in.

However, an hour before lunch, her husband asked if he and Elizabeth could be forgiven if they took a walk in the gardens before lunch.

Soon, they were strolling along through the rose garden. The scent was strong around them.

"I can smell autumn in the air," she said. "I suppose it comes earlier as we go north."

"Yes, you're right."

She smiled and tucked her hand in his arm and he supported her as they walked.

"It might be another cold winter. But there is

nothing better on a crisp cold day than coming in from the gardens to a roaring fire."

"It sounds wonderful," she said wistfully. "But do you not have to pass the Season in London?"

He glanced down at her. "Would you wish to spend it in London?"

"That depends where you are." She might as well be frank with him. "I would prefer Pemberley at all times, but I most assuredly wish to go to London if you have much business there."

His arm tightened around her hand and she saw him glance back at the house. Her heart beat rapidly within her, surely he would not risk propriety?

He did not. But he lifted her hand to his lips. "Provided you are able to undertake the journey, I will always wish you with me."

And with that, she had to be satisfied. They strolled on in quiet companionship for a few moments before he spoke again.

"Elizabeth, I have been wondering if you could enlighten me about something I am puzzled about. You are most observant and I am sure to have missed much of what you have seen. Perhaps you could share with me why the atmosphere between the parties confuses me."

She thought for a few minutes. She needed to

tell him, she knew that. But she did not want him to become angry and react precipitately.

"Might we sit down on that bench, Fitzwilliam?" she asked. "Then I can explain to you what I think."

He bowed and led her over to the bench.

She sat and thought for some minutes and he waited patiently. Finally she turned to him.

"Perhaps you could first tell me what you think about what you have observed and then I may expand upon your thoughts."

He looked over her head at the blooms nearby. "I think that Georgiana does not want to leave here at the present time, and after dinner last night, Cousin Richard was agreeing with that sentiment." He looked down at her. "I wondered perhaps, if the coach accident had caused her to fear another journey?"

She nodded. "It is a fair thought." She faced him. "But I think the answer is somewhat different. I will tell you, but might I caution you not to do anything urgently until we have fully discussed it?"

His eyebrows rose. "Is it of the import that you think I might?"

"I do," she said reluctantly. "You would do it out of love and concern. But I feel it might do more harm than good. And I hope that you will trust me for this little while."

"Madam, you have my full attention."

She drew a deep breath. Perhaps she could build on what he thought and it would be a way to prevent him misunderstanding what should be done.

"I think your thoughts about the fear of a new journey are sound, and I consider we should perhaps not rush to heal Georgiana's fears. But I think it has led to a strong feeling of safety within the house and for her hosts." She searched his expression. She needed to be careful.

"Georgiana told me of her rescue, how the servants lifted the coach and Mr. Peake carried her to his coach himself. He would let no servant do it." She smiled. "Of course she feels affectionately towards him, that he is her protector, and she feels safe."

His face turned thunderous. "You think she fancies herself in love? Again?"

Elizabeth put her hand on his arm. "Please, Fitzwilliam. You promised to listen to it all."

He sat back in the seat. "Pray continue."

"She is very young, Fitzwilliam. Very young and innocent. Young girls of that age always wish to think themselves in love, whether it be a local officer or a friend's brother. It is very normal."

She let her hand touch his. "My sisters have given me that experience, and you must have listened to the talk at the dinner table at Longbourn."

He smiled reluctantly, and she continued.

"I would be worried if she was unable to feel affection for anyone save for you. And she is trying to be discreet — after all, you suspected nothing. And I believe Mr. Peake is an honourable man. I do not believe he will take advantage of her feelings, if he indeed sees them." She gave a soft laugh.

"I do not believe he has noticed anything amiss." She glanced up, and laced her fingers through his. "I think if you insist on removing her precipitately, you will merely foster in her a resentment and a belief that she did love him after all, whereas, if we stay a few days, she may get over her temporary affections."

"And do you think it *is* temporary?"

She shook her head. "We cannot know, sir. Only a little more time might help me to ascertain that. But if it is not temporary, I can think that Mr. Peake is not the sort of man you might forbid from seeing your sister in the future, when she is older."

"Well," he said, rubbing his face. "I suppose you might be right. But I am dismayed that I did not see it for myself." A frown creased his brow.

"But do you think Cousin Richard has noticed it? He seemed reluctant to hurry her move."

Elizabeth laughed. "I am sure he is certain that it is not noticeable, but I think his own feelings have prevented him from observing Georgiana's."

"His own?" Mr. Darcy looked puzzled.

Elizabeth just looked at him with a knowing smile until he finally seemed to understand. "Oh! You do not mean … no, surely I would have noticed …" he shook his head. "And do you think the lady might reciprocate his feelings?"

"In my mind there is little doubt of that. But he is a reticent man, and he knows that, with no fortune, he is not an eligible man." Her fingers tightened around his hand.

"Please, Fitzwilliam, let us stay at least another day or two."

"You would not be afraid that Georgiana's affections will become stronger?"

"They might, but I think that outcome would be more certain if you took her away from here before she has more time." She stood up. "We must go in for lunch, or they will be coming to find us. Please do not betray what you know, and perhaps we might talk again later. I have more views which I would like to divulge."

He shook his head as if in a daze. "I am

surprised at how much you have divined in so short a time."

"And I could yet be wrong." Elizabeth tucked her hand back in his arm as they strolled back to the house. "Let us see whether your observations coincide with mine, now you are looking for the clues."

CHAPTER 57

M r. Darcy could not but feel admiration for his wife as they sat at lunch. Her happiness and gaiety lifted the mood of the whole party — but perhaps he was seeing more in her than the others, because of his love for her.

He tried to watch Georgiana and Mr. Peake, and also Cousin Richard and Miss Peake, but all he could see was the occasional glance.

There would have been awkwardness and uncomfortable silences had Elizabeth not been there. She changed the topic of conversation when necessary and soon had many of them happily involved.

He watched her, his heart full of love and pride. She would grace any company, and he knew she could accept the extra attention his honour would bring her.

"Darcy! You're being most inattentive!" Cousin Richard's voice was amused, and Mr. Darcy started.

"I suppose as a newlywed, you must be excused." Richard was laughing at him and he wanted to scowl with embarrassment.

But Elizabeth came to his rescue too, smiling warmly at him before turning her attention to Cousin Richard.

"Colonel Fitzwilliam, you have not told us what you found at Pemberley when you arrived there after your summons to London."

His cousin turned to Elizabeth. "I wonder if, one day, you will feel able to call me Cousin Richard," he teased her, and she inclined her head with a smile.

"So, what did you find?" she was not going to allow him to deflect the conversation away.

He grimaced and looked at Georgiana. "Perhaps we should not discuss it, since everything has turned out well, but I am afraid I left her in no doubt that Darcy would be most displeased." He glanced at Darcy.

"She told me that she was most displeased that you had left Georgiana *to be influenced by such an unsuitable young woman* and that *you would thank her in*

*the end for taking over the running of the household while
you were off wasting time while in France.*" His smile
was genuine, and Mr. Darcy's lips tightened.

"And is she still at Pemberley, waiting for me to
return home and be grateful?"

"No." His cousin shook his head. "She was
planning her return to Rosings Park. I am sure the
weather is warmer there, and Anne will be more
sickly if they remain in the north."

"I think I will need to speak with my aunt
soon." Mr. Darcy mused. "But I shall be in no
hurry about it, so that she is in no doubt that I
find other things more important."

He smiled at Elizabeth. "It would be as well if
she reads first of our marriage when it is in the
Gazette."

"You must be kind to her, sir. She is certain
that you will marry your Cousin Anne and our
news will be a great disappointment to her."

He gazed at her in surprise. He knew she had
suffered much at the hands of his aunt, who was
not known to care whether her words were cruel
or unkind. It became clearer still to him that her
innate kindness was genuine. How fortunate he
was to have found her.

He watched her, her grace and poise stirring
him and bringing his good fortune home to him.
She must have new gowns, suitable for her posi-

tion. It would not do for her to continue in those country print dresses.

How could he arrange that? He pondered. He could not ask Miss Peake, of her kindness, to travel to Leicester with Elizabeth. That would leave Georgiana here without a chaperone, and he would have to stay here with her. And he did not wish Elizabeth to go anywhere without him.

Perhaps Miss Peake could arrange a seamstress to visit Havenfield Hall? Or he could arrange for a London establishment to bring a selection of their gowns for her to try.

He smiled, Georgiana would enjoy helping her and suggesting which gowns would be the best choice.

"And what thoughts are amusing you, Mr. Darcy?" his host was watching him. He shook his head, smiling.

"I am sorry, Mr. Peake. You catch me at a most disadvantageous moment."

"You have much on your mind, sir. I understand." Mr. Peake's smile seemed a little wistful, and Mr. Darcy thought that Elizabeth had the right opinion of his affections.

He exerted himself to draw out the gentleman, to find out what he was really like. After all, if Georgiana wished to see him again, he must know what sort of man he was before inviting him to Pemberley.

AFTER DINNER, the gentlemen sat over the port again. Georgiana had walked from her chair to the door this time, supported by Elizabeth, and only then taking to the bath chair to go through to the drawing room.

"She is improving all the time." Mr. Peake was watching her too. "A very brave and courageous young lady."

"She is." Mr. Darcy poured his port. "After the death of her mother, she has been very shy and reticent. I have been concerned at her lack of experience in company, but if she does not wish it, it is hard to demand it of her."

"Especially as you do not like company either." Cousin Richard interjected with his usual dry humour.

Darcy jerked his head irritably. "But what are we to do about the danger she is in? We are most fortunate that she has not been discovered here — yet."

"Danger?" Mr. Peake's voice sharpened in apparent anxiety.

Mr. Darcy glanced at him and then looked at

Richard. His cousin swiftly gave the essence of the story more concisely than Darcy ever could have. His military experience was of help in this.

"So, what is to be done about it?" Mr. Peake was obviously concerned and Mr. Darcy wondered at the strength of the man's feelings.

He sighed heavily. "I have been hoping that Parliament might have been stirred into action. The Earl of Sandwich has been of great assistance. But we need a new law to protect the fortune of any young lady forced into marriage against her will." He shrugged.

"Until then, even if we do catch the perpetrators this time, they must have spread the thought of the crime amongst their fellow villains, and she will be in danger until she marries." He shook his head. "She is so young, both in years and in her maturity. But she is going to have to grow up very quickly, and I have to keep her safe until she is married."

There was nothing more to be said, although Mr. Peake promised to warn the staff of the Hall, and it was agreed that while Georgiana was indisposed, she was unlikely to be at immediate risk.

CHAPTER 58

*E*lizabeth was enjoying her time at Havenfield Hall, although she longed to be alone more often with Fitzwilliam.

But she treasured their stolen time together, their walks through the gardens; but most of all, at night when they were free to talk and be close. Each night she grew to value him more, and seemed to understand more about him.

Georgiana was improving each day, too, although Elizabeth was secretly sure that her new sister's injury was not now so bad as she made it out to be.

She smiled to herself, she was sure Georgiana was not deliberately dissembling, but Elizabeth was convinced that she was improving more slowly than she would have, had she not had reason to wish to stay in Leicestershire.

"What is amusing you?" Fitzwilliam sounded indulgent as they strolled through the woodland that bounded the estate.

"I am pondering on the situation here, Fitzwilliam." She glanced up. "Do you discover an increasing attachment of your cousin to Miss Peake? She seems to be a delightful lady — and I believe his affections are returned."

"I do." He nodded, and she returned her eyes to the path.

"What do you think Mr. Peake feels about the situation? Does he have another relative who would keep house for him if his sister marries?"

"I do not know that. But I think he would not stand in his sister's way of finding happiness." He sounded almost sad. "But I do not know if she has a suitable fortune. It is not something that arises in conversation."

"It seems unfortunate to me that the Earl could not make some sort of settlement on his younger son." Elizabeth was thoughtful.

"It would seem kinder to the individuals concerned, but in the event, the fortune should go with the main estate, for the upkeep of a large mansion and a London home can be very costly."

"You're right, sir. But it makes me sad.

Because having married me without a fortune to settle on our younger children, they might find themselves unable to follow their hearts."

He chuckled, and the warmth and richness of the sound warmed her through.

"I think we do not need to worry about that topic for many, many years yet, Elizabeth. And I have plenty of time to put away investments to settle on those of our children who need it."

"You are very thoughtful, sir." Elizabeth smiled up at him. "I am so very fortunate."

"The good fortune is all mine." He patted her hand and she thrilled to his touch.

They both heard their cousin's voice hailing them and looked at each other.

"We had better see what news he bears, Elizabeth." She nodded her agreement and they turned towards Colonel Fitzwilliam, who was striding towards them.

When he got close enough, he stopped, but he seemed unable to say a word, merely looking from one to the other.

"What is the matter? Has something terrible happened?" Elizabeth could hear her voice trembling and her husband's arm went round her.

"Be strong." His voice was a whisper and his head close to hers.

"Well, I … your Gr …" Colonel Fitzwilliam seemed utterly unable to finish the sentence.

"Oh." Mr. Darcy sounded resigned. "I take it the Gazette has arrived?"

Incredulity spread over the Colonel's face. "You knew? You knew about it and did not warn me?" He seemed to think better of it. "… Your Grace?"

Mr. Darcy turned to her. "This is when things change, I am afraid."

Her heart was beating fast. Your Grace? That must mean Fitzwilliam had been made a Duke. Or did they call a Marquess that too?

His arm tightened around her and he whispered in her ear. "Be courageous, my love. It will all soon settle down."

But Colonel Fitzwilliam was looking at them in surprise. "You did not tell Elizabeth, either?" He sounded completely astonished.

"No, I did not — mainly because of her fearing this stupid reaction, Cousin Richard. I am just the same and so are you. Now please let us go back to where we were before." He started striding back towards the house.

"We had better get the reactions over with. I hope things can then settle back to normal."

Elizabeth listened as the two men talked.

"If you think things can ever be normal again,

Darcy, I think you are sadly misguided." The Colonel turned to his cousin.

"Why ever did you agree to it? I thought you spurned the idea?"

Her husband sighed. "I did. You recall I persuaded my father to reject an Earldom from the old King. However the Regent is a different man entirely. He was very insistent, because I had already rejected one honour from him for a task I undertook last year." He smiled down at Elizabeth.

"But my main reason for accepting this time was in hope that I could make the woman I loved a Duchess. And so I have."

The Colonel didn't appear to have heard. "You did a task for him last year? I did not know that."

"I know." Mr. Darcy shrugged. "I was sworn to secrecy and I will never be at liberty to divulge the details. But the Regent assured me that if I accepted Portland, then he would not call on me again." He laughed.

"I am not convinced he will keep his side of the bargain, but I have been looking forward to anticipating Lady Catherine's reaction, once she knows where I am."

Elizabeth bit her lip. She must not laugh. The thought of Lady Catherine finding out that she, Elizabeth, was a Duchess, was most amusing.

Fitzwilliam leaned down to her. "Yes, I too am gaining great amusement at that. I wish I could be there when she discovers it."

Elizabeth gave him a mischievous look. "I hope she does not appear here, sir."

He looked disturbed. "I too, hope she does not appear here. It would be very difficult for our hosts."

"I do not know if she knows where we are," Elizabeth said thoughtfully. "Unless your uncle knows?"

Mr. Darcy turned to the Colonel. "I imagine your father knows where we are, Cousin Richard?"

Colonel Fitzwilliam nodded distractedly. "I think he will write to you. I cannot imagine he will appear here unannounced."

"But will Lady Catherine?"

"Oh." He looked dismayed. "She may do." He took a deep breath and straightened up.

"I think you have a duty to send her an express and tell her you will call on her at Rosings very soon. Then she will wait there, because she will not want to miss you."

"It is a plan," Mr. Darcy mused. "But I have

no intention of waiting upon her." He looked at Elizabeth.

"What do you think I should do for the best?"

She smiled. "Why not send her that express? Say to her that you are intending to travel to London imminently and when you are there you will be receiving everyone."

"It is well thought." He lifted her hand to his lips. "As always, you think of the right thing."

She felt her colour rising, and he chuckled. "And still so modest."

"But I do not understand the right forms of address, Fitzwilliam. Will you tell me what I should be saying?"

"Later will be soon enough, dearest Elizabeth. Now we need to go in and reassure everyone that I have not grown an extra proud head upon my shoulders and I wish to be just the same."

She squeezed his fingers, hoping for some little reassurance.

A Duchess! And only a week ago she had been plain Miss Elizabeth Bennet. She smiled to herself. How her mother would crow about it all!

CHAPTER 59

*H*is Grace, the Duke of Portland, lately Fitzwilliam Darcy, strolled with his cousin around the gardens the following morning. He felt it beholden on him to apologise for the upheaval of the previous day.

"Because I was not sure if the Regent would even keep his intention long enough to make the declaration," he said, swishing the long grass with his cane.

"But I am sorry I could not warn you without it seeming boastful if it never happened."

"Do not worry, Darcy. I have forgiven you." His cousin sighed deeply.

Darcy frowned. "But you are not content here, Richard. Can you not tell me what it is?" Darcy wished he had Elizabeth's way with words, able to gain people's confidences without seeming to gloat.

For he suddenly realised how unfair it must seem to Cousin Richard that he, Darcy, was wealthy beyond measure, had a wonderful wife, a great estate, and now the highest ranking peerage possible for a commoner.

His lips tightened. He had not considered it like that.

"Richard. Forgive me if I am talking out of turn, but I have seen the way the lady looks at you. Are you concerned as to financial matters?"

His cousin gave him a sharp look. "I have hoped ... but there is not much to say." He shrugged hopelessly. "What do I have to offer?"

"If this is what you want, Cousin, you must let me help you. I would wish for you the happiness my marriage has brought to me."

His cousin looked at him, disbelief and a dawning hope in his eyes. "I do not see that you are obliged, Darcy." He shook his head. "Sorry, I forget that I must refer to you now as Portland."

Darcy laughed. "When there is no one around to be offended or confused, then I would prefer Darcy." He shook his head.

"I have already been undone with the *Your Grace this* and *Your Grace that* from the servants this morning."

"It serves you right." Fitzwilliam sounded unsympathetic.

A few steps later he stopped. "I am sorry, Darcy. I should not have said that."

"You do not have to apologise. I think I understand, although I cannot feel how it must really be for you."

"No. I do not want to talk about it right now, Darcy. But if I cannot think of anything, then I might return to you to discuss any offer you might have been referring to." He grimaced. "I would not ever wish to admit it."

"And no one else would ever know." Darcy would not tell his cousin of the others he was already assisting, as he would never tell them of him. All he knew was that he could not possibly spend all the income from the Darcy estate, and it was beholden on him to use it wisely. He did not know of a braver man, or one more deserving.

"That's odd." The Colonel had stopped, and Darcy turned to where his cousin was staring at a makeshift camp almost hidden in the trees. A rough piece of canvas was strung between two of the trees, and several blackened cooking pots lay beside a deadened fire.

"I wonder who it might be?" the Colonel mused, and he bent to examine the heap of personal belongings.

"Warm." He tested the embers.

Darcy stood and began to look around, his whole body tense with suspicion. But he could not see anyone. He began to circle the camp, searching for any sign of those who might have been here.

"Aha!" his cousin's voice sent him back to the camp. He was waving a piece of paper.

"We must go back to the house at once, Darcy!"

Darcy seized the paper. A crudely drawn sketch, but the likeness was unmistakable. Georgiana.

Both men took off at a run to the house.

As they entered, Mr. Peake met them in the hall. "What is it? What is the matter?"

Darcy brushed past him, thrusting the paper at him.

"Is Georgiana all right?"

"Why, yes. What has happened? Where did you get this?"

Darcy heard his cousin begin to tell Peake in a low voice what they had found, but he followed the sound of the pianoforte into the drawing room.

He stopped in relief as he saw the three ladies grouped around the instrument, laughing as they each played a part on the keys they could reach.

His eyes locked on to his sister. She was most precious to him and he could not bear to think of the risk to her happiness and security.

"Fitzwilliam?" Elizabeth was rising to her feet. "What is it?" she came towards him, leaving the other ladies looking at her.

He drew her aside and spoke in a low voice. "We will be leaving as soon as we can, Elizabeth. We have discovered that the men who want Georgiana are camping nearby. It was by the merest chance we found their camp. We dare not stay another night." He glanced around the room.

"Please take Georgiana upstairs and stay with her while her maids pack her things. Then keep her with you while the maids pack your gowns too. Please do not let her out of your sight."

She touched his hand. "I know you will do what is right, sir. I will do exactly as you ask." She looked around, and lifted his hand to her lips for just the merest moment. Then she was as perfectly behaved as before.

A tiny smile which turned his heart over, and she whispered to him. "Try not to be too concerned. We will soon be home and safe."

He nodded, and watched her as she beckoned to the footman to bring the bath chair and she went over to speak to Georgiana.

He could watch no longer, the pain in his

heart as he looked at the two ladies he loved above all else emphasised starkly his failure to be able to rid the country of those who would harm them.

He turned on his heel and went back to the hall. Mr. Peake and his cousin were talking fast in low voices, and they looked over at him.

"Ah, yes, Darcy. Let us go into the library and we can make haste with the plans." Mr. Peake led the way and Darcy was glad when he poured whisky into three large glasses.

"I have ordered your coach be got ready, sir, and mine as well. I will also take the chaise, as it is good if we appear to be a large party. You can double up the servants on your coach with those who have been here since Miss Darcy had her accident."

He paced around the room. "If you do not mind, my sister and I will travel with you. I think the larger the party, the better it will seem. We can return here as soon as you are safely at Pemberley if you would rather be alone."

"No." Darcy had to stop and clear his throat. "I mean, you would be most welcome to stay at Pemberley. But we are going to London."

He saw the Colonel turn and look at him in surprise. He grimaced.

"I know. I would far rather go to Pemberley. But London will be safer, I feel. There are more constables than in Derbyshire, and they are better organised. I can also call on many more resources to protect her."

He turned to Mr. Peake. "I must thank you for your hospitality and assistance in this matter, and I am sorry it has come to such a swift ending. Might I trouble you for a small early luncheon to be set? We might then get to Woburn for our night stop. I know the inn there, and so do my servants."

"Of course." Mr. Peake nodded at the footman, who hurried away.

"I have also set my steward and a group of farmers to patrol the estate. They will burn and remove any belongings they find and detain any persons loitering in the area." He smiled. "I have an — understanding with the magistrate here. Anyone with evil intent will not be dealt with lightly."

Darcy nodded. "Thank you." He looked around. "Perhaps I will wait in the hall for the ladies to come downstairs."

CHAPTER 60

$\mathcal{H}$e paced up and down the hall, waiting for Elizabeth and Georgiana to come downstairs. Had he forgotten anything? He worked through the plans from beginning to end.

He heard their voices and watched as Elizabeth walked beside the bath chair as it was carried down by the servants. Georgiana smiled up at him from it.

He could see how anxious she was, but her resolve seemed that she would not show it, and she said, "Elizabeth and I have been deciding that I would try walking more around the house, but she thought that since I will get tired in the coach, it was better not to attempt too much."

He bowed. "I think that is very wise." He shared a look with Elizabeth.

Georgiana nodded. "I will miss it here, but I love Pemberley very much, too."

"We are not going to Pemberley, I am afraid, Georgiana." He hated to disappoint her, but he must tell her at once, and he sensed Elizabeth's surprise.

"We are going to London. There is a more organised constabulary and I can get a guard more easily." He smiled at his sister. "You will be pleased to know that Mr. and Miss Peake will be coming with us. We will be a large and cheerful party when we stop at Woburn for the night."

He caught Elizabeth's eye as Georgiana cried out with delight. Her partiality was easy to see.

He smiled at her. "You three ladies will all travel in my coach, if that is satisfactory to you. There will be extra servants on it as well. Mr. Peake's coach and chaise will make it seem a large party. Colonel Fitzwilliam, Mr. Peake and myself, as well as extra servants, will be riding alongside you."

"Oh, Fitzwilliam, I am so sorry. All this trouble is all my fault," Georgiana cried. "I have put everyone to so much trouble."

He crouched down beside her. "You were not to know, Georgiana. And there is nothing now to be done. I will keep you safe, and will not allow you to be left in the care of our aunt, ever again."

She smiled at him with swimming eyes. "But I can still be sorry about it. It is a pity that it is so many months until I am sixteen."

He was shocked. He had not realised she knew she must marry early. "You will still be my responsibility even then, Georgiana. We will have to see."

He rose to his feet again and looked at Elizabeth. "I am sorry, Elizabeth. It has hardly been the peaceful start to married life that I would have hoped for you."

She laughed. "I told you how I had complained to my sister about my monotonous, predictable life before I met you. I did not anticipate quite such excitement to fill my life quite so quickly."

He found himself smiling with her. "Thank you for your confidence in me. Now, let us have something to eat and we can soon be on our way."

HE WAS VERY weary when the whole party drew up in the yard of the Swan at Woburn. His head groom jumped down from the coach and hurried inside. Darcy hoped the innkeeper would be able to accommodate them all.

When the whole party was assembling for dinner in the largest parlour, Darcy went in search of the innkeeper.

"Thank you for finding enough accommodation for us. But I have one request from you tonight."

"Yes, Your Grace." The man bowed low. "May I congratulate you, sir, on your elevation."

"Thank you." He tried not to be irritated. "We believe my sister to be in some danger. The gentlemen will take our turn to stand guard outside her room. But I would also like two of my servants to stand with us, in case of trouble, rather than them all being accommodated in the servants' quarters."

Once that had been agreed, he rejoined the party.

IN THE MIDDLE of the night, he slipped quietly into the bedchamber where he hoped Elizabeth was sleeping, having seen Colonel Fitzwilliam arrive sleepily to stand guard in the hallway outside their rooms. A maid was sleeping in a cot by the window in Georgiana's room, and she was as safe as he could possibly make her.

Now to try and get some rest. It was a long

ride tomorrow. He prepared himself for the remainder of the night as quietly as possible, and slipped silently into the bed.

But he might have known Elizabeth would be awake and waiting for him. Her arms reached out to him.

"Come and rest, Fitzwilliam. You need to sleep."

"I did not wish to wake you, dearest Elizabeth."

"And you didn't." There was a hint of laughter in her voice. "I was already awake."

She smoothed back his hair. "Now you can relax. I have been lying that side of the bed so it is warm for you."

And she had. Not only was it warm, but her scent wafted around him, comforting. "Thank you."

She kissed him and drew him closer. "No more talking, just rest."

He lay quietly, the strain and aching sense of responsibility washing out of him. "Please ensure I do not sleep too late, Elizabeth."

"I will," she promised, and he relaxed. He could trust her absolutely.

But his sleep was punctuated by dreams and he jerked awake several times. Each time Elizabeth was there for him, calming him again, endlessly patient. Only once did he get up and go to the door and check on his cousin.

"Go back to bed, Darcy, and leave this to me!" Richard's harsh whisper sent him smiling back to Elizabeth.

HE HAD a difficult horse the next day, and he was glad of it, it took all his skill to keep the animal under control. Whenever he had the opportunity, he rode up beside the coach window and glanced in. Elizabeth was always watching for him with her loving smile, although Georgiana and Miss Peake seemed to be asleep much of the time.

HE WAS VERY, very relieved to get to Darcy House in the middle of the afternoon and get everyone inside safely.

As the servants hurried around with their belongings and the footmen brought in tea, he saw Mr. Peake talking to Georgiana. He wondered what was being said.

But Cousin Richard turned to him with a rather wicked smile.

"Should I send word to my uncle? He might arrange a guard with the Brigadier."

Darcy nodded. "Thank you. It is a good thought." He smiled. "Although I rather think he will expect me to turn up at Matlock House."

"Maybe, but you cannot be expected to leave Georgiana. No, he will expect me to go, so that he can quiz me on how you had the audacity to attain the Duchy." The Colonel laughed mirthlessly.

"Which is why I would prefer to send a servant in your name."

Darcy clapped him on the shoulder. "Good thought. Do it."

He watched Elizabeth as she rose and walked towards him. "Are you well?" he murmured as she reached him.

"Indeed. But as you see, Georgiana is out of spirits because Mr. Peake and his sister will be going to their London establishment shortly."

"Ah, I wondered what he could be saying."

She smiled. "I wonder if you might invite them back to dine with us tonight? That will please them both, I think."

"Of course. But this is your home, now, Elizabeth. You may extend any invitation you wish without consulting me." He smiled and she returned it.

"I keep forgetting. But I would not want to do so without your approval." Her eyes danced with amusement, and she turned and went back to their guests.

Elizabeth knew she would miss Pemberley, but it seemed that Darcy House was to be their home for the foreseeable future.

She was content with that, her husband was here and he seemed more at ease in his own domain, although she knew he had been happy to stay at Havenfield Hall when she had explained why she felt they should stay.

She had watched as he had exerted himself to become better acquainted with Mr. Peake, and had been amused as he tried to keep an eye on Georgiana and watch her at the same time.

For she knew his eyes were on her constantly, and while it had disturbed her at first, when he was Mr. Hudson and she just a friend to Georgiana; now she knew it was a result of his love and protectiveness toward her.

The only person she really missed was Jane and the first morning, she requested time of Georgiana to write to her sister and tell her where they were.

Dear Jane,
How very long it is since I wrote to you.

*Please forgive me, for so much has
happened in the last few days, I
scarce know where to begin.*

*But first, we are now in London and you
should write to me directly at Darcy
House. I think we will be here for
some time, almost certainly for the
Season, and I will ask Fitzwilliam
whether you may come and stay
with us.*

*As I said in my last letter to you,
Georgiana was not badly injured in
the accident and she is improving
daily. But she is not going to be able
to go out into town for some little
while, so your assistance to enlarge
her circle of friends will be
invaluable.*

She stopped to think. No, she would not
mention about her husband's new rank, it would
be difficult to write about without seeming to
boast, and she was not sure how to say it — it was
all so new to her understanding.

She smiled, as she sat at the writing desk. The
only ennoblement the Bennet family had known
was when Sir William was knighted. But it had
made no difference to Elizabeth's friendship with

Charlotte Lucas, and she was determined that
being a Duchess would make no difference to her
relationships with those she loved.

> *I am sure you will be dismayed to know
> that the villains who wanted to take
> Georgiana had found she was at
> Havenfield Hall. It was the merest
> chance that Fitzwilliam and his
> cousin discovered their hiding place
> and we have come to London to
> afford her better protection.*
>
> *She will be sixteen in the early summer
> next year, and Fitzwilliam is coming
> to the sad reality that she might have
> to marry as soon as she is of age
> before she is kidnapped by those who
> would force a marriage to gain her
> fortune.*
>
> *I think she knows that, but she is now
> thinking it is a good thing, because
> she feels most affectionately toward
> her rescuer and host, Mr. Francis
> Peake.*
>
> *He is a fine gentleman, and although
> Fitzwilliam is most protective to
> Georgiana, I think he is beginning to
> accept the idea that this may be the*

*best possible outcome, even though an
early marriage is not what he would
have wished for her.*

*Miss Peake keeps house for her brother
and is a kind and gentle person. I
think Fitzwilliam's cousin, Colonel
Fitzwilliam, is very taken with her
and she with him, but he is
despondent, because he has no fortune
of his own to offer. I cannot think
what I might do to help them. I
would dearly love to see them be
happy together.*

*But I suppose I must stop meddling in
other people's affairs and attend to
my own.*

*I am so happy in my marriage to
Fitzwilliam, dear Jane. I can only
wish you find equal happiness to
mine, you deserve such happiness
because of your goodness to everyone.*

*Please do write and tell me everything that
is happening at Longbourn. I do miss
it, even though I am very happy here.*

*Your affectionate and loving sister,
Elizabeth*

She dried the ink on her letter and folded it.

"Thank you for letting me write the letter, Georgiana, I have been most remiss in not keeping up with my correspondence." She sealed the envelope and wrote the direction.

"Now, should we practise our duets for tonight?"

Georgiana looked up from her needlework. "Yes, it is a good idea. Do we have guests tonight?"

Elizabeth watched the girl's shy smile and flushed cheeks.

"Why, did you not hear me invite Mr. Peake and his sister?"

"Well," Georgiana's flush deepened and she paid close attention to her stitching.

Elizabeth smiled and got up. Placing her letter on the table by the door, she went to Georgiana.

"Would it embarrass you very much if we talked about Mr. Peake?"

"Yes, it would, but I suppose we need to." She looked at Elizabeth and bit her lip. "It would be far more embarrassing to talk to my brother."

Elizabeth laughed. "I suppose it would. He would go to Mr. Peake and ask him if his intentions are honourable."

"Of course they are!" Georgiana looked up indignantly. "He is most proper."

Elizabeth laughed. "I am sure he is." She

became serious. "Have you had much opportunity to talk?"

Georgiana shook her head. "As I have not been able to walk, we have not been able to take a turn about the gardens, which would be the only opportunity." She smiled. "But we can talk a little, and Susannah is very kind and pretends not to be listening."

"She is a sweet, kind person," Elizabeth agreed. "She would be an ideal sister-in-law for you."

Georgiana looked at Elizabeth a little anxiously. "Do you think Fitzwilliam will allow it? He will say I am too young until I am about forty, I think."

Elizabeth nodded. "I think elder brothers are always protective of their younger sisters, Georgiana. But he knows that he cannot really keep you safe for a long time, and is coming to the conclusion, however reluctantly, that if you find a gentleman who is a good and honourable person, and that you have affection for, he must not stand in your way."

"Do you really think so?" Georgiana's eyes were alight with hope.

"I do." Elizabeth was pleased to see the girl's excitement. "Now, I know it can be difficult to guess, but do you think Mr. Peake returns your affections?" She was quite sure about it in her own mind, but she wanted to know what he might have said to Georgiana.

"It is difficult." Georgiana sighed. "Gentlemen have to be so formal and polite. But I think so." She looked pensive. "He has been telling me all about his family. Did you know his parents died together in a coach crash when he was only nineteen? I think that is why he was so determined to look after me very well."

"Oh, poor Mr. Peake — and poor Miss Peake, too! It is such a sad story, but I am glad they have had each other." Elizabeth picked up her needlework, the pianoforte could wait.

"I think perhaps Mr. Peake needs to make his intentions known to your brother. I know there can be no formal betrothal this early, but an informal agreement might make you feel better?"

"Oh, that would be wonderful," Georgiana breathed. "Are you sure Fitzwilliam will agree?"

The drawing room doors opened and a footman entered.

"The Earl and Countess of Matlock!" he announced.

Elizabeth and Georgiana got to their feet. Both curtsied deeply as their guests entered.

"Lord Matlock, Lady Matlock," Elizabeth greeted them.

Her uncle by marriage looked rather glum, but he bowed. "Your Grace." Then he turned to Georgiana and bowed again.

"Miss Darcy."

They all sat down. "I am afraid my husband is in Town at the moment," Elizabeth said. "But I expect him back shortly."

The Earl nodded. "Is my son Richard with him?"

"I believe so, sir."

Elizabeth nodded at the servants as they brought in the trays of tea and cakes. She hoped Fitzwilliam would not be very long. All she knew was that the guards in the street outside had been arranged by the Earl and she was very grateful.

She nodded at Georgiana to pour the tea, and observed the Earl out of the corner of her eye. He looked drawn and worried. The countess, too, was pale and sad. Elizabeth wondered what had happened. But she could not ask, she had only met the Earl very briefly the first evening they were in London and he had been cool and dismissive.

She hoped very much that her husband would be here soon.

CHAPTER 61

*D*arcy and his cousin dismounted in the
yard. They had called on the
Brigadier and discussed the guard on Darcy
House and how Georgiana could be protected
once she began to go out again.

Afterwards, they had wanted to go on to the
chief of the constabulary, but Darcy had felt a
certain disquiet. "I think we need to go home now,
Cousin Richard."

And now they were here, staring at the mono-
gram on the waiting coach.

"How long has the Earl been here?" he barked
at the coachman.

"Just over fifteen minutes, Your Grace."

Darcy felt a little ashamed of his tone. "Thank

you. Go to the kitchens and get some tea while you are waiting."

He and the Colonel hurried into the house and handed their hats and canes to the footman. What on earth had brought the Earl here?

They went through to the drawing room and bowed. He glanced at Elizabeth and saw her warning glance. Something was up.

"I need to talk to you both," the Earl said. "In private." He looked at his wife, still on her feet after rising to curtsy.

"You stay here, madam." His voice was still curt and Darcy saw her eyes were swimming with tears. But he had to hear what the Earl had to say. He caught Elizabeth's eye. She would find out what needed to be done to support the Countess, even if she had never met her before.

He led the Earl and his cousin to the library. The Earl planted himself in Darcy's comfortable leather library chair.

"Whisky, Darcy, if you don't mind. I don't care for tea."

Darcy poured him his drink. He wouldn't comment on the incorrect title; he could see the Earl was most assuredly not himself, and it was not a calculated rudeness — although the man was not past doing that, and Darcy knew he would call him out on it when it happened.

"Thank you," the man grunted as he handed him the drink.

Darcy looked at Richard, who raised his eyebrows. Something was certainly up. They drew up chairs and sat waiting. The Earl would tell him soon enough.

"David's dead." The Earl spoke harshly and suddenly. Darcy felt shock course through him at the unexpected news.

He glanced at Richard. It was not quite the way he should hear of the loss of his brother, and he would wish to comfort his mother privately, surely?

"I am very shocked to hear it, sir. Have you only just had the news?"

"Yes, it came through this morning. Wanted to get out of the house at once before the fawning flatterers come. And his creditors!" the man was scowling and angry. But Darcy could see the pain behind the harsh words.

"I am sorry for your loss, sir. How did it happen?" It was not surprising to him, he was only surprised that it had not happened before now.

"An accident when he was drunk, I think. Fell down the stairs at a brothel! Not a gentlemanly way to die, at all!"

Darcy winced. What a terrible way to be

remembered. He was not particularly saddened, he'd never been close friends with his Cousin David.

He turned to his cousin. "I'm so sorry at the loss of your brother, Richard. Would you like to use the small parlour to comfort your mother?"

He thought making the Countess visit here had been extremely harsh, she should have been permitted to take to her bed, with female relatives to provide comfort.

"Thank you, that might be best." His cousin seemed a little lost. "Would you …"

"But it means you're my heir now, Richard! I need to talk to you before you go to her!" The harsh voice held no sorrow or sadness, and Darcy understood that the Earl had been ashamed of his eldest son. But surely he must feel the loss?

He stood up. "You may talk to Cousin Richard in here, sir. I will leave you now."

He closed the door quietly behind him. Richard would make a good heir and a good Earl. He just needed time to get over the shock.

He grimaced, wondering how long it would take Richard for it to sink in that he too now had good prospects to offer in marriage. It could not have happened to a better man.

He went back to the drawing room. The Countess was still sitting, ramrod straight, staring ahead of her, but Elizabeth was sitting beside her now. Georgiana sat on the other sofa, looking distressed.

He went to the Countess. "I am so deeply grieved at your loss, Lady Matlock. Perhaps you could take a little tea in the small parlour, where Richard can join you in a few moments?" He glanced at Elizabeth.

She put her hand on the Countess' arm. "That is a good idea. Cousin Richard will wish very much to talk to you privately. Let me go with you."

The older woman looked at her as if she'd only just seen her, but she stood up and followed Elizabeth from the room. Fitzwilliam stood in the doorway and watched as they went to the parlour.

Then he went over to Georgiana.

"How did it happen, Fitzwilliam?" she sounded anxious. "Lady Matlock didn't seem able to say."

"No, she would not wish to think about it." He wondered if he should tell her, then realised she would undoubtedly hear about it anyway.

"It was most unfortunate. He had taken too much drink and fell down the stairs — at the brothel he was visiting."

Georgiana's hands were over her mouth. "How terrible!"

"Yes," he said heavily. "We must not talk of it again."

"Take some tea, Fitzwilliam. I suppose there is nothing to do but wait, now."

He sat down beside her. "I think you are right. But it was not good to bring Lady Matlock out of the house. She needs to go back soon and into formal mourning." He shook his head.

"I do not know what his Lordship was thinking of." But he did. He knew his uncle would want at the earliest moment to see his younger son, the new heir. And he would not have been able to sit still and wait for the servant to go and summon Richard.

"Perhaps we should let her go home in your coach, Fitzwilliam? Then Uncle Henry could take his own when he is ready."

"It is well thought of, Georgiana. Elizabeth could go with her and my coach bring her home when she is ready."

He got to his feet. He thought the Earl and Richard might be some time.

He knocked quietly on the door of the small parlour and when Elizabeth came to the door he spoke quietly.

"I imagine Lady Matlock is very shocked. His Lordship should not have brought her out, especially without mourning clothes. Might you suggest that she go home in our coach and you go with her and see that she is settled with her daughters?"

"Yes, that is best, I think, Fitzwilliam." Elizabeth looked deeply troubled. "Cousin Richard could call upon her there when he is finished with the Earl." She looked across at the library door.

"I wonder what there is to talk about?"

Darcy smiled. "He is now the heir. His Lordship will have that as his top priority now, to ensure that Richard is ready."

"Oh!" Elizabeth gasped. "I had not thought of that."

Darcy nodded. "That is for later. Could you tell her Ladyship, and I will call the coach round."

She nodded and gave him a small smile.

CHAPTER 62

*E*lizabeth hadn't been to Matlock House before, but Richard had two younger sisters still at home. They met her with reddened eyes and assisted Lady Matlock into the house.

Elizabeth spoke to the elder daughter and explained in a low tone what had transpired.

"Thank you for bringing her home," Lady Jane said. "I don't think Father was thinking straight at all. He demanded she go with him and he had to find Richard at once. He wouldn't wait at all while I prepared mourning clothes."

"You're right," Elizabeth commented. "It was obvious he could not quite bring himself to believe what has happened. But anyway, she is here now and I am sure it is for the best."

"Yes, thank you, Your Grace. I — I hope we might be friends in happier times."

"Indeed, I'm sure we will." Elizabeth said her farewells and was happy not to have to stay too long before she could get back into the coach. She was not at all comfortable being addressed as a duchess. She sank into the seat on the right. It was where Fitzwilliam usually sat and his scent rose all around her, comforting her. Surely nothing else could happen?

She sat there, thinking of the Colonel. She was so happy for him, as he was now the heir, she supposed he would be free to make an offer to Susannah Peake. She smiled; he would be so happy.

But of course, he would be in mourning for several months, so any engagement would have to wait.

She looked out of the window. They were nearly at Darcy House. Of course Susannah Peake would wait for him. Elizabeth had watched with delight their growing affection for each other and she knew they'd be very happy.

The coach pulled up outside the steps and the coachman jumped down and lowered the step before opening the door. Elizabeth got out, seeing her maid also climbing down.

She saw Fitzwilliam waiting at the top of the

steps for her. She was very pleased to see him and hurried up to greet him.

"Thank you for accompanying Lady Matlock, Elizabeth. Did all go well?"

"Yes, sir. Her daughters are with her now. They told me that when the news arrived, Lord Matlock would brook no delay or excuse. He was insistent on coming here to find Cousin Richard."

"I thought as much." Her husband offered her his arm and took her into the house. "He and Richard have gone together to Matlock House."

She smiled sadly. "I imagine there is much to be done."

He shrugged. "It is a great misfortune. David was a fine young man until he could not control his drinking and his licentious behaviour."

"Were he and Cousin Richard very close?"

"They were. But not recently. I hope Richard will be able to grieve in his own way and not find the duties of an heir too onerous."

"Perhaps it is wrong of me to say it so soon, but I think the duty of marrying and providing an heir might help him regain his happiness."

He glanced at her. "I have had the same thoughts. The lady will make a fine Countess in the future."

Elizabeth shook her head, smiling.

"What are you thinking, Elizabeth?" he asked, sounding interested.

"Just that all these titles and family interconnections are very hard for this simple country miss!" She laughed, and he did too.

He bent his head toward her. "This simple country miss is now a beautiful Duchess. And I am so proud she is my wife," he murmured.

Elizabeth felt her face go hot. She took a deep breath. "Let us go in to Georgiana." And she urged him forward.

He smilingly allowed himself to go with her and Georgiana looked up in apparent relief.

"Did everything go well, Elizabeth? I am happy you have returned."

"And I am too." Elizabeth sank down into the chair beside her. "Cousin Richard's sisters were there and I was able to leave reasonably quickly. But I confess I am quite tired."

"It is always difficult when family duties impose themselves." Fitzwilliam smiled. "Especially when so much has happened in so short a time."

He looked at the clock. "It is getting into the afternoon. I will call for a light meal as we have missed lunch and then perhaps you might like to take a short rest before dinner."

Elizabeth pretended not to see the blush on

Georgiana's cheeks and leaned back in the chair. "I think that is an excellent idea."

LYING on her bed an hour later, she shut her eyes as she tried to remember just what had happened each day. But events were blurring into one another and she couldn't remember who had said what to whom and whether it was important.

She closed her eyes, pulling the shawl up a little more. There was something she needed to tell Fitzwilliam. What was it? But she was tired, perhaps she would remember when she awoke.

She was just beginning to doze when the mattress tilted and she knew he had joined her. She rolled towards him with a sleepy murmur, too tired to open her eyes.

His arm went round her and she settled into his embrace contentedly, feeling his linen shirt beneath her face.

"Thank you for coming in," she murmured. He chuckled.

"We have so little time together, my Elizabeth." His warm breath fanned her hair. "Sleep well, I'm here for you."

She sighed contentedly.

She was woken suddenly by an urgent knock

on the door. "Your Grace! Sir!" His valet's voice was muffled through the door. "Urgent news from Havenfield Hall, sir!"

Her husband muttered irritably, but he gently disentangled his arm. "I'm sorry, Elizabeth, but I must go."

She lifted herself up on one elbow. "I will come down in a moment, sir."

He buttoned his waistcoat, looking at her. "Do not be concerned. I will only be assessing the news." She watched as he picked up his jacket, smiled again at her and went to the door.

CHAPTER 63

*D*arcy hurried downstairs, pushing back his hair. Perhaps he should not have gone up, but he had not been able to resist his chance to have a few minutes alone with Elizabeth.

Mr. Peake was waiting in the hall for him. "Good afternoon, Your Grace. I am sorry to call unexpectedly."

"It is nothing. Come through to the library, Mr. Peake."

He poured out a whisky and handed it to his guest, sniffing the redolent smell of cigars left by his morning guest. He wrinkled his nose.

"I apologise for the smell of these particular cigars, Peake. My uncle was here this morning." He poured his own whisky.

"Of course." Mr. Peake bowed. "I know you have many concerns and worries."

"It was news of which I will wish to appraise you in a few moments." He might as well tell the man now, and he could assess the importance to Miss Peake before he saw her. It would be better than learning of it another way.

"But first, you have news from Enderby?"

"I do." Mr. Peake took a letter from his pocket. "I have just received a letter from the magistrate in the town. Two men were apprehended for theft last night." He scratched his ear and smiled.

"When he questioned them this morning, they stated that a local landowner had destroyed their camp and their food and that is why they were starving."

He handed over the letter to Darcy. "Of course that will not excuse them. If they were a danger to Georgiana, then that danger will be gone if they are transported or hung."

"Indeed." Darcy read the letter rapidly. He wondered if these men were the ringleaders or merely hired villains. It seemed the magistrate had also thought that, and he'd offered to allow Peake and his guest at the time a chance to see and question the men.

Darcy waved the letter at Mr. Peake. "It was very good of you to bring this over immediately. Do you think it possible that I could intrude upon your time and call on this magistrate?"

"Of course, sir. I am at your disposal whenever you wish."

"Hmm. I wonder if the Earl of Sandwich is in Town?" Darcy thought it would be incredibly good luck if he was. He would be invaluable.

"If you would allow me a moment to send a note?"

He turned to his writing desk and wrote hastily. Sealing the letter, he rang the bell, and when the servant arrived, handed it to him.

"Get this taken to Mayborough House for the Earl of Sandwich, and enquire if he is at home. If he is not, bring me the note back. If he is, hand this in and wait for a reply."

The footman bowed and went away again. Darcy turned to his guest and waved the whisky decanter at him.

"Another?"

Mr. Peake nodded. "Thank you." He held out his glass. "What was the other news you said you had?"

"Ah." Darcy took his own drink and sat in the comfortable chair opposite his friend.

"Yes. I think it has relevance for you, Peake. But it is difficult news. My uncle, who called this morning, is Colonel Fitzwilliam's father, the Earl of Matlock."

Mr. Peake nodded, but didn't interrupt.

"He had some unfortunate news. His heir, my Cousin David, Viscount Renham, was killed in an accident in the early hours of the morning."

Mr. Peake sprang to his feet. "I am so sorry, sir! Let me go away, and I apologise for intruding at this sad moment."

Darcy waved his glass at him. "Sit down, Peake. It is sad news, yes. But my cousin was not … close to any of us, and so it would be deceitful of me to be too sad." He watched as Mr. Peake sat back into his chair, but sitting on the edge of it.

He smiled wryly. The man had understood the import of the news as regarded his sister.

"Of course, Colonel Fitzwilliam will have to remain with his family for the time being. The first day of mourning — he will not be able to join us for dinner."

Mr. Peake nodded. "I will send a letter of condolence to Matlock House."

Darcy nodded. "It will be appreciated." He caught Peake's eye. "He is, of course, now the heir to the Earldom, and will be in the Gazette as appointed Viscount Renham forthwith." He sipped his drink, still looking him in the eye.

"How do you think your sister will feel about the news?"

Mr. Peake looked away. "She will, of course, sympathise very much with Colonel Fitzwilliam on his sad loss."

Darcy sat forward. "Let us, between ourselves, at least, be clear on this matter. I am as fond of him as if he were my own brother and I am delighted that he will now be able to buy out his commission and be safe from this infernal war." He put down the glass, when had he finished it?

"He now has prospects enough to be able to seek a wife. I am aware of his affections to your sister and am asking, as if I were his brother, whether you can see any impediment that might cause him sorrow in those affections?"

Mr. Peake smiled thinly. "It is as well we understand each other, Your Grace. I have, of course, been aware of the growing affection between them, and I have been troubled by it. I know him as a good and honourable man, and he would not be seeking my sister's fortune alone. But, while adequate, it would not have been enough to afford them a good standard of living."

He put down his own glass. "However, my sister is of full age and I know that she is able to make her own decisions." He smiled.

"I think I knew what that decision was likely to

be in any event. But this news will make it easier, once the mourning period is over." He stood and bowed.

"I will tell my sister that you are in mourning and therefore dinner this evening will be postponed."

Darcy rose too. He shook Peake's hand. "Thank you for your understanding."

"If you need to go to Havenfield Hall tomorrow and see the magistrate, I am free to accompany you, sir, and I will wait to hear from you."

"Thank you, Peake. For bringing me the news of these men, and for our conversation on the other matter."

He saw him to the door and waited while he mounted his horse and rode off. A fine man. He could raise no objection if Georgiana wished to wed him.

He turned in again and went through to the drawing room to see if Elizabeth was up. He would not have wished his sister married at sixteen, though. She needed time, but time was not available to her.

CHAPTER 64

*S*ummer was definitely over. Elizabeth shivered a little as she dressed that morning, enjoying the heavy satin fabric. It was so much warmer than the cotton dresses she had been wearing when at home at Longbourn.

How long it seemed since she had been there. She stopped and gazed pensively out of the window. It was nearly six months since their wedding and she had become a little more used to living as the wife of a wealthy man. She smiled. But she had loved Fitzwilliam since he had been Mr. Hudson, she knew that now. He was the kindest and most generous of men.

And today was another wedding. She would be able to stand beside her husband and listen to the words of the vows and remind herself of when she had said those words in that hurried ceremony in the sitting room at Longbourn.

She knew Fitzwilliam was acting as groomsman for Cousin Richard, but when he was standing with his bride, Fitzwilliam would come and stand beside her.

She sighed with happiness. Richard and Susannah Peake had taken a little while after his mourning was over, but they had become engaged and he had grown in confidence with her by his side.

Even with the disapproval of his father, who had firmly instructed him to marry one of his cousins, Richard hadn't faltered.

"No," he told Elizabeth. "I told my father that I would never marry Cousin Anne. He was insistent that Rosings Park added to the Matlock estate would ensure more security for the estate; but when I reminded him that she was likely be too unwell ever to produce an heir, he thought again." He smiled reminiscently. "And then, of course, he had nothing but praise for Miss Peake."

"And that is quite right, too." Elizabeth smiled. "She is a most amiable and accomplished lady and very beautiful."

"Yes, yes! You are so right." The Colonel sighed. "I am so fortunate in being able to offer her all I would have wished to."

And now their marriage day had dawned. Fitzwilliam had rented this wonderful house in Leicester, as they would be marrying in the cathedral there. It was the only church large enough within an hour's drive of Havenfield Hall, and the bride would marry from her home.

Elizabeth wished them all the happiness that she herself had known in hers. They would be living in a house owned by the Matlock estate, and would be there in time for their first Christmas together.

She smiled, and it was close to Pemberley.

"Elizabeth! Elizabeth!" She heard Georgiana's voice in the gallery.

"I am here, Georgiana." She looked through her door. "Oh, you look delightful, dear sister. Come into my dressing room while I finish getting ready."

Georgiana sat on the window seat and watched as Elizabeth's maid carefully threaded the tiny beaded ribbons through her hair.

"That looks really nice, Elizabeth. Almost like the flowers we can get in the summer." Her brow furrowed.

"But I am concerned, Elizabeth."

Elizabeth swung round in the seat. "What distresses you, Georgiana?"

"I'm thinking about Mr. Peake. He will find

his house very empty tonight. And what about Christmas next week? I know he is not family, but do you think Fitzwilliam will permit you to invite him for at least part of the day?"

"I think it is a very good thought, Georgiana." Elizabeth turned back to the glass for the maid to continue her work. "I will speak to Fitzwilliam later this afternoon. I won't see him before the wedding starts."

"I know, but I wanted to tell you." Georgiana leaned against the window frame.

"I am glad I will be getting married in the summer. I cannot imagine shivering on my wedding day."

"Ah, but you would happily marry in the winter if that was when it was possible to do so, wouldn't you? If your sixteenth birthday was in January, you wouldn't wish to wait until July?"

"Oh, no! I definitely wouldn't." Georgiana smiled complacently at the mirror where she could see Elizabeth's reflection.

Elizabeth glanced at her. "Well, we need to wait and see, Georgiana. You must remember that Fitzwilliam and the Earl of Sandwich believe there is now no danger to you being unmarried and a target of gold-diggers. You might agree with him that you should gain some more experience of the world before you marry."

"No!" Georgiana sat up at once. "He would not do that to me! We have an arrangement that if I did what he said to keep me safe, he would let me marry Mr. Peake as soon as I was sixteen!"

"I know that, Georgiana, but you must remember that things are different now. Please consider over the next few months whether this is what you really want."

"It is what I want! Fitzwilliam will not stop me, will he?"

Elizabeth shook her head. "No, he won't. He always keeps his promises. You may marry on your sixteenth birthday with his consent if that is what you wish. I just want you to be very sure."

"Don't you like him?" Georgiana sounded childishly disappointed.

"Of course I do!" Elizabeth swung around again, beginning to wish she had not begun this conversation today. "I think he is a true and kind gentleman."

Georgiana looked puzzled. "So why don't you want me to marry him?"

Elizabeth shook her head. "I didn't say that. What I meant was that the urgency to marry is not there any more, and you might wish to take your time."

"Oh." The girl sank back in relief. "Oh, yes. But I know nothing will change. He is the perfect man for me, and I love him so much — and I can't bear to think of him living all alone any longer than he has to."

Elizabeth smiled at her. "Well, let's go and see his sister get married, then it will seem that your wedding will come all the sooner, won't it?"

CHAPTER 65

*D*arcy sat in the coach with his cousin as it made the short journey to the cathedral. His cousin had been a brave and resourceful officer. But he was reduced to silence by his apprehension.

"I wish this whole day was over, Darcy!" he groaned. "I suppose you did not have time to be uncertain, as there was no time to anticipate the occasion."

Darcy smiled. "You have met Mrs. Bennet. How do you think I felt, standing up in her sitting room to marry her daughter at not a moment's notice?"

"Oh." Richard had obviously not considered the matter. "Yes, I can see that might have been difficult."

"Never mind, Richard. It will all be over sooner than you think, and you will be very happy. She is a lovely lady."

"She is, isn't she?" His cousin turned towards him with eagerness.

"Yes, she is. She will make a fine Countess when the time comes." Darcy was not inclined to talk much, but he supposed it was part of his duty as groomsman. He just wanted his part to be over, then he could return to Elizabeth's side where he belonged.

And he knew she was there, the moment she came into the cathedral soon after they had taken their pew at the front of the cathedral. He sat, facing the front, a reassuring presence for his cousin, not looking round. But he knew she was there, a few rows behind. Her gaze warmed him, and he waited until he could rejoin her.

AND IT WAS ALL OVER. His coach took him back to their rented home with Elizabeth and Georgiana, after the bride and groom had left for Matlock.

As he got into the coach, he looked around the grounds of Havenfield Hall. It had all begun here, when Mr. Peake had rescued Georgiana from the coach on the main road, and brought her here. The very isolation of the place had protected her long enough for them to find her, but then they could again have nearly lost her.

But now she was safe. Peake was a good man, and knew how to arrange matters for her safety. When they had come back here to see the magistrate, they had talked in the coach afterwards. The men who had been detained were the main perpetrators, and had both now been transported to the colonies for theft. No statements or witness appearances had been necessary by him or Georgiana, for which Darcy was very thankful.

Darcy had been able to relax, although he still harboured hopes of getting the law changed so others would not be at risk as she had been.

And this wouldn't be the last time they were here. Undoubtedly he and Elizabeth would do their share of visiting when Georgiana was mistress here. He shook his head. He still couldn't believe that she was ready for this, she was so young.

Elizabeth slipped her hand into his arm. "Is all well?" she whispered and he forced his mind back to the present.

"It is well." He offered his hand for her to get

into the coach and join Georgiana. Then he turned and bowed to Mr. Peake.

"Thank you for your hospitality, Peake."

"You have been and will always be most welcome, sir."

He swung up into the coach and into his favourite seat, next to Elizabeth. Georgiana caught his eye. She looked very content. "Weren't they lovely? They looked so happy."

He nodded. "Yes, they did. I think Cousin Richard, at least, is glad that it is over."

Elizabeth laughed. "He was so nervous, anyone could see it."

"Please don't tell him that when we see him again." Darcy had to hide a smile. "I am sure he thought his apprehension was well-hidden."

Elizabeth sighed and relaxed back against the seat. "I must admit, although Huncote House is very nice, I will still be glad to get to Pemberley tomorrow."

"It is a long day, though." Darcy looked at her. "If you would prefer to rest at Huncote for a few days, we can do that."

"Thank you, Fitzwilliam. It's very thoughtful of you, but I do want to go home."

"Then we will start as soon as you're ready in the morning." He smiled at her. He would do whatever she wanted — and when she wanted the same thing as he did, he was even happier.

"Will I be getting married from Pemberley or Darcy House?" Georgiana sounded thoughtful.

Darcy drew a deep breath, but Elizabeth put her hand out to him.

"It's not quite the right moment, Georgiana."

Darcy was grateful to let her take over the conversation.

"We have Christmas to think about, and then the winter to enjoy."

Georgiana gave her a meaningful glance and she shook her head warningly at her. She had not had time to ask if they could invite Mr. Peake for Christmas, and she would not do so until they had reached Pemberley.

Georgiana stared out of the window, looking put out and Elizabeth smiled. She knew her husband was looking at her for clarification, and she gave a tiny shake of her head. She knew he would understand.

IT WAS after they had retired to their bedchamber much later when he asked what had affected Georgiana.

"I was not going to trouble you with it for a

day or two, Fitzwilliam." Elizabeth smiled at him and went into his arms.

"She is merely concerned that Mr. Peake will be all alone for Christmas, now his sister is married. She wanted to ask you if you might invite him to join us for the occasion."

Her husband's arms tightened their embrace. "I love you very much, my dearest Elizabeth. If you think it is the right thing to do, then tell me if you wish me to extend the invitation."

She sighed with happiness. "I am so fortunate to have you as my husband, dear Fitzwilliam. I could not wish for anything more." She raised her face to his.

"I think it a good idea. Georgiana needs to see much of him before a formal agreement is announced to ensure she knows her own mind."

His finger traced her lip. "I cannot think she is old enough to marry next year."

She raised her own finger to his lips. "Hush. Please invite him to Pemberley for Christmas and we must let time work its own tricks. I am sure that either Georgiana will find someone she prefers more, or her affections for Mr. Peake will strengthen more." She pressed her body closer to his. "So our conversation now will not be material."

"You are right. I must learn to try not to

control the future." He smiled and kissed her forehead. Heat seared through her at his touch and the look in his eyes.

"But as for the here and now …" He took her hand. "Come to bed, loveliest of all ladies."

CHAPTER 66

*I*t was spring, and the days were longer and warmer than ever. Elizabeth walked out onto the great stone terrace and gazed out over the landscape she had come to love, whether covered in snow, or carpeted with spring flowers.

She was happy that they had stayed here in Derbyshire for the whole winter, despite urgent and angry communications from Lady Catherine, the Earl, and several other members of the family; all saying that Georgiana should be in London for the Season, that Darcy was being very selfish, not allowing his sister to attend the Season's balls.

Elizabeth smiled. Georgiana did not want to go to London, not while Mr. Peake was welcome at Pemberley. He stayed often with his sister and

Cousin Richard at the house in Matlock and called most days.

And she herself hadn't wanted to travel south — until she found her husband having to travel down increasingly frequently on business as his influence with the Prince Regent was sought by the Government.

Two mornings ago, he had come into her bedchamber to say farewell before making another early start to the long journey, he had surprised her in tears.

"Elizabeth!" He had been aghast. "What is the matter?" He had hurried across the room to her and knelt in front of her chair.

"Please do not weep, my darling Elizabeth. I cannot bear it."

She had dashed away the tears, ashamed he should see her crying. "It is nothing, Fitzwilliam. Do not be concerned at all."

He got to his feet and drew her up into his arms. "You must never tell me untruths, Elizabeth. Never. Something must be the matter, I have never seen you weep without good cause."

She laid her head against his chest and felt his strong, steady breathing through his garments.

She took a deep breath, and pushed herself upright. "I am sorry, Fitzwilliam. I would not wish to cause you any anxiety, especially before you have to leave here." She looked down.

"It is only that I know it will seem like many days before I see you again, and I dread the moment of your leaving."

He had listened to her without speaking and had claimed her lips in a searing kiss. Then he had embraced her again.

"I had no suspicion that you felt this way, Elizabeth." His voice was heavy with sorrow. "I should have guessed. I am ashamed that I did not."

She had hurried to spare his feelings. "It is my doing, Fitzwilliam. I was determined not to show weakness when you have to go — it is your business and your duty. I must not drag you back or make you unhappy."

But today he was coming back. He had gone then, after they had had a long conversation between each other, and he was returning today, as soon as his business was over.

Then, next week, when he had to return to London, she and Georgiana would go too, and open up Darcy House. She could be with him and she was content.

She smiled out at the hills. Georgiana had been less happy. Elizabeth was content that the girl was more confident and able to express her disappointment, but it did mean that she had had to work hard to sweeten the blow.

True to her word, when Cousin Richard and Lady Renham had called yesterday with Mr. Peake, that gentleman had immediately — and conveniently — said that he also had business in town and was likely to be opening his London home quite soon.

After that, Georgiana objected to London no more, and Elizabeth had hidden a smile as she reached out to pour more tea. As she looked up to hand the cup to Susannah Renham, she caught Cousin Richard's eye. He too, had appeared amused by what had been said. She suddenly felt quite old.

Elizabeth glanced at the fading light over the far hill. Fitzwilliam should be home within the hour and she turned to go up to her bedchamber to refresh herself.

But she could hear the sound of the coach and horses along the drive, and her heart began to race. He had hurried home to her. Refreshing herself could wait, she smiled and smoothed down her gown. Now she would hurry down the great, sweeping staircase to greet him.

CHAPTER 67

*I*t was high summer and London sweltered. Darcy scowled as he rose at dawn to gain fresh air in the gardens.

He longed for the cool fresh air of Pemberley again. But it could not be, just yet. It seemed that Georgiana was really attached to Mr. Peake, and that gentleman had been most proper and restrained. Darcy could not think of a better husband for her, and so he had reluctantly accepted that it would not be right to make Peake or Georgiana wait any longer.

Elizabeth had kissed him. "I know it is difficult for you to accept, dear Fitzwilliam. But I believe they will be happy and you will see that for yourself very soon."

He strode down the gardens, breathing in the fresher air.

"Fitzwilliam!" he turned at the sound of his name, and watched as his wife hurried towards him.

He extended his hand and she took it and he raised her hand to his lips. "Dear Elizabeth. Are you well?"

"I'm perfectly well, Fitzwilliam. You must not be concerned about me."

"But I am. I wish you had told me the news sooner, so that I could …"

"Be uneasy even sooner than you could now?" she teased him. "Oh, dear Fitzwilliam, there is so much that can go wrong in the early days. I wanted to be very sure it was settled before I told you."

"You are much stronger than I." He chuckled. "I certainly would not have been able to keep the secret for so long." He tucked an escaped tendril of hair behind her ear.

"What can I do to make life easier for you?"

She smiled. "Everything is going well with the wedding preparations. It was well that we announced the date very early, it has meant all the gossip about her has died down and it has been quite accepted now." She tucked her hand into his arm, and they turned and strolled along the path. He could hear her light breathing as she tipped her head to listen to the birdsong.

"I wish we could have arranged the marriage to be from Pemberley," he grumbled.

"I do too," she said regretfully. "But you know it would not have been possible, because of the length of journey time for the older members of your family."

"That is true." He sighed. "Still, next week it will all be over. Georgiana and Mr. Peake will go back to Havenfield Hall at the earliest opportunity, and perhaps you and I might leave London."

"I'd like that," she said quietly. Then she drew a breath, as if to say something, but she did not.

"What did you wish to say, Elizabeth?" he asked.

"It was just … well, I wondered, before it becomes impractical, if you and I might visit somewhere, just the two of us, where business matters cannot demand your attention?"

He turned to her. "But will you be fit for travelling? In your condition?" He felt uneasy. "Be not alarmed, it is not that I would not like to accede to your suggestion. I just do not wish to put you at any risk."

She smiled and reached up to kiss him lightly.

"It is the best time of all, sir. I no longer feel unwell when travelling, and I am not yet so big as to draw attention to my state." She gazed into his eyes.

"Please say we can go. Soon we will have other matters taking up our attention."

"Scotland," he said thoughtfully. "I promised you Scotland. It is very beautiful, and it is close enough to Pemberley that you will not have to travel many days to get there."

"Thank you, Fitzwilliam. I would love to visit Scotland. You know I have never been there."

"Then that is what we will do." He looked down at her. "Your family arrives the day after tomorrow, if I recall correctly?" he tried hard to keep any trace of his worry out of his voice.

"Yes, that's right." She had noticed, he was sure. She was so observant of his mood. "I have arranged it all, and I hope their behaviour is not too shocking to your family." She smiled. "At least Lady Catherine will not meet them, being still too incensed at you marrying me and the impertinence of you becoming a Duke to attend."

"I could even bear that with equanimity, Elizabeth. But I do not wish you to feel embarrassed."

"I don't want you to worry about that. I have been used to it all my life." She smiled. "I am more concerned about seeing you embarrassed."

"Then, if I promise not to be embarrassed, you will promise not to be, either?"

She laughed, and he warmed at the sound.

"If that is what you want, then it is a firm agreement."

They turned and began to walk back to the house. "It is well that Lady Catherine is not attending, I think," she said thoughtfully. "It might otherwise be quite exhausting keeping her apart from my mother. But I do feel that we might need to repair the relationship when you might bear to. It is not good to remain offended."

He nodded. "I think that you're right. But she must temper her language to you. I will not have her rudeness continue." He thought for a moment.

"It is this morning that Mr. Bingley is calling with his sisters, isn't it?"

She nodded, but he was sure she showed the slightest expression of distaste.

"Yes, sir. Your friend is a kind and amiable gentleman."

"He is. We have known each other a long time. But I think you find his sisters a little diffi-cult, do you not?"

She smiled ruefully. "It must be hard for Miss Bingley. I understand she was quite certain of gaining your hand. And our sudden marriage must have made her think I ensnared you."

"And so you did." He slipped his arm around her waist. "You enchanted me and ensnared me, from the moment you showed your beauty and thoughtful nature at Bayford House when you thought I was just a nobody."

"Oh!" She coloured a little. "Thank you for saying that."

"It is true."

She laughed. "It is also true that she would have loved to be a Duchess, and the pain of losing you is therefore much harder to bear."

He could laugh openly at that. "Miss Bingley wishes to marry someone with a great fortune, and a title too, if possible. She is unconcerned who that person might be. She has no interest in me as a person, or Georgiana, except as a means to gain my attention and affection." He shook his head.

"She would never have been able to get an offer from me, never."

"Poor Miss Bingley." Elizabeth was pensive as they climbed the steps up to the terrace. "I hope she will find happiness with someone."

"You are very generous, Elizabeth. I know Miss Bingley has not been kind to you."

"It is of no import, sir. After all, I have all the

happiness I could ever wish for. I can feel compassion for her."

"As I said, you are very generous. There are few who could be so." He smiled. "Enough of that. Let us take breakfast, and then I will attend to my correspondence until our guests arrive."

CHAPTER 68

*E*lizabeth stood at the front pew, watching as her husband walked Georgiana down the aisle towards Mr. Peake. Cousin Richard stood beside him as groomsman, both looking at Georgiana as she walked, radiant, beside her brother. She showed not a sign of the nervousness and shyness that had characterised her when Elizabeth had first known her and she felt very proud of the progress the girl had made. It helped, of course, that she knew Mr. Peake very well now, and had the utmost confidence in his kindness and gentlemanlike behaviour.

Fitzwilliam reached the altar with her, and as she stood beside the groom, he stepped back and entered the pew to stand beside Elizabeth.

The bishop stepped forward and began the service.

"Dearly beloved, we are gathered together here in the sight of God, and in the face of this Congregation, to join together this man and this woman in holy Matrimony …" and the huge vaulted roof of the great cathedral echoed the words.

Elizabeth sighed. What a magnificent setting for Georgiana to remember this day all her life.

She felt her husband's fingers steal into her own. He must know what she was thinking and she turned and smiled at him. She regretted nothing, whatever he felt, and she did not want him to even think she did.

SOON ENOUGH, it was all over, and back at Darcy House, Elizabeth welcomed the guests for the wedding breakfast.

Her serenity was helped by the knowledge that her family was represented only by her father and Jane; the other members of her family having been struck down by a short but violent illness. She felt a little guilty that she was happy her mother and other sisters were not here, and she promised to herself that she would invite them when they were well again. But today was easier because of it.

"Jane." She embraced her sister as she came into the hall. "Stay with me."

Jane smiled her usual serene smile. "I had better go and make sure Father has somewhere to sit down comfortably. Then I will come back to you." She looked at her properly.

"Darling, Lizzy. You look tired. Come and sit with us as soon as you are free to do so."

Elizabeth smiled. "I am not sure when that might be, but I will do what I can."

She watched her sister affectionately as she steered Papa to a chair in an alcove.

She turned back to the receiving line, next to her husband. He gave her a little smile.

"Are you well?"

"Yes, sir. Thank you." His warm concern strengthened her and she straightened her back.

"Mr. Bingley! How wonderful to see you! And Miss Bingley, Mr. and Mrs. Hurst."

He bowed to her. "You are as beautiful as ever, Your Grace. And you have organised the most wonderful occasion for Georgiana."

"Thank you, sir." She noticed Jane standing a little away from him and had an idea. "May I introduce my sister?" She drew Jane forward.

"My sister, Miss Jane Bennet." She turned to

Jane "Jane, Mr. Bingley, a friend of the Duke, and his sister, Miss Bingley." She saw the Hursts had walked off. She wasn't the only person here with embarrassing family.

Mr. Bingley's face was a study to behold. He looked completely captivated by Jane, who curtsied politely.

"Good morning, Mr. Bingley. I am delighted to meet you." She smiled at the lady behind him. "And Miss Bingley."

He bowed deeply. "Miss Bennet, I am honoured to make your acquaintance. Would you do me the honour of introducing me to your family? Perhaps …"

Elizabeth watched them as they walked away. What did he wish to say to Jane? She wished she knew.

Fitzwilliam leaned over towards her. "He will ask if they might sit near to her family for the meal." He sounded amused.

"How do you know?" she glanced at the glint in his eyes.

"Because he will not want to allow another gentleman to speak to her. You'll see."

"Oh." She had to allow that he knew Mr. Bingley better than she did, and it would be good for Jane to get some flattering attention.

She turned back to her duties as hostess,

wishing she would be able to sit down soon. But of course no one apart from Fitzwilliam knew of her condition yet, so she must not show any sign of weakness.

"YOU HAVE BEEN AMAZING." Fitzwilliam reached and took two glasses of wine from the servant's tray. "We may rest a few more moments, and then it will be time to see Georgiana and Peake away in the coach." He handed her the glass. "Are you well?" his voice was barely a murmur.

She nodded. "You have taken great care to take on much of the entertaining. Thank you." She knew he disliked the task, but he was very good at it, and he'd taken much of the strain from her.

She sipped the wine. They would see the happy couple off in the coach. Then it would be the rest of the guests. Only Jane and Papa had been staying here and though they had thought they would not leave until the next day, they had decided to leave at the same time as the rest of the guests and get home to see how the invalids were doing.

Elizabeth smiled. She was certain it was Jane who wished to go, and her father who would be happy to stay away another night or more. However, the decision had been made and their trunks were packed and on the coach.

"Oh, Lizzy!" Jane sat down beside her. "What a wonderful occasion you have given Georgiana." She smiled. "Who would have dreamed the shy girl who was Miss Hudson at Bayford last summer would be such a beautiful, confident bride?"

"Who indeed?" Darcy reached for another glass of wine and offered it to Jane. "Wine, Miss Bennet?"

A few minutes later, Mr. Bingley joined them. It was very clear to Elizabeth that his partiality to Jane was instant and deep. She smiled, Jane could not do better. But he was expressing sincere and anxious concern that they were leaving almost immediately.

"As soon as you have ascertained that your family is recovering, you might come back and visit your sister here?" he said hopefully.

"Alas," Darcy said. "Elizabeth and I will be leaving within a day or two for Scotland. But you have been saying for many months now that you would be seeking an estate in the country. There can be nowhere better than Hertfordshire." He smiled at Elizabeth.

"I remember when you castigated me that I had not taken Netherfield Hall instead of Bayford

House, because it was much more suitable for a gentleman."

Elizabeth could see that if Mr. Bingley could have done, he would have leapt to his feet and been signing for the place tomorrow. She smiled. Certainly Jane would not have a more assiduous suitor.

CHAPTER 69

*D*arcy helped Elizabeth out of the coach and she gazed up at the incredible peaks on the skyline and the deep blue loch which filled the valley.

"Oh," she said softly and stood silent, drinking in the beauty of the scenery. "It's the most beautiful place I've ever seen, Fitzwilliam."

"Apart from Pemberley, of course," he teased.

"Of course." She smiled. "What's this place called?"

"Kinlochleven." He stood behind her and she leaned back against him. He wanted to protect her from everything and anything that could do her harm.

"We will have lunch here, looking out over the loch. I thought you might like to take a gentle stroll along the lakeside before we drive on to Glencoe for the night."

"It is so beautiful here, and the air so clear." She sighed. "I could not be happier."

He nuzzled his face down into her shoulder. "I am glad you are enjoying it. It was an inspired idea of yours to come here after our busy summer in London."

She looked up over her shoulder at him and her eyes were dancing. "But it is good to hear the news when it catches up with us, is it not?"

He laughed. "And which news would that be? The news from Bingley, or from your sister? Or the news from my uncle, repeating what Lady Catherine has said?"

She bit her lip and he felt his breathing catch. She was so lovely to him.

"I enjoyed it all. Even Lady Catherine's opinion seems unable to hurt us while we are here."

He took her hand in his arm. "Let's go to the inn and you can sit down while we wait for lunch. I do not want you getting tired."

"You look after me too well, Fitzwilliam. But I will be happy to sit down if I can still see the hills."

"I will ensure it." He turned with her on his arm and they crossed the path to the inn.

"So, what did you think of Mr. Bingley's news in his letter?" Elizabeth glanced up at him.

"I have to admit that I laughed." Darcy smiled wryly. "Mr. Bingley is known to act precipitately and without thought. To have rented Netherfield Hall on merely our words that afternoon, without even seeing it, must be the height of folly."

She seemed determined to see the good in his friend. "Perhaps it shows a depth of his affection that you have not yet seen?"

"Perhaps." He would not tell her of Bingley's constant changes of affection. Perhaps this one would stick. Darcy knew that Bingley was intensely loyal. Once he did marry and settle down, he would make an attentive and affectionate husband.

Elizabeth sighed. "But I think that once they marry, Netherfield might be too close to my mother. You must encourage them to move closer to Pemberley. I would love to have my sister living closer."

"I will do as you suggest. Are you certain that they will marry, then?"

"Oh, yes! Anyone can see it in his eyes. And I could see that my sister very much admired him."

He laughed comfortably as they approached the door of the inn. "We must be sure to give Lady Catherine much more to complain about."

He delighted at the sound of her laugh.

"Indeed we must, Fitzwilliam."

THAT EVENING he watched her as she stood looking out of the window at the great peaks that surrounded the whole village. He loved her with every fibre of his being and he promised himself he would spend the rest of his life making sure he gave her everything she could possibly want.

"Oh!" she suddenly winced and he was by her side in an instant.

"Elizabeth!" He thought his heart would stop.

She put out her hand, stopping him, the other hand on her belly, just beginning to show.

He was beside her, waiting until she would let him assist her.

"What is it?" he whispered, in an agony of not knowing.

"It is all right, everything's all right." But her hand still kept him at bay.

Finally, after what seemed an age, she looked up and let him hold her.

Her lips twitched. "Your child just kicked me — from the inside." Her voice turned dreamy. "What a strange feeling."

He felt suddenly lightheaded with the relief

from fear. "*My* child? What happened to *our* child?"

"When he kicks me, it's *your* child," she said firmly.

"Oh, no. I'm not having that." He took her tightly into his arms. "Boy or girl, good or bad. It is our child — the fruit of our love."

She murmured agreement and laid her head against his chest. He could feel her heart beating fast against his own.

But he had to know. "What does it feel like?"

She laughed. "I can't possibly explain it. But — suddenly it's real."

"Of course it is. Real love, a real child. Our happiness. It's all real, Elizabeth." He lowered his lips to hers. "I love you so very much."

ABOUT THE AUTHOR

Harriet Knowles loves writing about Jane Austen's wonderful characters from Pride and Prejudice.

She is the author of several other novels and novellas, including

- Mr. Darcy's Stolen Love
- The Darcy/Bennet Arrangement
- Compromise and Obligation
- The Darcy Plot
- Mr. Darcy's Change of Heart
- Hidden in Plain Sight
- Her Very Own Mr. Darcy

Harriet Knowles' books can be found in paperback and ebook formats on many online stores.

32306923R00301

Printed in Great Britain
by Amazon